Lilac,
I love the cover?

SpaceBook Awakens

by

Stephen Colegrove

Book Three of the Amy Armstrong Series

Copyright Information

Cover design by Lilac

Find out more about the author and upcoming books
at the websites below:
stevecolegrove.com
amishspaceman.com
twitter.com/stevecolegrove

Also by the author:
The Girl Who Stole A Planet
Empire of the Space Cats
The Amish Spaceman
The Roman Spaceman
A Girl Called Badger
The Dream Widow

Table of Contents

Cast of Characters

Amy Armstrong: A fourteen-year-old thief from 1995 California. Accidentally flung two thousand years into the future, she is trying to find a way back to her own time

Philip Marlborough: A seventeen-year-old boy from late nineteenth-century England also trapped in the future

The Lady: An ancient human cyborg and corporate head of a business that specializes in trans-dimensional theft, who gives Amy Armstrong a ship. Revealed at the end of Book One to be a dimensional twin of Amy Armstrong.

Sunflower: An orange shorthair tabby who worked for the Lady and accidentally brought Amy Armstrong into the future. His wife disappeared while on a similar mission. Bone strengthening and other cybernetic implants have changed his body from that of a normal cat.

Betsy Jackson: A male Jack Russell terrier who formerly worked for the Lady. Dim-witted and easily distracted. Bone strengthening and other cybernetic implants have changed his body from that of a normal dog.

Nick: A female sprite who formerly worked for the Lady in the gem-sorting department. Sprites are a bio-engineered species of five-inch-tall humanoids with transparent wings that allow them to fly.

Nistra: A former officer of the sauropod prison system. Ordered to help Amy Armstrong find a way back to Earth, but secretly plots to steal her ship, since his home world powers the ship's drive. Sauropods are a bio-engineered species of seven-foot-tall bipedal lizards, similar to a fat crocodile walking on its hind legs

George, Plastra, Astra: Sauropods who have secretly hidden themselves in the cargo hold of Amy's ship.

Kepler Prime: Nistra's homeworld, secretly miniaturized by the Lady and installed as the power source for Amy's ship

SpaceBook Awakens

Alligators are legendary throughout the galaxy as the dumbest creatures to ever fog a mirror, and that includes teenage pop stars of any species. With more teeth than brain cells, the myopic monsters thrashed freely through the swimming pools and sewer systems of an ancient land called Flory-Duh, swallowing anything and everything in sight. A cursory attention to politics and current events would have alerted these scaly morons to imminent war among the humans, who were also blasting experimental ships full of cats and dogs to the stars––the inheritors of true civilization and your ancestors. However, instead of picketing the launch sites of the colony ships or creating a political action committee to elect alligator-friendly representatives to Congress, the swampy reptiles continued to burst through toilet bowls and chomp away at anything that moved, guaranteeing extinction as the mushroom clouds and radiation destroyed all life.

Centuries later, one particular megalomaniac was not content with the absence of such an illiterate, boneheaded species from the galactic gene pool. A circus owner and former bioscience researcher, Doctor Furrykins, mounted an expedition to Earth, returning from the dead world with the DNA of what he claimed were 'alligator,' but which many suspect were cell samples from a mutant lizard slash radio deejay called Alan living in a nice two-bedroom condo on the outskirts of a radioactive Miami. Intending to clone the species and add them to his many carnivals traveling around the planet Gliese, the cat scientist Dr. Furrykins made a decimal point error in his calculations. Infused with too much human DNA, the giant reptiles developed brains ten times larger than normal, and could even drive a stick. This became useful when a band of the monsters escaped from Furrykin's lab in an off-road vehicle, taking fertilized eggs and a recipe for quick cloning. A guerrilla war with the local cat police quickly turned global, culminating in the War of Ten Armies. Although the artificial creations––now called "sauropods"––lost the war, enough of the beasts escaped to Kepler Prime and quickly covered that planet.

In summation, the next time you meet a sauro in the street, don't kick them in the shins and run away. Just point and laugh at the idiots, because they used to live in the sewer.

[Excerpt from Wank & Fugnalls Galactic History, Four-Hundred Seventeenth Edition]

War is hell, and you'll see that real quick if you surprise a platoon of sauropods without armor or air support to back you up. The bastards wear metal sheathing on top of their already-thick hide, and run and jump like grasshoppers on a hot stove. With all that weight they still carry automatic rifles that would break the back of any cat just picking it up, and I've served with some of the best cats in the Empire. Some say it's the reptile rage they go into; others say it's because they're as dumb as two rocks in a bag. I say, nuke 'em from orbit.

[Major Mittens Wallace, 6/7 Third Cat Infantry, *Remembering the Gliese Conflict*]

The government of Tau Ceti has many reasons for sending Class-A convicted criminals to the orbital prison on Kepler Prime. First of all, no one has ever escaped. Imagine yourself locked in a room with a horde of scaly monstrosities pacing outside. That cell is no longer a cell––it's a safe house! Other reasons ... sometimes they eat the prisoners. Not for enjoyment, mind––it cuts down on cost.

[Sooka Black, Preceptor of the Glorious Imperial Homeworld of Tau Ceti]

Amy paced the navigation room, her fingers rubbing the burnt edges of a hole in her blouse right over her heart. If not for the six-inch rip in the silky material and the pink circle on her skin, it would have been impossible to tell from her appearance––slightly mussed, long blonde hair, long-sleeved white blouse, black leather vest, pleated skirt in tartan blue, dark navy tights, and leather Mary Janes––that she had just come from a battle between murderous tentacled robots and a regiment of furiously leaping armored cat tanks.

Philip had changed into the embarrassingly tight uniform required by the ship. Apart from the black skullcap, the crimson color of the stretchy spandex material matched the shade of the teenager's face when he was first ordered to wear it. The dark-haired boy leaned over a low black cylinder in the center of the room and stared at a mess of text and numbers scrolling across the flat upper surface. The walls, floor, and ceiling of the room that surrounded the pair of teens were in reality featureless and gray, but the ship projected a panoramic view of the exterior into the minds of the two humans, making it seem as if they and the control console were flying through the night sky with nothing but clouds around them. Below their feet, the moon shone on the Pacific Ocean, the dark coast of Monterey Bay, and a grid of houses with only a sprinkling of yellow lights.

Amy shuffled to a stop next to Philip. "I should be dead," she murmured.

Philip looked up from the data scrolling across the table and hugged her tight. "Still fretting over that, darling? I rather think we should be concerned with how and why we've come to be in the wrong California."

Amy shrugged. "Oh, I know how that happened––I dropped a screwdriver in the transmat drive." She pulled together the edges of the wide hole in her blouse and stared up at the stars in the sky. "Blanche, should I be dead?"

"Despite her attempts to the contrary, my Lady is experiencing nominal health for a fourteen-year-old human female," said the motherly voice of the ship, "Blood pressure, pulse, and glucose levels are within range, although reproductive hormones are––"

"Stop! All I want to know is, did I survive because of my blouse?"

"Most likely, my Lady. I have been informed that several thousand nanites in the affected cloth perished while absorbing a high-energy particle beam."

Amy glanced down. "Wow. I feel bad now."

"My Lady would not be feeling anything if the nanites had not sacrificed themselves and the surrounding material. My Lady would be dead."

Philip smiled faintly. "Perhaps we should hold a memorial service."

"The honorary services have long since ended," said the ship. "The offspring of the heroic nanites are preparing to attend nanite college on scholarships established for this purpose. The span of life and temporal awareness on a microscopic scale are much faster than a human's."

Philip leaned forward and touched the cloth of Amy's blouse. "Allow me to ponder this for a moment, my dear. You're walking around with an extremely small university in your garments?"

Amy held up her hands. "I don't want to know. I'm very grateful that the nanites saved me, but I really don't want to think about tiny bugs living in my skirts."

"Nanites are neither bugs nor insects, my Lady," said the ship. "They are nano-elemental organisms on the hadron scale."

"I don't care!"

Philip raised a finger. "Let's focus on the current situation. I would like to point out that flying a large silver spacecraft in full view of everyone who lives along the seaside is not the wisest of actions, even at night."

"Are you afraid they'll shoot at us? Nobody ever looks up. This is before UFOs and little green men."

"Yew-eff-oh? Is that Spanish?"

"Unidentified Flying Object. Blanche, is there any way to find out the year? I don't want to land and get eaten by the natives."

Philip pointed down at a dark line that followed the coast north and south. "They have a railroad, so I doubt we'll find any cannibals."

"From the decay of the nearest SpaceBook signal, the approximate year is between 1910 and 1920 C.E.," said the motherly voice of the ship. "By analyzing Earth's distance from Sol, I would estimate early April of the Gregorian calendar."

"Good gravy," whispered Amy. "That's a long shot from 1995."

"In vastness of space and time, it is quite close," said the ship. "The accuracy of transdimensional travel is lessened when my overrides are disabled and a tool is dropped into the elemental array."

"Sorry! I said I was sorry."

"No need for apologies, my Lady. I am merely stating fact."

"In my opinion we should move this ship to a more discreet location," said Philip. "At least until this MacGuffin character can calibrate the transmat drive. He said that it wouldn't take long."

Amy sighed. "Right, sorry. I've been focused on myself. Blanche, take us further south. We can land in the mountains and not bother anyone."

"Or not have anyone bother us," said Philip.

A bright circle appeared in the night sky and an orange tabby cat and a brown-and-white Jack Russell terrier jumped into the navigation room. A six-inch-tall blonde woman flew through the opening after them, her transparent dragonfly wings buzzing loudly. The two animals wore the ship's tight red uniform, their fur sticking out from the leg and neck openings, and the tiny woman wore a short red dress of the same stretchy fabric.

"Are we there yet?" barked Betsy, the terrier.

"That is the dumbest and most predictable thing you could have said," growled Sunflower. "You wouldn't know where 'there' was if 'there' came up and hit you with a steel pipe!"

Betsy blinked at the cat. "Hey! You just did that, Sunnie. Thanks for knocking my implant back into place."

"My pleasure."

The tiny blonde woman landed on Amy's shoulder.

"I'm bored! We've been stuck in this ship, like, forever. Can't we go shopping like you promised?"

Amy watched the dark line of the coast fly beneath her feet as the ship moved inland. "I don't know, Nick. We're in the right place, but the wrong time."

Sunflower's green eyes grew wide. "What? I thought that idiot Macwhatshisname fixed everything."

Amy nodded. "He did, but this idiot—me—dropped a screwdriver on the transmat drive."

"Fantastic. You know, blowing up your entire civilization was the best thing humans did for the galaxy."

"What about Alpha Centauri?" asked Betsy, tail wagging. "Lots of humans there."

"Have you seen them play football? They might as well be dead, the way those zombies stagger around the pitch."

Betsy giggled. "That's right! Humans can't play at all. They're funny."

Amy ran her fingers through her hair and walked through the holographic night sky to the hatch.

"This conversation has been so interesting that I hate to walk away," she said. "But I need to take a bath."

"My Lady, your garments are self-cleaning," said the ship.

"Well, I'm an old-fashioned girl who likes to take a bath the old-fashioned way."

"I don't think there are any buckets on the ship," said Philip.

Amy turned and spread her arms. "Not THAT old-fashioned!"

ASTRA SET two *poona* next to the wall of the container. One had brown fur with white patches, and the other was gray. He pointed a sharp claw at the hamster-like rodents and turned to the group of giant lizards behind him.

"Five hundred mao to the winner. The one that makes it to the corner."

A huge brown sauro shook his head. "Why are you telling them? *Poona* can't talk."

"I'm not talking to them, George! I'm talking to you!"

"Oh, okay. That's fine."

Astra slapped the metal deck behind the *poona*, and the small mammals shot along the wall on their four tiny legs. Astra and the half-dozen sauro watching the race screamed and hooted, perhaps in a belief that the already panic-stricken rodents would become even more panic-stricken.

The brown-and-white contestant reached the far wall first, and a few of the sauros groaned, including Astra. George tromped in his big-clawed feet to the corner, snatched up the gray poona, and tossed the squirming rodent into his jaws like a circus peanut.

"You egg-brain!" yelled Astra. "Why?"

George shrugged and swallowed. "He lost."

"Now we've only got one. You can't race one *poona* against himself!"

George blinked at Astra. "Sorry. Want me to eat the other one?"

"No. Go and sit in the corner."

Plastra and three other giant lizards sat in a circle around a small shipping crate, each holding five cards in front of his scaly snout. On top of the crate lay a pile of cards.

"Stop making so much noise, you two!" yelled Plastra, staring at the cards in his hand. "I'm finally winning."

His yellow eyes opened wide as the air condensed into a straw-colored gel, trapping everything in the shipping container like a fly in amber. A sweet odor mixed with carbon entered the narrow nostrils of the sauro, smelling like a box of sweet rolls covered in flame, and warmth spread over his scaly hide. The heat changed suddenly to a searing cold, and everything disappeared in a blinding flash.

Plastra blinked. The amber, the smells, and the cold were gone, and the inside of the container was the same as before. He growled and stamped his foot.

"George!"

"I didn't do it, I swear!"

"Probably just the engines slowing down," said Astra. "It means we'll stop soon."

George rubbed his clawed hands. "That means killing! Can we start killing now?"

Astra clapped a scaly green hand on George's shoulder. "When Nistra gets us out of this stupid box. Don't worry—–it will be soon."

An evil, sharp-toothed grin spread across George's long snout, like an alligator who'd just eaten a very tasty cat.

"Good," he whispered.

AMY WASHED her hair with something she hoped was shampoo and stood for a long time in the tiny shower-closet, her forehead pressed against the wall and a stream of something she hoped was hot water pouring down her neck and back. It could have been baby oil for all she cared. The only important thing was that it was hot.

She took a deep breath, turned, and the water gushed over her face.

"Off."

Amy slid open the tiny shower door. The sight of a dog and orange cat in red uniforms standing in her bedroom caused her to scream and rip a towel from the wall to cover her dripping body.

"Did we scare her?" asked Betsy.

Sunflower shook his furry head. "I think she saw herself in a mirror. You'd scream too if you looked like that."

Betsy nodded. "I get it! That's why they wear clothes."

Amy tightened the towel under her arms and smiled grimly.

"Thank you for breaking into my room and watching me take a shower."

"You're welcome!" said Betsy.

Sunflower shook his head. "You said not to bother you no matter what. That's what we were doing––not bothering you. We've been here five minutes doing nothing but not bothering you."

Amy sighed. She grabbed another towel and began to dry her blonde hair in front of the bathroom mirror.

"Speak, my good and helpful friends. What's the problem now? Run out of Meow Mix? Someone knock over your water bowl?"

"No need to be patronizing," said Sunflower.

Betsy stared at the cat. "What's that mean?"

"It means, she's treating us like we're stupid. That's true for only one of us."

"Me, right? You're always calling me that, Sunnie."

Amy waved a hand. "Hello? Can one of you tell me what's so important that you waited outside my shower door?"

"The ship has picked up some kind of emergency signal," said Sunflower.

Amy shrugged. She leaned close to the bathroom mirror and touched the circular pink burn in the middle of her chest. "Worse things have happened at sea."

"Like what?"

"Like cats getting thrown into the airlock, falling into the ocean, and eaten by sharks. The signal's probably coming from a ship in trouble. Lots of wrecks along the coast in the old days."

Sunflower shook his head. "That's a nice theory, but the radio signal is coming from the hills to the east, and it's in Cat French."

AMY FELT GUILTY about changing clothes that were supposed to be "self-cleaning," but she also felt that the nanites in the damaged white blouse or their descendants needed a break. She chose a long-sleeved button-up in pale pink cotton, a lined, knee-length skirt made from god-knows-what but which felt like soft corduroy, and white tennis shoes.

"Are these made from the same material? With tiny robots and crap?"

"Indeed, my Lady," said the ship's voice. "A nanite division of the 'Fighting Fifth' are at your command. How is your injury progressing?"

"Feels better. Thanks for the lotion." Amy paused. "You didn't put any nanites in it, did you?"

"Very few, my Lady."

As Amy entered the navigation room, Philip, the tiny sprite Nick, and the sauropod Nistra looked up from the black cylinder of the command console. A dark panorama of the coastal mountains was projected around the walls, ceiling, and floors. In the light of the moon the dry earth and the tumbleweeds appeared in pale shades of gray, but the stars above were as bright as those in orbit.

"Captain on deck!" yelled Nistra. He touched a scaly claw to his forehead in salute, then immediately looked sheepish. "Sorry. Bad habit."

Philip stepped one foot back and bowed. "As pretty as a painting, my dear."

Amy rolled her eyes. "I just changed my clothes. What's wrong with that? People change their clothes all the time."

Philip kissed her on the cheek. "Thank goodness all people are not you, my love."

"Stop it or I'm going to be sick everywhere," said Sunflower. The cat followed Betsy into the room. "Her hair looks awful, all dangly and wet like that. No female cat would be caught dead with damp fur."

Amy shrugged. "Sue me. I couldn't find the blow dryer."

"I volunteered to lick it dry but she wouldn't let me," said Betsy.

Philip spread his hands. "How the devil would that even work?"

The terrier blinked for a second. "I don't know."

Amy walked up to the central console. "Show me this radio signal that's got everyone's panties in a bunch."

"As you wish, my Lady," said the ship. "Approximately twelve minutes ago, a supersonic object passed through the lower atmosphere, and I detected this signal."

A waveform appeared on the top of the console. A white line wriggled up and down as a robotic voice spoke through pops of static and distorted noise.

"Ijans ... tanpree ede ... peelot en danjay ..."

The voice repeated the phrases several times, until Philip swiped his hand over the screen, turning it off.

"Apart from a series of numbers, that's the entirety of the broadcast."

"What's it saying?" asked Amy. "Somebody translate."

"Emergency, help me, pilot in danger," said Sunflower.

"The numbers in the message are galactic coordinates for a SpaceBook repeater," said the warm voice of the ship. "Not the closest repeater, nor one of any significance that I can determine."

Nistra snarled, baring rows of sharp teeth. "We've been followed!"

Amy nodded. "For once I have to agree with space——I mean, with Officer Nistra. I know they had radios back in the olden days of Earth, but I don't think they'd randomly broadcast Cat French and a SpaceBook location. Those didn't exist."

"You're right about Cat French, but not Space-Book," said Sunflower. "It's always been around."

"Whatever. I'm still right."

"Curiouser still," said Philip, brushing his fingers across the control screen. "Is how close we are to the source of the signal. It's a mere three miles away."

All eyes turned to the eastern horizon, where a column flashed bright crimson.

"That makes it easy," said Amy, and rubbed her damp hair with both hands. "Lift off, Blanche, and we'll check it out."

Nistra's eyes bulged. "What?!! It's a trap!"

"The statement of the crew member is within reason, my Lady," said the ship. "Statistically speaking, this object has a higher chance of being a golden coconut full of toys and candy than a random encounter. The originator of the signal has either followed our transmat, or has detected our presence in this dimension. In either case, it is likely they wish either to capture myself, the crew, or an unknown cargo I am carrying."

Betsy jumped high in the air and barked. "Did you say candy? I love candy!"

Amy adjusted the cuffs of her pink blouse. "So it's a trap. Who cares? You're the fastest spaceship in the galaxy, Blanche. We'll just run away."

"Some traps close around the mind," said Sunflower quietly. "And take the form of a job offer you can't refuse, when all you wanted to do is sell catnip from the back of a van."

"Way to bring the mood down," said Amy. "Head for the signal, Blanche."

"As you wish, my Lady."

The long ship rose on a column of dust and cruised through the mountains like a hundred-meter arrowhead, the moon gleaming on her silver skin.

After a few seconds of flight, a thin stream of smoke appeared over the mountains. The column boiled straight up and flattened to the east as it hit an inversion layer.

Nistra jabbed a sharp claw. "Down there––a craft!"

Something had carved a kilometer-long path over a ridge and across the flank of a hill, plowing a deep channel through the loam and shallow brush. The scar ended in a pile of smoking dirt and broken trees at the bottom of a draw, and there rested the ship.

It was shaped like an egg, but an irregular, blocky egg designed by a committee of robots who had never seen one in person. The nose was covered in black streaks of carbon, and the white skin of the egg was marred with scratches, dents, and cracked panels. Three small exhaust nozzles were set on the rounded back in a triangle. A trail of thin white ropes lay in the channel and led to the ripped fragments of a yellow parachute. A red light flashed at the top of the egg.

"Skippy dippy," whispered Betsy. "A golden coconut!"

"Looks like an escape pod," said Sunflower. "The big question is, from what ship?"

"According to the bit code on the identifier beacon, it is from an interstellar, Gliese-flagged craft called *Hare Twist*," said the ship. "I have no records of this craft, but that is not uncommon with Gliese."

Sunflower shivered. "Cats from Gliese––a planet of scum and scoundrels to the last kitten."

Amy smiled. "But I thought you were a scoundrel, too."

"No, I'm a rebel," said the orange tabby, twitching his tail. "A confused, hippie rebel."

"More like a confused hippie lover."

"Yeah!" squealed Nick, buzzing above the cat. "I saw what you did when you were emperor!"

Sunflower flattened his ears. "Back off, butterfly."

"You guys keep fighting," said Betsy, and scrambled toward the exit. "I'm getting that candy!"

"Betsy, stop!"

Amy ran and grabbed the terrier, but he wriggled out of her arms and darted into the corridor.

Sunflower shook his furry head. "If it's a bomb and explodes Betsy, at least there won't be any loss of life. Intelligent life, that is."

Amy brushed dog hair from the front of her blouse. "Blanche, can you see if anyone is inside the pod?"

"Negative, my Lady. Significant thermal energy is radiating from the craft as a result of recent atmospheric entry."

Amy walked toward the exit. "All right. I'm going outside."

Philip rushed up and blocked the hatch opening. "Amy, no! It's too dangerous."

"At least wait to see if Betsy keels over and dies," said Sunflower.

"Very funny, especially after you tried to save him at the spaceport." Amy pulled Philip's hand away from her arm away gently. "I'll be fine. Have Blanche land near the crash site."

"Let me go with you."

Amy stood on the tips of her toes and kissed him. "If anything happens, I promise to let you come and save me."

Philip shook his head. "Amy, if anything happens to you ..."

"I know," she whispered, and left through the open hatch.

Sunflower turned away and made a retching sound.

"Hairball?" asked Nick.

"I wish it was only a hairball. Humans are so squishy and dramatic."

Nistra bowed and walked rapidly toward the exit. "Allow me to excuse myself. I have to visit the little sauro's room."

Sunflower blinked. "If you need to use the bathroom, just say it. We'll just be happy you're gone."

Nistra grimaced. "Thank you for that consideration."

***

AMY GRABBED a handhold inside the starboard air-lock and waited. She realized she didn't have a weap-on, not even a thimble, and looked down at the wag-ging tail of the brown-and-white terrier at her feet.

"You'll protect me if there's anything bad out there, won't you Betsy?"

The dog looked up at her and blinked. "Protect you from candy?"

"No, but maybe there's something in the dark that wants to steal all the candy."

"That's no problem," said Betsy happily. "I'll rip his face off!"

Amy sighed. "Right."

The floor of the airlock shivered and thumped, and the red light above the hatch leading outside turned green.

"Planetfall complete," said the calm voice of the ship. "Safe egress is now possible, my Lady."

"Thank you, Blanche. One question––is there a way for me to talk with you when I'm outside? Apart from screaming and waving my arms like a crazy per-son."

"Indeed, my Lady."

The wall clacked and a tray slid out to display a dozen key chains, each with a white rabbit's foot and a large pink crystal.

"Are you kidding? That's a space walkie-talkie?"

"The communicator does not work in a vacuum. Power is generated from bio-electric contact and routes through the human cerebrum."

"We're going to 'think' to each other?"

"Unfortunately, my Lady, your mental flexibility has not developed to the point at which you may transmit without the physical act of vocalizing. You will, however, be able to receive messages from me, or any others who are within a kilometer of the ship."

Amy scooped a keychain from the tray.

"Awesome! I have to give Philip one. Wait—he won't be able to read my thoughts, will he?"

"Only if you concentrate on sending a message, will any message be sent, my Lady. Contact must also be maintained with the crystal."

Betsy scrabbled his front paws on the round exterior hatch. "Candy!"

"Yeah, Betsy, I get the message."

Amy pushed on the center of the metal hatch. It popped out with a sudden hiss, a gust blowing Amy's hair and skirt from behind as the air equalized with the outside atmosphere.

The cold air smelled of dust and charred plastic as Amy held Betsy with one arm and descended the ladder. She stepped onto dry yellow grass but kept one hand on the rung of the ladder, as she scanned the arid hills and scrubby brown bushes for trouble.

"Grizzly bears used to eat people in the old days," she said. "Too late to turn around now."

Betsy squirmed free and darted toward the huge battered egg at the end of the ditch carved along the top of the ridge, the little dog tumbling through the dry brush and sliding wildly through the lightweight, soft loam. Amy took a more cautious approach, walking slowly and watching the darkness for hidden dangers. Blanche had turned on her landing lights, illuminating the area with a hazy white glow, but every few seconds, the beacon on the escape pod flashed and turned the surrounding hills bright red. With each step of Amy's leather shoes, tendrils of white smoke curled up from the plowed-up mess of earth and roots and yellow grass.

A phrase floated through her mind, as subtle as a billboard floating two inches from her forehead.

—[Are you receiving, my Lady?]—

"Whoa!" Amy laughed and held up the keychain. "That is ... strange. I hear you, Blanche, but I'm not sure if I like it. It's painful, like I'm having a brain freeze from eating ice cream too fast."

—[Understood.]—

She caught up to Betsy, who had climbed on top of the pod and was barking at something. The small dog activated the manos bracelet around a front paw and used the artificial fingers to tug at a small handle.

"Quiet, Betsy! Everybody's going to come running if you keep barking."

The terrier stared at her with wide eyes. "Sorry," he whispered. "I didn't think about that."

"Looking for a way to open the hatch?" asked Amy, scanning the dented side of the egg. "What's 'emergency' in Cat French?"

——[Louvri Ijans.]——

"Thanks, Blanche. Here it is——a red lever with that stuff written on it. Are you ready? Hold on to your butt!"

Betsy blinked at her. "How?"

Amy shrugged. "It's just a thing people say."

She fiddled with the circular handle, at last twisting it ninety degrees and pushing it down. Betsy jumped off the top of the pod as a curved section hissed and swung up to the night sky. The tiny cluttered space inside the egg contained a pair of very narrow reclined chairs and a figure in an orange pressure suit, its head and features obscured by a bubble helmet with a reflective face shield. The human-sized figure had wrapped its arms around its knees and held them to its chest with thick gloves. The cramped interior of the escape pod had obviously been designed for a much smaller creature.

Betsy sniffed the air. "Where's all the candy?"

"That's your theory, Betsy, not mine. Just don't start barking again."

Amy grabbed a splintered branch from the ground and poked the figure in the pressure suit.

"Aw, this is boring," said Betsy. "I don't smell any candy at all and that thing is dead."

"Don't run away! What if it's still alive?"

Amy leaned over the folded-up creature and examined the neck of the pressure suit. She used both hands to press a pair of buttons on either side of a metal ring at the neck, and then twisted the silver helmet ninety degrees to the left.

"I saw that in a documentary about the space program," she said, and pulled up on the helmet. "Lucky guess ..."

The helmet dropped from her hands and rolled away through the dirt as Amy stared at her own face, only a year or two older, framed by blonde hair identical to her own.

The girl blinked slowly and her blue eyes wandered lazily around the inside of the egg. When they came to rest on Amy, the girl smiled with perfectly white teeth.

"Hello, Amy Armstrong."

2

Amy stepped back from the escape pod.

"You're … me? How's that possible?"

Her twin slapped the harness release at her chest and climbed out of the pod.

"No time to explain!"

She grabbed a small black case from behind the seat and jogged up the hill toward the lights of the *White Star*, her pressure suit making loud, rubbery squeaks with each step. Betsy scrambled after her along the trail of scorched earth, barking up a storm.

Amy grabbed the pressure helmet at her feet. "Wait!"

She quickly caught up to her doppelganger, who had slowed due to a combination of the heavy suit and the terrier dangling from her back, his teeth clamped onto a loose strap.

"Please call off the little monster," said the twin. "It's going to rip my suit. I'm not even going to ask about that little red outfit you made it wear."

"Betsy, stop!"

The terrier let go and tumbled to the ground. He shook his coat and flung gritty brown dirt everywhere.

"But she's a stranger! I'm supposed to bark at strangers––it's dog law."

"Dog law is officially suspended. Don't attack her."

Amy's double turned away and continued to jog up the hill.

"Where did you come from?" Amy yelled after her.

"We need to get away from here!" shouted the twin. "The others are looking."

"What others?"

"The people I'm running from!"

The twin climbed the ridge and stopped. She raised a gloved hand to her forehead to block the glare from the landing lights.

"Holy bag of hammers," she whispered.

The ship gleamed against the darkness; a long, hundred-meter blade of liquid metal, standing on edge without any visible openings or markings apart from the spidery landing legs and their small ports.

Amy stopped next to her twin. "It's nice, right? The Lady gave it to me as a sort of consolation prize because of that whole going to prison for stealing a planet thing."

The blonde girl stared at her. "Gave you a ship? Either she really liked you or we're talking about the dumbest woman in the galaxy."

"I wouldn't say that. She was me. I mean, another version of me. I guess that means she was you, too."

The doppelganger jogged toward the ship. "I'm my own person, sister. Where's the airlock?"

"The other side!" yelled Amy. She grabbed Betsy and followed her twin under the wide silver keel of the ship. "What's the rush?"

On the starboard flank of the ship a circle glowed on the silver skin. The airlock hatch swung out with a hiss and the ladder ratcheted down. The twin grabbed a rung and stared at Amy.

"The people that are after me, you don't want to stick around to meet them," she said as she climbed. "They don't play with dolls and have tea parties and crap."

Amy looked down at Betsy. "Tea parties? Does she think I'm four years old?"

The terrier blinked. "Dog years or people years? I just hope she knows where the candy is!"

He extended the artificial "manos" hands from the bracelets around his front paws and climbed the ladder.

Amy sighed. She slapped at a cloud of tiny insects around her face and looked around one last time at the crashed pod and the grassy hillside framed in the landing lights.

Inside the airlock, her twin had already unzipped her orange pressure suit, revealing more skin than clothing with her tiny white tank top and tight gray shorts. Colorful, flashy tattoos covered both arms: a tiger baring his fangs, a spray of orchids, and vertical Chinese writing. Across her shoulder blade, a huge tattoo of a golden fish leapt from the water, a red butterfly inches from its gaping mouth.

"Wow," said Amy. "Where did you get those? Did you have to kill someone?"

Her twin looked up. "Get what? Oh, the ink. It's nothing special. Everyone has them where I'm from."

"And where's that?"

"Phobos. You know, Mars." She frowned and brushed a hand through her hair with stubby, black-painted fingernails. "It's been a long time since I've thought about that stupid place. Geez, what a bunch of losers."

Amy opened a locker and pulled out a red spandex uniform. "You have to wear this. That spacesuit and helmet should fit inside."

Her twin hooted with laughter. "You're kidding, right? I'd rather run around naked."

"That's exactly what'll happen if you don't wear a uniform. This ship is allergic to people and normal clothing catches on fire."

The blonde girl pointed at Amy's blouse and skirt. "How come you're not wearing one?"

"My clothes are made from the same stuff as the uniforms."

The twin shrugged and grabbed a pile of spandex. "Okay, whatever. Burning alive is not my scene."

"This is ... strange," said the ship in a halting, nervous tone. "In a thousand years of dimensional travel, I have never had more than one Amy Armstrong on board. The statistical chances of this happening are quite remote."

The twin pushed her blonde head through the neck of the stretchy red top.

"It wasn't chance, Grandma Talking Voice. The others followed you here. If we don't leave now they'll shove those statistics in places you don't want them to be shoved!"

Amy frowned. "Blanche, close the airlock and prepare to lift off."

"What should be done with the damaged craft, my Lady? Should I open the cargo hold and grapple it inside?"

The twin held up her small black case. "Leave it. I've got all my stuff."

"No, I think we should take it with us. Might find something useful."

"As you wish, my Lady," said the ship.

The airlock hatch shut with a hiss and the floor vibrated as the ship's engines increased thrust.

"Prepare for decontamination procedure," said the ship.

"You might want to hold on," said Amy. "We're about to get plastered."

The twin looked up with one leg in the spandex trousers. "Get what?"

"Stinky wind!" barked Betsy.

The antiseptic tornado blew all three against the curved walls of the airlock like bugs on a windshield.

NISTRA STOOD in the cargo hold and jabbed at a keypad at the end of a tall rectangular shipping container.

"Unlock, you stupid cat-made piece of poona dung!"

The sauro banged on the keypad with his fist. The metal and plastic shattered and fell to Nistra's feet in hundreds of tiny pieces.

"What's going on?" came a faint voice from inside the container. "Get us out, already!"

"Murder," said another muffled voice.

Nistra pressed his jaws close to the corrugated metal. "Nothing's going on. Now keep quiet!"

He found a large crowbar in a locker and began to pry at the edge of the container's door. The metal squealed in protest but didn't budge.

"Holy hairballs," gasped Nistra.

The floor vibrated and the air hummed as the ship's engines increased thrust.

"What's happening?" screamed one of the voices inside the container.

"Nothing," Nistra yelled through the door. "We're probably leaving this disgusting planet."

The vibrations in the floor increased and a red light flashed in the ceiling. A wide, empty space of the floor behind Nistra split in two, and the high-pitched roar of the ship's engines assaulted his ears. The giant lizard scrambled to the side of the shipping container to keep from falling down to the grassy hillside visible through the opening in the cargo floor, and covered his eyes from the fine dirt and grass swirling through the air.

"Cat's teeth!"

A pair of claws attached to thick cables dropped from the ceiling of the cargo hold and pulled up the dirt-covered, carbon-scored egg of the escape pod, gently placing it next to the shipping container. Four smaller clawed cables emerged from the wall and secured the egg to the floor and ceiling as the floor slid shut.

"Do you require assistance, crew member?" asked the ship's voice.

Nistra dropped the crowbar and backed away, his claws up in surrender.

"I was, uh, just exercising. I'll be going now."

AMY'S DOUBLE tossed the stretchy black cap into the airlock behind her and brushed her fingers through her blonde hair.

"Not wearing one of those if you don't," she said. "We're sisters, right? We do everything together."

"Someone I met five minutes ago hardly counts as my sister," said Amy. "I don't even know what to call you."

"'Amy' doesn't work? I guess not," said the twin. "How about 'Three'? That's what the others called me."

"That's about as strange as calling you 'Amy,' but okay."

Three glanced around the corridor. "Talking about strange, where's that dog?"

"Probably the kitchen. He's always looking for food."

"I'm starving, too. Lead the way, friend. It's your ship."

Amy straightened her pink blouse and walked toward the kitchen. The featureless gray metal of the corridor walls faded and was replaced by the loamy sights and sounds of a redwood forest.

"Blanche, have we left the mountains yet?"

"Affirmative, my Lady. I am passing one-thousand seven hundred meters in altitude––"

"Cancel that and drop down to the surface," said Amy. "We can't leave the atmosphere yet."

Three nodded. "Smart move. Let's find a cave or barn to hide somewhere."

"A hundred-meter ship inside a barn? Not happening. Blanche, take us north to the bay. There's an underwater trench a mile deep very close to shore."

"This is an interstellar craft, my Lady. I am designed for the vacuum of space, not for extreme pressure on my exterior."

Three giggled. "How about your posterior?"

"I do not understand the question. Is it rhetorical?"

"Ignore that, Blanche," said Amy. "How deep can you go?"

"To avoid environmental intrusion, I recommend no more than fifteen meters."

"Good. Find a spot in the middle of the bay and take us down that far."

The path split in the "forest." Amy turned left and kept walking with Three beside her.

"We could try running for orbit," said her twin. "This ship looks fast enough."

"Maybe, but we've got a problem with the trans-mat drive," said Amy. "I want to make sure that thing is fixed before any running or jumping or laser blasting."

"I get it! That's why you parked in the mountains."

"What?"

Three shrugged. "Nothing."

The kitchen area was empty and Betsy was nowhere to be seen. Three walked to a refrigerator mounted to the wall and opened the chrome door.

"How about I make a sandwich? Do you have any soy butter?"

"Probably not."

The blonde girl leaned further inside. "Skeksi cheese? Tomatoes? Poona loaf?"

"No, yes, and mother of god I hope not."

Three sighed. "All right. I'll try to make something that won't kill both of us."

She put together a pair of sandwiches from sliced vegetables and unknown strips of meat. Amy grabbed two cups of ice water and joined her at the kitchen table.

"Interesting," Three said after a few bites of the sandwich. "I've never had a red tomato. Tastes the same."

"What color should a tomato be? Purple?"

"Of course! Red is freaky--it's like I'm eating alien babies or something."

"Speaking of 'freaky,' what's going on with you and this escape pod? Did you follow me from Tau Ceti?"

"The others did," said Three. "They slapped a tracker on your ship and followed your demat from the last dimension. Ask grandma in the control room if you don't believe me."

"She's not my grandma. It's the ship's voice."

"What? That's weird. I thought she was real."

Amy looked up at the ceiling. "Blanche! Is there anything strange on the outside of the ship? A beacon or something?"

"Commencing a scan of foreign objects," said the warm voice of the ship. "Preliminary scan negative. Secondary--ah, yes, a magnetic micro-tag on my starboard flank. Applying a negative charge ... device is non-functional."

"One of those inspectors must have put it there during the battle at Cheezburger," said Amy. She watched Three bite into the sandwich. "Who are these others and why are they looking for me?"

"You should be asking, who could possibly follow me through another dimension?"

"The Lady? But her asteroid was about to explode like the Death Star."

"The who and the what?"

"The Lady is a really, really old version of me. She's the one who gave me this ship."

"You're on the right track, but the person I'm talking about never gives anyone anything, unless it's a one-way ticket out the airlock," said Three grimly. She took a drink of ice water and wiped her mouth on the sleeve of her red uniform. "Two hundred billion galaxies with billions of planets in each. Through all the infinite combinations possible in each dimension, there is only one constant. You. Me. Amy Armstrong. We're the spinning hub in every dimension: the basis point, center of the wheel, and patient zero. In some of these places, Amy Armstrong is a mousey, boring churchgoer who doesn't break the rules, in others she's a totally rad party girl, and in others ... in others, she's the stuff of nightmares, the boogey man, the story that scares children. Only she's real."

The floor vibrated.

"Surface contact, my Lady," said the ship. "Submersing to fifteen meters."

Amy stared at Three. "All these versions of me. Are you saying––"

"What the devil?!!" said Philip.

The dark-haired teenager stood in the open hatch staring at the young women with his mouth open. "Amy?"

"Philip!"

Three jumped up, ran across the kitchen, and threw her arms around Philip. She kissed him on the cheek with a wet smack.

"My word," said Philip. "I meant the other Amy."

"Three, let go of my boyfriend," said Amy dryly.

Her twin pulled back from Philip in reluctant, clingy stages, moving her hands away from his neck, down to his hands, and finally stepping back, her fingers the last to let go.

"Sorry," she said. "I just ... I didn't expect this. It's been a long time since ... never mind."

"She bears a remarkable resemblance to you, Amy," said Philip. "Perhaps a bit older and slightly taller. I saw that someone had come on board, but I never expected this."

Amy stood shoulder-to-shoulder with Three and crossed her arms. "You really can't tell the difference? Say that again and I'll throw something at you."

Philip smiled. "Of course I can tell the difference, my love. But please, could you explain?"

"What's to explain? She's a copy of me from another dimension."

"I'm certainly not a copy," said Three. "I'm my own person. Right, Philip?"

The teenager glanced down at Three's tight-fitting uniform and hurriedly brushed his hands down his spandex trousers as if he wanted to jam them into non-existent pockets.

"Umm ... quite so. One question, if I may. This seems absolutely impossible. Am I dreaming?"

Three smiled coyly and leaned forward. "Do you want to be?"

Amy stamped her foot. "Enough with the flirting already! Philip, I don't know why you're so shocked. Did you forget what happened in England?"

Philip nodded. "You're absolutely right, of course. So this is the Amy Armstrong for this dimension? The egg-shaped conveyance we brought on board doesn't seem to be from Earth, although I suppose it's possible."

"It's not my home," said Three. "Did you see orbital billboards on the way in, or a space elevator? I don't have a clue about this Earth, but it's definitely not where I'm from."

"She was telling me a story about escaping an evil Amy Armstrong," said Amy.

Philip nodded. "Sounds familiar. Didn't we do that last week?"

"I'm not just running from one Amy Armstrong," said Three quietly, and bowed her head. "I'm running from three."

Amy rested a hand on the teen's shoulder. "Finished with that sandwich? I'll show you more than three copies of us. Come on, both of you."

Philip and Three followed her through the ship to the memorial room filled with shelves of old objects under glass, and which contained a wall covered in faded photographs.

Amy stood in front of the wide assortment of paper, plastic, and digital images. "Hundreds of Amy Armstrongs," she whispered. "I'm sure some of them were nasty and maybe even kicked a cat once or twice."

"For sure," said Three, staring at the photos. "But nothing like the ones I know. They wouldn't tape anything to the wall unless it was to scare the crew."

"Pardon my ignorance," said Philip. "But I don't understand exactly what's going on."

"Me neither," said Amy. "Why are you running from these other Amy Armstrongs? They want you to join the Columbia Record Club or something?"

"Torture, more like," said Philip.

"That's what I said——the Columbia Record Club."

Three glanced between the two teenagers. She opened her mouth for a moment, trying to form the words, and then looked down at her bare feet.

"They want to destroy us. Completely."

A low tone sounded from the ceiling.

"Incoming hail on a low frequency wavelength," said the ship. "A request to open two-way communication."

"From who? This is old-timey California with cowboys and railroads and crap. Radio hasn't been invented."

"I am not certain of the proper response to that question, my Lady. To put it broadly, the message is from you."

EVERY SURFACE of the navigation room glowed deep blue from the artificial projection of the waters of the Monterey Bay. On the ceiling, the ocean's surface sparkled in a fainter shade, while long shadows moved in the holographic darkness below the floor.

Amy stepped through the hatch. "Spooky! Glad I can swim."

Behind her, Philip cleared his throat. "I'm afraid that when it comes to my particular case, that statement is not true."

Three elbowed the tall boy in the ribs. "What's the matter, Phil——afraid of getting naked? You Martians are all the same."

"Pardon me, but I'm from England, not Mars."

"Sorry. You talk exactly like a Martian. That's probably why I keep confusing you with him."

A long shape flashed across the walls from left to right.

"Was that a shark?" asked Amy.

"A bottle-nosed dolphin," said the ship.

Philip pointed at a similar shadow below his feet. "Another dolphin."

"That's a shark," said the ship.

"I hope it doesn't know how to open an airlock," said Amy. "Blanche, is this copy of me still broadcasting?"

"Yes, my Lady."

"I don't see any shark," said Three. "What the fox ears are you two talking about? This place has no decoration and barely any lights. Tape up some posters of Sailor Twit and hang a few lava lamps, is all I'm saying."

"The ship has a mental projection system," said Amy. "Called T.H.E.——Total Happiness Environment."

Three shrugged. "The dumb thing is broken. All I see are gray walls and a black table in the middle of the room."

A rectangular holoscreen materialized above the central console. The upper body of a woman appeared on the screen, framed by low-tech control panels covered in switches and old cathode-tube displays. Cats wearing headsets sat in front of the displays or moved behind the woman pressing switches. The woman seemed to be in her late forties or early fifties. The ends of her blonde hair touched her shoulders, was streaked with gray, and faint lines showed at the edges of her eyes and mouth. Her razor-sharp bangs, deep red lipstick, collared white shirt, and the confident way she stared at the camera gave the impression of a corporate executive, an image that sharply contrasted with the jagged pink scar that sliced down her pale face from forehead to chin. An artificial limb clicked and whirred from her right shoulder, taking the place of her flesh-and-blood arm. With silver mechanical parts and exposed wiring, the arm was more crude than any technology Amy had seen on the Lady's body. This woman was not the Lady, but even with makeup and the weathering effect of age, her face was still Amy's.

"My word," said Philip. "She's you."

"She's not us," said Three. "Maybe she started out the same as me, maybe not, but there's no way I'll turn out to be such an evil, back-stabbing control freak. And I'd never be caught dead wearing that outfit. It's so 'corporate vice president.'"

Philip leaned over the navigation console and stared at streams of data. "How are we receiving this? I thought the ocean provided a shielding effect."

"The audio transmission is on a low-frequency band," said the ship. "198 kHz. After detecting the broadcast, I found a limited video signal on a higher frequency."

Amy shrugged. "Her lips are moving but I don't hear any sound."

"Activating," said the ship.

"——is a dangerous criminal wanted in fourteen dimensions for violent acts of terrorism, sedition, and love crimes. Under the authority——"

Three hooted with laughter. "Listen to that! She's piling it high and wide this time."

"What's a love crime?" asked Amy.

"A crime of passion, I suppose," said Philip. "They have those in France."

Three giggled. "Oh, boy. It's when you do something bad——you know, like blowing up a building—— but because you had SO much fun doing it, some fat, stupid judge calls it a 'love crime' and he gives you ten extra years in the poke."

"Did you actually do any of these things?"

Three shrugged. "I've stabbed plenty of jerks and blown up a few space bars on the asteroid belt, if you know what I mean, but none of that terrorism crap she's blabbing on about."

Amy crossed her arms. "Right."

"What? She's just fishing for an easy catch. You don't get it! If she knew where this ship was, she'd fly in with cannons blazing. This one looks like us, but trust me——she's the Lady Hitler of all the Lady Hitlers in the universe!"

"——agree to meet at a planetfall location that is distant from any local culture in this time-dimension. An additional option is to deposit this Amy Armstrong on the surface, and contact my ship with the coordinates. As mentioned, the reward is twelve million mao of iridium bars transferred to any location you provide. If you can receive this message, respond immediately on this frequency."

"I'd rather not contact this individual," said Philip. "I don't know what a Lady Hitler would be, but it doesn't sound pleasant."

Amy rubbed the back of her neck and sighed. "Right. Doing nothing seems like the best option at this point."

Three punched the air. "Sweet!"

"Don't get cocky," said Amy. "If you stab any of my crew or steal a paper clip, I'll push you out an airlock myself. That goes double for love crimes."

"Yes, One––I mean, Amy. Captain Amy."

A bright circle appeared in the wall of deep blue ocean, and Sunflower trotted inside the navigation room.

"That stupid MacGuffin," grumbled the orange cat. "I don't see why you thought he was so smart. Still working on the transmat ... at ... at ..."

Sunflower stopped and stared open-jawed at the floating holoscreen.

"... at her ..."

"He hasn't met your double," said Philip. "Sunflower, allow me to introduce Three––a slightly older Amy, and on screen, Lady Hitler––an even older Amy."

"Her ..." whispered Sunflower, his yellow eyes still locked on the screen.

Amy knelt beside the cat. "Snap out of it! You should have expected one of my twins to show up sooner or later. It was your job to travel through dimensions."

"Not her," whispered the cat, still staring at the screen. "Her."

"That's what I'm talking about. That's a copy of me, just much, much older."

"Not HER her," growled Sunflower. "Her!"

On the holoscreen, a shorthaired gray cat wearing a headset stood behind the fifty-something twin of Amy, constantly blinking and clasping and unclasping her front paws.

Three laughed. "The gray cat? She's a nobody; a personal assistant."

Sunflower dashed to the central console and slapped the top surface. "Where are they? Open a channel now!"

Amy held up a hand. "Stop! Blanche, disable all radio traffic. Sunflower, we're not going to talk with her or broadcast our location. She could be dangerous."

Sunflower looked up from the controls. "Dangerous? She's my wife!"

"Ah, yes," said Philip. "I see the misunderstanding––he's talking about the cat."

"Andy Nakamura? That's impossible."

Philip pointed at Three. "Quite so, dear, but I said that only a few minutes ago when I met this one."

The blonde teenager shrugged. "You might be right. She could be called Nakamura or something like that. We kidnap––I mean, pick up cats from every dimension, so it's hard to tell. Anyway, they all look the same to me."

"You stupid, specist Centaurans," growled Sunflower. "Give me back the controls! That's my wife. You know it, I know it, and even this taller, better-looking version of you knows it."

Amy shook her head. "Better looking? The Lady said––in front of all of us––that Andy Nakamura disappeared without trace. I know it's hard to accept, but this cat is just a copy of your wife, if anything."

"She's definitely something and you're wrong!"

Sunflower darted out of the room.

"Awkward," said Three. "Anyone for a snack? I just realized I didn't finish lunch. Philip?"

"You two do what you want," said Amy. "I'm going to check on the repair job."

3

The gigantic steel tiger lay dormant in the cargo hold, blunt gray head resting on its front paws. Even when lying prone it was taller than a man, and stretched from nose to tail longer than a box truck from Old Earth. Black stripes down its flanks and a blood-red paw print on the shoulder identified the machine as a former unit of "The Reds"––the emperor's elite First Armored Brigade. A web of steel cables held it to the diamond-patterned floor of the cargo hold, as if someone were afraid the feline-shaped vehicle would wake from its slumber and escape. To the left of the huge machine stood Nistra's rectangular cargo container, and to the left of that, the escape pod in which Three had arrived, both held to the floor and walls with the same type of steel cables.

The circular hatch spiraled open and Sunflower stepped inside the cargo hold. The orange tabby turned and watched the corridor behind him for a moment, and then trotted to the armored cat. He stood on his hind legs and pressed a switch concealed in the neck of the giant machine.

Servos whined and tight cables creaked as the blunt head lifted and revealed a clear, curved window where the mouth would be on a real tiger, between fierce white fangs painted on the nose. With a heavy click, the head split horizontally below the window and opened to a forty-five degree angle. Inside the small and narrow cockpit sat a pair of seats in tandem, both sized for cats.

Sunflower slid into the rear seat and rapidly flipped switches. A red glow and a faint hum filled the cockpit as control panels flickered and shone with pinpoints of light. A half-dozen rectangular holographic displays materialized above the front and rear control panels.

"Good morning, navigator," said a male voice with a serious, military tone. "No pilot detected. Would you like me to scan the local area for pilot, starting with space bars, holo-theaters, and clip joints?"

"No, no, no," said Sunflower, and lowered his voice to a murmur. "Holy Saint Fluffy, I hate automated systems."

"Would you like me to spin up turbines? You are not a pilot; it is understandable you would not be aware of the most basic of steps in the pre-flight sequence."

"Disable auto start, disable voice prompts," hissed Sunflower.

"How can voice prompt notify navigator I am disabled if voice prompt must activate to notify navigator I am disabled?"

"What kind of refurbished, dropped-at-the-factory junk are you? Don't say one more word or I'll rip out your central processor and turn you into a refrigerator thermostat!"

"How dare you—my mother WAS a refrigerator thermostat. It's a good job."

Sunflower shook his furry orange head and sighed. "Now I see why they gave me this one."

He stuck his paws into wide tubes set in the control panel, and began to flip the holographic display through several screens of information, stopping at a bright green, horizontal line.

"Now to find the right channel," he murmured. "It was in the megahertz band ... one-ninety something."

"Hey, Sunnie!"

The familiar voice caused Sunflower to jump and bang his head on the ceiling of the cockpit. Betsy's brown-and-white head and floppy ears poked into the opening below the curved front window.

"Whatcha doing?"

"Number one—-I'm busy, and number two—-none of your business."

Betsy giggled. "You said number two."

Static crackled through the cockpit speakers, and the straight green line on the holographic display changed to a violent up-and-down squiggle.

"Under the authority given to me by the Centauran planetary government, I am authorized to arrest the individual known as Amelia Earhart Armstrong for the express purpose of transporting her to a detention facility on Alpha Centauri. Individuals providing information leading to her capture will be awarded twelve million mao or a lifetime supply of space burgers, dependent upon availability. Respond on this frequency—-"

"That sounds like Amy," said Betsy. "But old, like her mom."

"Quiet," said Sunflower, and leaned close to the controls. "This is Sunflower of the *White Star*. Can you hear me?"

"Yes," said Betsy. "Why are you whispering?"

"Shut up for one second, will you? Broadcasting source, can you read me? This is Sunflower of the *White Star*. Please respond."

Betsy climbed into the cockpit and shoved his furry rear into the seat in front of Sunflower.

"I know what you're doing! You want that lifetime supply of space burgers. Amy's my friend and I want the burgers!"

"That's not what I'm doing, you idiot."

"Good morning, pilot," said the male voice of the armored cat's computer. "Would you like to begin the start-up sequence? I'm ready to spin up turbines."

"No, thank you," said Betsy. "I'm talking to Sunnie and we're about to eat space burgers."

"Acknowledged. Start-up suspended."

Sunflower groaned. "Can both of you geniuses please be quiet?"

The speakers crackled and a squiggly blue line flashed across the holographic display.

"Sunnie, are you there?" whispered a female voice.

"Andy! It's me!"

"Don't talk! Switch to encrypted channel 192."

Sunflower moved his paws in the control tubes. The holographic display changed to a full-color video feed of a gray shorthaired cat with a black headset over her ears and the pipe of a small microphone in front of her whiskers.

"Sunnie! Is it really you?"

"I want to ask you the same question," said Sunflower. "Are you a copy, or are you the real Andy Nakamura?"

"I'm not important enough to be anything," whispered the cat. "I was snatched up by these horrible fake copies of the Lady and I never thought I'd see you again."

"Ask her about the burgers," said Betsy.

"Shut up."

Andy's yellow eyes widened. "What did you say? That's how you treat a wife trapped in another dimension that you haven't seen for a year? My mother was right about you and your hippie family!"

Sunflower sighed. "Dear, I was talking to a dog, not you. A stupid, stupid dog."

"I'm okay with being stupid," said Betsy. "I don't get blamed for anything."

"Oh! I hear his voice now," said Andy. "He sounds nice. Sorry about that thing with my mother."

Sunflower shook his furry head. "What are your coordinates? I'm coming to get you."

"You can't do that! Just leave, Sunnie. Get out of this system before they kill all of you!"

"Not without you, Andy. Do you know how long I've been looking for you?"

The holographic display flickered. Sunflower's wife disappeared, replaced by the face of the older, scar-faced version of Amy.

"Well, well, well," mused One. "What do we have here? A reunion of star-crossed lovers. Or shall I say, traitors? Thank you for allowing me to triangulate your location. With the few precious minutes of freedom you have left before my fleet arrives, I suggest you power down your systems and prepare to surrender. After all, we don't want the husband of dear Andy Nakamura to be violently murdered, do we? That would mean it wasn't true love the whole time."

The video feed snapped off.

"That makes me sad," said Betsy. The small dog rested his chin on the cushioned back of the front seat and stared at Sunflower. "Not a word about burgers."

Sunflower pulled his paws out of the control tubes and sighed.

"Aw, poop."

A metallic whoosh came from outside the armored cat.

"Someone's coming," hissed Sunflower. "Watch your tail, I'm closing the cockpit."

"Got it," whispered Betsy. "This is fun! We're like secret agents."

Sunflower moved his paws inside the control tubes and the fiercely-painted jaws of the armored cat whined shut. The blunt head silently lowered down to the paws on the cargo deck.

Nistra froze in mid-stride and stared at the giant steel tiger.

"Could have sworn that thing moved," he murmured. "Need to get my prescription checked when I get back to Kepler Prime."

The large sauropod walked to the cargo container. He stuck a crowbar into the side of the container and pulled back on the metal bar, straining his huge, scaly arms to try and pry the door open.

Inside the escape pod on the other side of the cargo hold, a digital timer continued to count down.

PHILIP BUMPED against the wall of the kitchen, his hands raised in surrender.

"I did not say that, Miss Three. Please behave yourself and stop being outrageous!"

The older twin of Amy touched Philip's chest and rubbed the slick spandex of his uniform.

"Stop being so shy," she said with a smile. "I'm taller and better-looking than her. If you're worried about getting caught, just say you were confused. Pretty girls always get a man confused, everyone knows that." She wound an arm around Philip's neck and pushed her face close to his. "How about my eyes? Are they just as blue?"

"Miss Three, this is scandalous!"

"Think so? I'll show you scandalous."

In a flash, Three pulled her stretchy red top over her head and tossed it across the kitchen. She shook out her curly blonde hair, put both hands on her waist, and pulled back her shoulders.

"I'm a real woman, not a girl," she whispered.

Philip stared at the tank top and the tattoos up and down Three's muscular arms.

"Miss Three, it pains me to say this, but I have the feeling that you're not a very good person."

Three waved at the orchids and Chinese characters on her arms.

"What––because of these? Everyone has them where I'm from."

"Not at all. It's your behavior. You're simply far too aggressive for a young woman."

Three gave him a broad, nose-wrinkling smile. "I know! It's great, isn't it? Bad is rad and stuff." She flexed her arms. "Let's not waste time, honey. I'm a girl, you're a boy, let's you and me give it a whirl."

"You and I."

"What?"

"You and I give it a whirl, not you and me."

Three furiously grabbed Philip's uniform top with both hands and kissed him hard on the lips.

Philip pushed her away. "I beg of you, please stop!" He backed across the room, keeping the dining table between himself and Three.

"Stop what? Just let it happen," said Amy's twin, and banged on the table with both fists. "Everyone loves a bad girl, especially good boys!"

The hatch spiraled open with a swish of air, and Amy stepped in from the corridor. She stopped and stared at the pair of teenagers.

"What's going on here?"

Philip cleared his throat. "I, um ... simply having lunch, dear."

"Why does Three have her top off?"

"Um ..."

"Because it's really hot in here," said Amy's twin, a smirk on her face. "Right, Philip?"

The teenager turned red. "Quite."

"Strange," said Amy. "I thought the temperature was self-adjusting. I wonder if it has something to do with the transmat drive. MacGuffin is still holed up in there banging on it and won't give me any clear answers."

Philip nodded. "Very likely."

Amy crossed the room and touched Philip's lower lip with an index finger.

"Did the 'really hot' temperature kiss you on the mouth?" she asked, rubbing red lipstick between her finger and thumb. "That's not very likely, is it?"

"Ah," said the dark-haired boy. "No, it's not, but I'm entirely innocent. She attacked me!"

Three spread her arms wide. "What a monster! I would never betray the sisterhood like that. He pushed me against the wall!"

Philip stared at her. "I beg your pardon?"

"I'll ask Blanche," said Amy. "She watches everything. Hey, Blanche!"

"My Lady, we are being hailed."

Amy shrugged. "It's that repeating broadcast. I said to ignore it."

"This is on a different frequency, my Lady. From the beam variance, it appears to originate from a craft bearing twenty-seven degrees and traveling one-hundred twenty two meters per second."

"She's still fishing," said Three. "If you say anything over the airwaves, she'll know our location."

"That information is no longer secret," said the ship. "Our coordinates are included in the broadcast."

"Show me," said Amy.

A holographic screen appeared in mid-air and displayed the scar-faced, older version of Amy.

"This is Captain Armstrong of the *Hare Twist*, approaching your position of thirty-six point seven two six six seven by negative one twenty-two point zero five five. Respond immediately."

"Are those our coordinates?" asked Amy.

"Indeed, my Lady."

"Give me a microphone or something. I want to talk to her."

Three stared at Amy. "What?"

"She knows where we are. How can it hurt?"

"I don't know if this is wise," said Philip. "I thought we wanted to avoid contact. We should leave the area post-haste."

Three nodded. "What he said!"

"We ARE going to leave," said Amy. "Just let me talk to my dimensional twin for a second. It's not every day you meet one of 'em."

Three blinked. "Um ... hello?"

"Two of 'em. Blanche, is the connection ready?"

"Yes, my Lady."

Amy brushed blonde hair back from her face and straightened the front of her pink blouse.

"This is Amy Armstrong of the *White Star*. Can you hear me?"

The image of the scar-faced woman flickered. She leaned forward, her eyes wide and red lips parted.

"I can, child, I can," she whispered. "So young and so lovely ... was I ever like you? Full of energy and promise, daylight and dreams? Old age has worn away the memories, like pebbles in the river of time."

Three crossed her arms and grumbled quietly to herself. "Lovely? What a load of crap."

Amy chopped a hand down. "Skip the philosophy, and tell me what you want."

The scar-faced woman smiled. "Direct and to the point, just like the rest of us. Miss Armstrong, I would like nothing more than to invite you and the sister copy standing behind you to have dinner on my ship, the *Hare Twist*."

Three stamped her foot. "It's a trap!"

"I assure you, dear sister, it is nothing of the kind."

Amy shook her head. "What about these stories about kidnapping Three? From the list of charges and 'love crimes' you've been broadcasting I expect that at the end of dinner, you'll want to slap a pair of hand-cuffs on her."

The scar-faced woman smiled grimly. "We are not so medieval as that, but you are very perceptive for your age. What are you? Sixteen? Seventeen?"

"Fourteen."

"Remarkable. In any case, the young woman you know as Three has a large Centauran bounty on her head and must be returned to the planetary authori-ties."

"Thanks for the offer, but I'll pass. Three reminds me of a wild animal and might be trying to steal my boyfriend, but I sort of like her. She reminds me of me."

The scar-faced woman leaned back and crossed one leg over the other. "A funny girl, I see. How about a swap? I trade you a cat that one of your crew claims is his wife, and you give me the Centauran criminal."

Amy glanced at Philip and Three. "His wife? That's why Sunflower was so upset. He tried to con-tact her, didn't he?"

The scar-faced woman shrugged. "Names are ir- relevant at this point. Before you reject my offer with another pithy, off-hand comment, be aware that I am known as 'One' among the rest of the sisters. I am al- pha and omega; the first and the last. I have out- smarted, out-charmed, and out-fought more queens, generals, and mercenaries across more dimensions than you can imagine. I have plans upon plans ready and waiting for any action you take. Make it easy on yourself and accept my invitation to dinner."

"Four craft rapidly approaching from bearing twenty-eight, my Lady," said the ship.

Amy made a slicing gesture across her throat. "Cut the transmission, Blanche! Get us to orbit."

The holographic screen disappeared. Silverware and plates rattled in the sink as the entire kitchen be- gan to vibrate.

Three gave Amy a tight hug. "Thanks for trusting me, sister."

"Promise me you won't smear any more lipstick on Philip, and we're even."

"But he's so cute!"

Philip cleared his throat and walked rapidly to- ward the hatch.

"I believe my attention is required by matters on the opposite side of the ship," he said.

THE DISPLAY ZOOMED into a long, barracuda- shaped craft framed against the black surface of the midnight ocean. As it rose into the sky, waves burst over it and white streams of moonlit water cascaded from the hull of the silver ship.

A black cat wearing a headset over his furry ears pointed at the display.

"There she is, Captain! Have you ever seen a ship like that? With those engines, I bet she goes like lightning."

The scar-faced copy of Amy frowned. "Thank you, Wilson, but I don't pay you for your opinion."

The black cat shrugged. "You don't pay me at all, actually."

"What an impertinent thing to say. Remind me again why I haven't locked you in a punishment cube?"

Wilson held up a paw. "Because one——you just threw Andy Nakamura in a punishment cube, and two——I'm the only other cat on this ship who knows anything about anything. Nobody else wants to be your first officer!"

One sighed and rubbed her eyes. On the display screen, the silver craft picked up speed, its narrow hull skimming above the waves.

"Activate the rescue teams and salvage drones," said One. "Hold on tight, Amy Armstrong. This is going to hurt you more than it hurts me."

"Ugh," said Wilson. "So cliché."

"Shut up."

One pressed a button on the arm of her command chair. A thin bar swiped back and forth across the display.

"That's the camera cleaner, my Lady," said the black cat. "I'm guessing you actually want to activate the secret thingy? That's the button to the left. The one covered by a plastic shield? No, the other button. You almost pressed the drive flush——I can't tell you how BAD that would have been."

"This one?"

"Yes! Finally."

One flipped up a small plastic cover and stabbed a red button. The silver ship on the screen disappeared in a blinding flash.

SUNFLOWER STOPPED in the midst of cleaning his furry face with a paw.

"Seriously, Betsy. Start acting like a dog that cost the Lady millions of mao in cybernetic implants, instead of a fizz-brained *kribich* who just fell off the plate."

The brown and white terrier whined. "But I'm bored, Sunnie."

"We can't leave until sergeant poona breath is done playing with his cargo container. Saint Mittens knows how long that will take. It doesn't matter because I don't want anyone to know I was down here."

"I know you're down here!"

"You'll forget about it the minute I mention 'space burgers.'"

"Ooo! Space burgers. Do you think I'll win some?"

"Definitely," said Sunflower, and went back to cleaning his fur.

"But Sunnie——how long is a lifetime supply?"

"A couple of days, in your case."

"That's awesome!"

The terrier yawned and began sniffing around the tiny cockpit. He reached down to the floor and pulled out a green pilot's helmet.

"Look what I found!" Betsy stuck his furry head into the helmet and fastened a strap under his chin. "See, it fits."

"Fantastic."

Betsy turned forward and faced the control panel. "These are almost the same as my bomber controls. I bet I could fly this thing, too."

"It doesn't fly," said Sunflower. "Cat armor runs and cat armor jumps. No flying."

"Sounds the same. Computer, power up electrics."

The small control panel flickered to life and a curving slice of holographic displays materialized in front of the terrier, displaying engine data and status of systems on the armored cat.

"Stop," hissed Sunflower. "I turned it off for a reason."

"Welcome, pilot," said the voice of the flight computer. "Welcome, navigator."

"Hi!" barked Betsy.

"Thank you for wearing a protective helmet, pilot. Navigator is not in compliance with Imperial regulations for wearing a protective helmet. Would you like a protective helmet to be provided to the navigator?"

"Yes!" barked Betsy.

A metal arm jerked down and squashed a red flight helmet over Sunflower's furry head. This would have been fine, if it weren't for the fact that the helmet was facing backwards.

"Idiot machine!" came the muffled voice of Sunflower, as he pulled and scratched at the sides. "Get it off!"

"Navigator is attempting to communicate, but I cannot understand," said the flight computer, a hint of amusement in its electronic voice.

Betsy searched the front seat. "Where are the belts? Safety first, you know."

"Deploying harness restraints," said the computer.

Strips of bright red fabric emerged from the top and bottom of the seat and clicked into a metal buckle at Betsy's furry chest. In the back seat, the webbing pulled Sunflower's paws from his helmet and wrapped him in a tight cocoon.

"I can't move!" he yelled. "I can't see and I can't move! Take this thing off, you stupid motherless garbage can!"

Betsy flipped the sun visor up and down on the front of his helmet. "Sunnie, that's not a very nice thing to say. Do you think it's a nice thing to say, computer?"

"I have no opinion on the matter," said the electronic voice. "But I agree with the pilot."

"Gah!" yelled Sunflower. "I'll take both of you apart, piece by piece!"

Betsy giggled. "Say please and I'll let you out."

"Please!"

"I can't hear you ..."

A deafening boom threw the cat and dog hard against their restraints, their pilot helmets bouncing in all directions as the world spun in circles of gray and black. After a second impact, the cockpit window was covered in dark blue water and trails of tiny bubbles.

"Explosive impact on port flank," said the flight computer. "Negative damage. Negative sealant leak. Low oxygen environment present. Recommend battery power."

"That was fun," said Betsy. "Can we do it again?"

"What in the name of Saint Fluffy and his seven lives just happened?" hissed Sunflower's muffled voice. "Did a stupid little dog in the pilot's seat accidentally shoot off micro-missiles and blow up the entire ship?"

"If I see a stupid little dog, I'll ask him," said Betsy. "I don't know what happened, but I think we're upside down."

A thruster fired, turning the armored cat upright, and the steel claws sank into the muddy ocean floor.

"Inertial movement halted," said the flight computer.

"Now I have to look for that other dog," said Betsy. "Do you think he's outside?"

Sunflower sighed. "Please get this helmet off my face."

Betsy leaned toward the glass and stared as hundreds of yellow fish with black vertical stripes swam past the cockpit.

"Hey, Sunnie ... does this thing swim?"

THE BLAST threw Amy against the ceiling. She fell back to the kitchen floor with a painful smack, her arms around her head. Three had tumbled against the nearby wall and lay crumpled with hands pressed to her side. She winced under a mess of blonde hair over her face.

Locker doors had burst open, spilling pans and boxes of dried food over the diamond-patterned metal deck. A series of high-pitched beeps pealed from somewhere, and the light from the overhead panels had changed from pale white to deep crimson. The floor shivered and the entire ship pitched unevenly in all directions.

"Blanche! What's going on?!!"

"Detonation in cargo hold. Starboard impeller compromised. Third bulkhead compromised. All crew abandon ship. Repeat, all crew abandon ship."

A line of tiny red lights flashed on the deck, forming arrows that pointed to the corridor.

"I don't believe it," groaned Three. "She's trying to kill me!"

Amy helped the girl to her feet. "Why are you surprised? You said she was Lady Hitler."

"Yeah, but she's not supposed to kill me!"

"Welcome to the club, because I don't want to die either. Blanche, where's Philip?"

"All crew abandon ship. Repeat——"

Three groaned. "Even your ship has abandoned ship. Where's the shuttle craft?"

"We don't have one."

"How about escape pod? Let's go!"

"Um ..."

Three stood and hobbled across the vibrating deck. "This is your ship, and you don't know where the escape pods are?"

Amy grabbed Three under the arm and helped her walk to the exit. "I didn't expect to use them!"

"Talk about a death trap," murmured Three. "This place is worse than the bucket of bolts One flies around in. Wait! Let me grab my makeup kit." She stuffed the small black case in a cargo pocket.

Outside the kitchen the gray walls of the corridor gleamed red in the emergency light.

"Projection system is off," said Amy.

"That's not our biggest problem, sister! Where's that water coming from?"

Water sloshed and foamed at the far end of the corridor. As they watched, Philip sprinted around a corner and splashed through the flood toward them.

"Philip!" shouted Amy and Three together, and both waved at him.

The dark-haired teen slid to a stop in front of the girls. He was bare-footed and his red uniform was completely soaked.

"Are you hurt?" he asked. "Doesn't matter—follow me!"

The deck pitched left and right and an inch of pale blue water swirled around the feet of the teenagers. Three had a sudden recovery of health, and both girls chased after Philip.

"What happened?" Amy yelled after him. "Was it a missile?"

"Don't think so," shouted Philip over his shoulder. "It was the cargo we took on board at Tau Ceti or that escape pod. That's my guess!"

"Don't blame me!" yelled Three, as she splashed through the water beside Amy. "I'm not stupid enough to blow up your dumb spaceship when I'm inside!"

The line of blinking red lights led them to the port-side airlock. Philip slapped the center of the circular hatch and helped the two girls inside. Water swirled around his calves as the hatch shut behind him, silencing the bubbling roar of water and squeals of tearing metal from the corridor.

"What about the others?" asked Amy. She felt her entire body start to shiver from cold or fright or something, and crossed her arms to try and hold it in.

Philip hugged her tight. "I thought Nick was in our bedroom, but I couldn't find her. I don't know about everyone else. I hope they find an airlock."

"The ship can float, right?"

The deck tilted wildly, and the teenagers grabbed for handholds along the curved walls.

"There's your answer," said Three. "What now, Philip? Hold hands and kiss until the air runs out? I call first!"

Philip shook his head. "We have to escape and swim to safety. How that happens, I have no idea."

Amy began opening the narrow cabinets around the circular chamber. "This is an airlock, right? It's got to have spacesuits or oxygen or something!"

Philip opened a locker and held out a small red cylinder with an attached mask. "Found something."

"Only one?" asked Three.

"Don't worry, I found your suit," said Amy. She tossed the red pressure suit and clear bubble helmet to Three.

Metal groaned and the floor pitched at a sharp angle. Philip handed the red cylinder with the mask to Amy.

"There's no time!" he said, and turned a bright orange handle near the wall. Water began to fill the airlock. "The ship is sinking fast! You have to leave now, or you'll never make it to the surface. Two people can share the oxygen."

Amy grabbed his arm. "I'm not leaving without you!"

"Philip, don't do it!" yelled Three.

Water swirled around their waists, tinted red from the emergency lights. Philip pushed the pair toward the outside hatch.

"I'll get out another way!" he yelled, and pulled the lever to open the hatch. "I love you, Amy! Don't give up!"

"No!" shouted Amy. A blast of freezing water hit her in the face, and something pushed her into the deep blue emptiness outside the ship.

The long silver craft sank toward the depths, streaming bubbles like a wounded fish. Amy swam as hard as she could at a right angle, to escape the suction caused by the massive object. Her vision pulsed red, and a hand pressed a mask over her face. Amy sucked in a lungful of air and gave the air cylinder back to Three. Below their feet the silver ship faded into the black depths, leaving the pair of teenagers surrounded in a haze of sapphire nothingness. Amy and Three swam up, toward the lighter part of nothing.

4

The tiny air cylinder died, the last traces of oxygen fizzing dryly into Amy's mouth. She let it tumbled into the deep nothingness of the ocean depths and kicked for the surface. Beside her, Three swam up just as hard, her tattooed arms pulling at the cold water.

A pair of bright points flickered above the struggling teenagers. The lights glowed yellow and red like the eyes of a devil, one that seemed to laugh as it looked down at the pair of desperately swimming girls.

Amy's heart pounded in her ears and her chest burned for air. The recent past flashed before her eyes: walking with Philip in Hyde Park, meeting his mother, feeling his strong hands around her before the explosion in the quarry. She felt the churn of Three's arms in the ocean nearby, and swam harder.

The eyes of the devil bounced and winked, close enough to touch. Amy reached up and a mesh of white string twisted around her fingers. She pulled away, but the cords wrapped around her wrists and arms. Amy thrashed in the cold water for a moment, but her arms and legs turned numb and wouldn't move. Everything turned dark.

She woke to the splash of waves against wood, the quiet murmur of a man's voice, and the creak of ropes being pulled tight. Her fingers touched wood and she realized that she lay on rough planking at the bottom of a boat. A heap of white fishing net covered her arms and waist, and a pair of strange figures were framed against the night sky. One of the men reached over the gunwale of the narrow boat and lifted a cage of embers that turned his face orange. The man was Asian in appearance: almond eyes, black hair, and oval face.

He wore a close-fitting black cap and a plain brown jacket that fastened down the front with knotted bits of cotton instead of buttons.

The man glanced down at Amy and blurted a string of incomprehensible words. She shook her head.

"Ship?" asked the man in a thick accent. "Ship gone?"

Amy sat up from the boards. "Yes! My friends. Please help them!"

The Asian man nodded and spoke to another figure standing in the bow. The two men untangled Amy, and then leaned over the sides and pulled more of the long fishing net into the boat. A pair of glowing metal cages hung over the left and right sides on wooden poles. The men doused the cages in the ocean with a hiss and set the steaming metal cylinders beside Amy's feet. The fisherman in the rear of the boat lifted a pair of oars into the gunwales. He turned his back to Amy and used the long wooden bars to pull against the ocean.

As the man rowed, a handful of orange lights rose and fell with the gentle roll of the sea. A brilliant horizontal beam flashed through the dark. The beam rotated around in a dozen seconds and Amy realized it was a lighthouse. To the left of the bright signal lay the scattered glow of dozens of blue-tinged lights, but that was the only clue that anything existed in the entire universe outside of these two fishermen.

Amy cupped her hands around her mouth. "Philip!"

The fisherman in the bow touched Amy's shoulder and pointed at one of the other wooden boats. It rowed closer and Amy saw the drenched figure of Three sitting on a wooden crate, waving both arms.

Her hair was plastered to her head and darkened to black by the water.

"Hey, sister!" yelled Three. "Are you okay?"

Amy sank back onto the pile of nets without responding and hugged her knees tight. Not because she was cold--somehow the nanites in her clothing had warmed up and dried her blouse and skirt--but because she was scared.

The Asian fisherman in the bow reached back and wrapped a thin blanket around Amy that smelled entirely of dead fish.

For a few minutes there was only the sound of the waves slapping against the wooden hull and the oars dipping into the sea. A distant thrum from the eastern side of the bay grew in volume, burbling and deep-throated like a gigantic mechanical frog. The fisherman at the rear paused in his rowing and pointed into the darkness.

"Big fish," he said. "Find ship."

Hoots of excitement occasionally broke through the slap of oars in the water, but Amy couldn't understand what the Asian men were saying, and the other boats were too far away to see what they had found.

"Friends?" she asked the rower.

He shook his head. "Treasure. Floating thing."

The man in the front yelled and reached over the side. He held up a clear plastic bag full of puffy white cylinders.

"Marshdevils," said Amy. "Definitely not treasure. Do not eat."

Long, sustained thunder rolled across the sky from west to east. The fishermen continued searching for a few moments, but after another strange rumble, lifted oars, spun their wooden boats, and pulled for the lights of shore.

Amy struggled to sit up. "What are you doing? We have to stay here and find my friends!"

"Bad," said the man in the bow, and pointed at the sky. "Storm bad. Home want go."

"It's not a storm, it's a spaceship!"

The man nodded. "Ship sink. Storm bad."

Amy sank down and lay on her side on the wet boards.

"Not a storm," she whispered.

THE BLACK CAT raced through greasy, cramped corridors that smelled of stale lubricating oil, dodging teams of dog engineers and a platoon of cat soldiers with gray packs and rifles across their backs. He paced in circles in front of a metal hatch while a cat guard unlocked and pulled it open, and jumped into the noise and light of the command center.

"We found a survivor, my Lady!" he blurted.

From the comfortable position of her command chair, One stared at the cat and then crossed her legs.

"I know that, you pan-faced idiot," she said, and pointed to the wall of displays. "We've got cameras everywhere on this ship. We finally caught that disgusting pig, MacGuffin."

The black cat Wilson blinked for a moment. "He's a cat and not a pig, my Lady. It's a common mistake, as a wet feline looks the same as a gigantic hamster who is also wet."

"You know what I mean, you thick-headed stream of lizard vomit!"

Wilson bowed. "Of course, my Lady. I simply had to see for myself."

"How about the diffraction screen? Is it still operational?"

Wilson jumped to a nearby control panel and tapped the display with his furry paws.

"Yes, my Lady. Our recovery efforts will be hidden from the local humans. Not absolutely necessary, as their technology has barely advanced past the wheel." The cat chuckled. "Think about it--they don't even have radar!"

One brushed her gray-streaked blonde hair over an ear and jabbed a button on her armrest.

"Two and Four, report in. How's the recovery?"

A pair of large displays showing the dark Pacific coast flickered and two versions of Amy Armstrong flashed into view--a blonde in her thirties and a twenty-something Amy with dark hair and a black turtleneck.

"We've raised the ship to the surface," said the blonde copy. "The flotation devices are working properly, and drainage should be complete within a few hours."

"Good. Comb it from top to bottom for anything useful. Four? Any more survivors?"

The black-haired twin of Amy glanced away from the screen for a moment.

"My rescue team has found a human body in a pressure suit," she said. "Hare Twist is stamped across the shoulder."

"Is it Three?"

Four shook her head. "Male. From the height and weight I think it's--"

One jumped from her command chair. "Don't say it! Have the rescue team bring him to the ventral pressure lock."

"But it's my turn," said the black-haired Amy. "You had the last Philip! We talked about this--it's been months since I had any fun."

One spread the fingers of her mechanical right hand and examined the chrome tips of the sharp, talon-like fingers.

"I didn't say I was going to do anything to him. I'll talk to the boy, and if he doesn't have anything interesting to say, I'll send him over. At least try not to murder him in the first five minutes like the last one. Not that I care one way or the other, it's just extremely messy to put a body in the transfuser that's been abused like that."

Four scowled and jabbed something in front of her. Her image on the display screen snapped to black.

The older blonde version of Amy on the other screen shook her head. "She's got a temper, that one, but can you blame her? Tragic."

One pointed a mechanical finger at the blonde. "Keep working on the recovery of that ship, Two, or you'll be the tragic figure."

With a squeak of leather, she stood from her command chair and walked briskly out of the control center. The black cat Wilson followed her at a gallop.

"What's the point of keeping another human?" he asked as One ducked through security hatches. "He'll cause problems!"

One waved dismissively. "Don't have a kitten, Wilson. It's just a bit of fun. Trust me, this human will be dumped out a pressure lock before the day is over——whoever or whatever he is."

A cat guard spun the wheel on the last security hatch and pulled it open. A steady breeze of salt and the ocean blew into the faces of One and her feline assistant. Both covered their ears against the deafening crash of waves and the roar of powerful engines.

The sounds came from a three-meter, circular opening in the deck. A taut steel cable swayed in the center of the opening and was connected to a spinning cylindrical hoist above their heads. Three white cats in yellow wetsuits stood at a small control panel at the wall. All saluted One and turned back to the controls.

The steel cable lifted a beagle in a red wetsuit and scuba mask through the opening, right above the dangling limbs of a human body in an orange pressure suit and fogged-up bubble helmet. Both were attached to the cable by a fluorescent yellow rescue sling. The arms and legs of the human hung down limply and dripped with ocean water. As the beagle and his human cargo cleared the deck, the circular opening to the outside world spiraled shut, silencing the powerful roar of waves and thrusters with an oily click.

One clapped sharply. "Get that suit off! Where's the LifePack?"

The three white cats unclipped the lifeless body from the cable and helped the beagle lower him to the deck. They twisted the helmet and pulled it off, revealing Philip's pale face as water poured from the bottom. The teenager's dark hair was plastered to his ghostly gray skin, his mouth was open in a slack-jawed expression, and his eyes were closed.

One knelt beside Philip and touched the boy's forehead gently, using the human fingers of her left hand. She stared at his face for a few seconds, as if forgetting where she was, then jerked her head up and glared at the white cats.

"LifePack!"

A cat slammed a large orange box on the deck and pulled out a nest of colored wires and giant stickers from the side. The limp body became a swirl of activity as hands and paws exposed Philip's chest and slapped, poked, and dug needles into the limp body of the teenager.

The beagle had pulled off his breathing mask and oxygen tank. He stood with a paw over a large button on the face of the orange box.

"Stand clear! Watch that puddle!"

One and all the cats moved back. The beagle punched the button and Philip's entire body jumped as all of his muscles contracted. He coughed and wheezed. The cats lifted his arm and rolled him to his side, where he vomited a stream of water.

"Vital signs normal," said the beagle. "Wait! Let me check––yes, normal for a human."

Wilson twitched his furry black ears. "What's that sound? Does anyone hear that?"

"You're having a flashback," said One. "I just pulled you out of a punishment cube. It does things to a cat's brain, which is sort of the point."

The beagle raised a paw. "I hear it, too! A female scream, but from far, far away, as if a thousand souls cried out for justice and were suddenly silenced. Justice ... raaah."

One stared open-mouthed, and shook her head slowly. "I hear a wet dog who really, really wants to see the inside of a punishment cube."

Wilson stood on his hind legs and waved his paws over his head excitedly. "He's moving!"

The orange sleeve of Philip's pressure suit bounced up and down, causing his limp arm to slap his side with a wet smack. A bulge in the shiny material squirmed up his arm to the shoulder, and a tiny woman in red spandex shot from the neck opening, her wings buzzing like an angry dragonfly.

"Are you people insane?" she yelled, pointing at the blonde hair plastered across her face and neck. "It took me ages to get this hair right, and you come along and ruin it!"

One stared at the tiny flying creature. "What the five suns is that?"

"I'm a sprite, and the best gem specialist this side of Gliese. Right, Philly-Billy?" Nick glanced down at the motionless body of Philip. "You killed him!" she screamed. Her tiny face turned red. "I'll murder every stupid person on this entire stupid ship!"

She buzzed and bounced around the room, kicking at eyes and pulling fur. The cats and beagle frantically scrambled into action, knocking over equipment and crashing into each other in an effort to catch the lightning-fast, flying woman.

"Watch it!" yelled One. "Grab it. Over there! Don't open the hatch, you fool. She'll get into the ship! And now it's gone. Don't stand there gaping at me, you globs of steaming cow spit––go catch that thing, whatever it is!"

After a series of effusive bows and hasty saluting, her feline assistant Wilson, the three cats, and the beagle dashed out of the airlock.

One shook her head and sighed as the hatch closed. She turned back to the soaked figure of Philip lying on the rubberized deck.

"I don't know why I keep expecting results from sewer-born scum of motherless pirates," she murmured. "Tell me, boy––is that thing of yours a cleaning robot? A tiny friend? A tiny girlfriend?"

Philip groaned and coughed as he rolled onto his back. His eyes were still closed, but a healthy pink flush had returned to his skin.

"Wakey, wakey, dear," whispered One. She leaned down and kissed his cheek.

Philip wiped seawater from his eyes and blinked at the strangely familiar voice.

"Amy? Is that you?"

One smiled. "Yes ... and no."

5

Dawn crawled up behind the mountains and slowly turned the clouds orange. As the rowboat inched toward the coast and the sky lightened from black to slate-gray, Amy stared with numb shock at the shore.

The Pacific Grove she remembered from 1995 was a tourist mecca and bustling retirement center–– nothing like this village of dirt streets and three-story Victorian houses. No condominiums rose above the rocky coastline; in fact, they probably hadn't invented the word. Green pastures spread below Lighthouse Avenue, and a thick forest separated the village from the orderly Army fort of The Presidio and empty green fields of New Monterey. The black rocks of the coast were barren of any piers or overhanging restaurants, apart from several wooden structures at Lover's Point, not the least of which was a two-story structure that looked like a Japanese temple. A railway only a few meters above the shoreline linked the fishing piers of Old Monterey to the sleepy Victorian town. Eighty years later, the two towns would be an indistinguishable swath of concrete urban development, but at this moment they were as separated by distance and purpose as a sardine factory from a Carmelite monastery. As the boats pulled closer to the shore, smoke from burning wood and coal mixed with a breeze of rotting fish and creosote. Black and green Model-T Fords rattled along the dirt streets, clanking and grinding on wire wheels and narrow tires. To Amy's left, a floating menagerie moored off the Monterey wharf–– schooners, Chinese junks, and tall wooden ships with furled sails.

The Asian rowers in the boats aimed for a beach between Monterey and Pacific Grove, the bluffs over the pale sand populated by a collection of gray, sun-beaten shacks. Large wooden racks stood on the beach, like temporary scaffolding. As they approached the shore, the men jumped into the surf and pulled the boats out of the foaming water. Women and children ran barefoot over the cold sand to help, all wearing jackets and pants similar to that worn by the men, but in dull shades of red and blue.

The two fishermen in Amy's boat yelled a stream of foreign words. An older woman and a girl of maybe eight or nine ran up to the side of Amy's boat and helped her climb out and onto the damp sand. The girl was barefoot, and her black hair was split into a pair of braids wound tightly at the sides of her head.

She stared wide-eyed at Amy. "You're a girl!"

Amy shrugged. "What else would I be?"

"Father brings squid and fish in the morning, not people."

The Asian fisherman who had saved Amy blurted out a stream of words at the girl. She nodded and bowed to Amy.

"I understand," she said. "You're from a shipwreck. Come to my house and be warm."

Feet squished the sand nearby and Amy glanced over at Three. The teenager was shivering, arms crossed and stringy wet hair dangling in front of her face. Both followed the young girl without a word.

A narrow trail twisted for a short distance, climbing above the high-tide line through huge boulders, and ended at the faded gray planks of a shack. Strips of red paper had been pasted on either side of a flimsy-looking door, and were covered with vertical streaks of squiggly black lines. Amy guessed it was Chinese writing.

Inside, the girl motioned for Amy and Three to sit on a narrow bed. The hard surface felt like the rough planks at the bottom of the boat, and wasn't softened a bit by the pink blanket embroidered with flowers that covered it. Steam curled from a teapot on top of a very small and very black pot-bellied stove in the center of the dirt floor. Wooden crates covered in colorful but thin cloth sat around the inside of the shack. Pages of old newspaper were glued to all four walls as decoration, but whatever news or product that had once streaked the tissue-like paper had faded away completely.

The Asian girl poured steaming water into a pair of clay cups, and smiled as she carried them to Amy and Three.

"Drink, please," she said.

Three took the cup and frowned. "Plain water? Don't you have tea or coffee?"

The Asian girl bowed. "I'm sorry. We do not have these things. I can run outside to purchase them if you wish."

Amy took a cup. "No, thank you. Water is fine with us. What's your name?"

"Lim Chow."

"Nice to meet you, Miss Chow. I'm Amy."

Three took a sip of hot water. "You can call me Three. It's a strange name."

"It's not so strange," said Lim. "I have four cousins in China and they are called by numbers, just like that."

"So you're Chinese?" said Amy.

The girl nodded. "Of course! Many Chinese live here and catch fish. Please——drink up. I will find you warm clothes and father will take you to the harbormaster."

"I don't think that's necessary," said Three.

"But your family will be looking for you," said Lim. "This is why we go to the harbormaster."

"I don't have any family," said Amy, staring down at the cup. "Not in this time, and not in this place. All of my friends were on that ship, and now I can't even go home."

"I'm very sorry to hear that," said Lim. "But many ships come here every day. The harbormaster or the police will help you."

"It's probably best if we don't talk to officials of any kind," said Three. "Especially police."

Amy nodded. "Right."

Lim's mother and father entered the shack and shuffled around the stove, talking to Lim in rapid Chinese. The small girl turned to Amy.

"My parents say normally there would be a huge crowd on shore searching for bits of the ship, but many people go to see submarine stuck on sand at Watsonville."

Amy stood up suddenly. "A submarine? What color is it? That could be my ship!"

Lim giggled and covered her mouth. "You're so funny! Girls aren't allowed on submarine. It's the American navy."

"I still need to see it."

Three nodded. "It's too much of a coincidence."

Lim's father watched them carefully. When they stopped talking, he spoke to Lim in a long burst of Chinese. The young girl listened and nodded.

"If you don't want to visit the harbormaster, Father says you can see the wrecked submarine. Uncle Shu is going to drive his truck there. After that, you should go to Bennie's house in Pacific Grove."

"Who's Bennie?" asked Amy.

Lim smiled and bowed. "It is not a who, but the Benevolent Society of Methodist Women. It's a charity for girls with sudden troubles. After you have warm clothes and breakfast, we can leave."

"I'm sorry, but we can't pay you for the clothes," said Amy. "We don't have any money."

"That is not a problem for you to worry," said Lim.

AFTER A MEAL of fried sticks of dough and hot porridge that smelled of eggs, Lim brought out a Chinese-style brown jacket, trousers, and a pair of boots for Three to wear, and brushed and braided the blonde hair of Amy's twin. The warmth and self-drying quality of Amy's nano-clothing amazed the Chinese girl. She wouldn't stop asking about the material until Amy told her it was from Paris.

A Model-T truck with an open bed rattled to a stop on the dirt road behind the shack. Chinese kids burst from every corner of the small fishing village, screaming and shouting, and climbed onto the truck. Lim pulled Amy and Three by the hand into the back of the truck, and the girls were soon squeezed in like cargo on the flat bed, pushed on all sides by chattering, staring children.

Amy winced as a boy elbowed her in the back.

"I feel like a sardine in a tin can," she said to Three. "I guess that's appropriate."

"Why?"

"Because Monterey is famous for sardines."

Three shrugged. "If you say so. At least we're warm, and not walking."

The truck's engine popped and roared, and began to bounce along Oceanfront Avenue. The young Chinese riders screamed and cheered at the apparently auspicious development.

The morning was cold and clouds covered the gray sky. A strong breeze whipped up the waves on the bay, turning the crests foamy and giving Amy painful memories of the crash and her desperate swim during the night. She turned to look up the hill and watched the lower gate of the Presidio pass by, guarded on each side by helmeted soldiers in white belts and wool uniforms the color of wet mud. Each of the young men rested a rifle on his right shoulder and wore white spats over his boots.

The wharf was busy with fishermen with nothing to do because of the stormy weather. Most stood around in clumps of conversation and tobacco smoke. Old Model-T cars and trucks dropped puffs of blue smoke as they clattered along the packed dirt of the Monterey streets. Along the sidewalks strode well-dressed bankers in bowler hats, deliverymen in rough blue coats and patched trousers, and Chinese in their strange outfits and round skullcaps. Instead of bill-boards to advertise their services, the businesses along the street relied on large, hand-painted facades at the top of the buildings and boys on each corner screaming at the tops of their lungs about malt beer, fish dinners, and tobacco products.

Amy was surprised at how busy the city seemed and the number of trees along the street. Smells of molasses and soap mixed with acrid exhaust fumes from the black, red, and green Model T's and the smell of fish in all stages of life and death. The Del Monte Hotel rose over them as the tallest structure in the city, its gleaming white tower standing in the midst of manicured gardens and curated ponds like a temporary Xanadu for the permanently wealthy. As they continued bouncing along the street to the north, the space between the houses widened and spread apart into artichoke and strawberry fields. A musty wind of loam and manure replaced the industrial smells of the city. The truck continued to rattle north along the coast, past gigantic sand dunes covered with the pink-flowers of ice plants.

After what seemed like an hour of jolting and elbows jabbing her in the ribs, Amy began to calculate the chances of jumping out without breaking a leg. She pushed through the kids and leaned over the wooden railing at the side of the truck, the wind whipping her blonde hair across her face.

Someone grabbed her arm and Amy turned.

"I wasn't gonna!"

Lim blinked at her. "The other side. Please look."

A railway from the east cut through the vegetable fields and crossed the dunes to a wide pier on the ocean, where several steamships and a submarine were tied up. Not far away, an identical submarine lay higher and parallel to the beach, waves crashing against a dark gray hull tilted away from the sea and toward the mountains. Crowds of men and women lined the beach and the long wooden pier, watching as a tugboat with a blat-blat engine churned the water and tried to pull the beached submarine with a thick steel cable.

"That's not my ship," said Amy.

Lim giggled. "Of course! I already told you it was American Navy. It's something fun to see, right?"

"Looks like it was tied up to the pier like the other one, but came loose," said Three. "That didn't work out so well."

Lim nodded. "Big storm a few days ago."

"What was the name of your ship, anyway?" Three asked Amy. "I was on board the thing for like five minutes, and nobody ever told me."

"*White Star.*"

"Strange name for a ship."

Amy shrugged. "It's even stranger for a cat. That's what I called my first one."

Three shook her head. "You Old Earthers with your pet cats. That's slavery in my day."

"How is 'White Star' a good name?" asked Lim. "All stars are white."

"Some stars, but not all," said Amy.

Lim's uncle parked the truck along the road behind a long line of Model T's, and the Chinese kids tumbled over the sides like soldiers storming a beach in reverse. Amy, Three, and Lim climbed down and followed at a safer pace.

Three watched the laughing children dash across the sand, where a large crowd stood watching the effort to move the submarine. She shook her head.

"I guess you kids don't get too many vacations."

Lim held a hand to her forehead and squinted at her. "What's a vacation?"

Amy left the two girls staring at the beached submarine and walked south along the cold sand. She passed under the round, creosote-stained pillars of the pier and wandered along an empty stretch of sand and waves. The distant, cloud-capped mountains to the south curved in a fishhook, with Monterey at the bottom and Pacific Grove at the sharp western barb to the right. The haze of smoke over the settlements could be easily mistaken for the last scraps of morning fog. Apart from the sails on the bay and the hillside of the Presidio cleared with military precision, it was strangely hard to pick out signs of modern life.

Amy sat on the sand above the high-tide line and folded her bare legs under her, covering them with her skirt. She smiled faintly as she watched the waves hiss over and over up the beach, and patted the beige material over her legs.

"Thank you, nanites, for keeping me warm and dry. You're the only friends I have left, even if you can't talk to me."

She felt a mild electric tingle in every place the cloth of her blouse and skirt touched her bare skin.

"That's enough! I didn't say I wanted a chat. You're the best and I appreciate that, but talking to your clothes is a short road that ends with me living alone with forty cats, or someone who collects spoons from every state."

The tingle went away for a few seconds, then came back with a warmth that counter-acted a cold breeze that whirled over the tops of the waves and into Amy's face.

She stared at the horizon where the ship had sunk. It was truly a guess, because the sea and sky were as cold, gray, and featureless as a bucket of dirty mop water. The waves roared and fell away, roared and fell away. A dozen tiny birds with white bellies and gray backs ran above the surf, legs moving so fast they were invisible, chirping and stabbing at the sand with black beaks. The waves came and went, the birds ran tiny marathons, and nothing changed them. Kingdoms fell, cities turned to ash, and everyone that mattered to a young woman could exist or not exist—— none of it mattered in the crushing whirlpool of time. A tear rolled down Amy's cheek.

"I'm sorry," she whispered. "Betsy, Sunflower, Nick ... and Philip. Especially Philip. If I wasn't so stupid none of this would have happened and you'd still be alive."

Three sat on the sand beside her. "Who'd still be alive?"

Amy wiped her eyes. "Nothing. Nobody."

"You're blaming yourself for the crash? That's stupid."

"Calling me stupid for thinking I'm stupid is not the best way to calm me down."

Three took a circular compact from her pocket and a cylinder of lipstick. "Sorry. I don't know what to say to people half the time. I'm not good at that stuff. You're sitting next to a stone-cold freak who's more Pirate Jack than Barbie. Ignore the fact that I'm staring into a tiny mirror and re-applying my lipstick."

"Where did THAT come from?"

Three shrugged. "Probably from being abandoned at birth. It does things to people."

"No, the makeup!"

Three waved a black rectangular makeup case in the air. "This? I grabbed it before we left the ship. You can't expect a girl to fight the universe without slapping on a little war paint."

Amy sniffed and watched the white birds run above the surf.

"Yeah, I know."

Three slapped her on the shoulder. "Don't get all weepy on me! You're better than that, and I'm the same way. In fact, we're the same person, me and you."

Amy sighed. "No, Three. We are not the same."

"That's fine," said the blonde girl. "But don't blame yourself for any of it. It was my escape pod that blew up. Seriously, think about it––One with her stupid, secret bomb could have killed me. If she and the others thought I was out of control, why didn't they say something? What's up with that? Safety first, I always say. Actually, I never say that."

Amy hugged her knees and stared at the waves.

"Right," she murmured.

Three waved her lipstick at the beached submarine half a mile down the beach. "Don't you think it's weird that your ship sank last night, and now we're staring at another one? Also, if you squint and look sideways at it, that thing looks like One's spaceship."

"If you say so."

Three finished applying the pale pink lipstick and put away her beauty tools. She watched Amy for a long moment, then picked up a tiny piece of driftwood and began to trace slow lines in the sand between her spread legs.

"Want to know what I think about this whole messed-up situation?"

Amy shrugged. "Knock yourself out."

"I've been to wild dimensions and seen things you wouldn't believe, where up is down and right is left. But no matter how crazy things get, there's always an Amy Armstrong and there's always a Philip. Sometimes they grown old without meeting each other, and sometimes they're born two streets apart. No matter what happens in whatever wacko time and place, if those two meet they'll be like yin and yang, chocolate and peanut butter, bread and jam, plasma rifle and charging core. They always love each other, no matter what happens. Like I said, you're lucky."

"What about you?" asked Amy. "Were you lucky?"

Three smiled and dug into the sand. "I stopped on Phobos to sell off some cargo I stole from the Alliance. There was a bar like there always is, and a fight like there always is. I got tossed through a window, and five seconds later, this dark-haired scarecrow lands on top of me." She sighed. "Philip. Never good in a fist-fight. Great pilot, though, and the best shot with a taze-gun. I don't remember much about the first two days or what happened, actually. He says I punched him first and threw a chair, and that's why we got thrown out of the bar, but it doesn't matter. The Alliance had a contract on his head for piracy, and he hid on my ship. We were a hot number for a few months ... a pair of goofy lovebirds. He wanted me to sell the ship, move to Fiji with him and raise chickens or something, but I was thickheaded and stubborn. I was stupid."

"It happens," said Amy.

"A huge Alliance cruiser caught us refueling at Europa. Philip was in the cockpit and I was in a pressure suit changing out the engine igniters when they started shooting. I never even ... I never got to say goodbye, you know? One minute I'm yelling at him about the cost of the engine parts, and then he was just ... gone. I should have been in the cockpit instead of yelling at him, and we'd have been blown into space together."

"I'm sorry."

"One found me in prison and paid the bounty to have me released. She thought I was cool and mean enough to join her crew of inter-dimensional space pirates slash wackos. There's not much else to it, and here we are!" Three spread her arms. "Sitting on a beach. Life is great, right?"

"But you said this 'One' version of me wants to destroy us," said Amy. "Why would she pay your bounty? She could have just left you in prison."

"It's a long story."

Amy waved at the long and empty stretches of beach to the north and south. "We're stuck here for the rest of our lives. Is that long enough?"

Three adjusted the collar of her brown Chinese jacket. "I guess it's not that complicated. She's doing it for love."

"What?!!"

"I said every Amy Armstrong has a Philip, right? One had hers, and she lived with him for years. 'Had' is the important word."

"I guess we've got that in common, too," said Amy.

"She shot him," said Three. "Stone dead. Accused him of cheating on her with a cute little research assistant. This is all second-hand, you know, and it happened before I met her. Turns out One was completely wrong about the cheating, and he was just spending long nights in his lab with the assistant researching trans-dimensional physics."

"Ouch. Burn."

"Exactly," said Three. "Because of that, she wants to travel back through time to the moment before she pulled the trigger on her Philip."

"That's impossible. You can't go back."

Three shook her head. "One found a way to link quantum constants in the universe––SpaceBook satellites, Amy Armstrong, and Philip––and thinks that will give her the ability to travel anywhere and any time she wants. SpaceBook is everywhere, it's how we navigate through the different dimensions. By using a 'quantum attenuation transfuser,' One is triangulating the frequencies of different copies of Amy Armstrong on the quantum level, and thinks she'll be able to find the creator of SpaceBook. Access to the origin point means complete dimensional freedom. The only problem with all of this is that triangulating the frequency means breaking down one of the constants on a quantum level."

"I have no idea what you're talking about."

Three rolled her eyes. "She shoots a big laser at us and we die. End of story."

"A laser? How does that help her travel back?"

"I thought you were smarter than this. I just told you——she breaks her copies down on a quantum level, shrinking us back through time to an embryonic spark of life. That's what I meant when I said she wants to destroy us. I didn't mean on a psychological or emotional level——I meant that she literally wants to change us into pure energy."

"Why go to all this trouble? Can't she visit another dimension and fall in love with another Philip? God forbid she could find someone whose name doesn't start with 'P.'"

"One is not the speed-dating type," said Three. "Or the any-kind-of-dating type. Every dimension is slightly or wildly different. Believe me, she's tried other Philips, usually for embarrassingly long weekends. It never works out, probably because they recognize that she's a dimension-hopping Lady Hitler, and only a dimension-hopping Stalin would want to hang out with her for more than two minutes before jumping out the nearest airlock."

"Or just a Hitler."

"Don't be silly. Hitler was definitely a woman, and I've seen her up close. Anyway, One and these other Philips never 'click' but it's not for a lack of trying. These days we just take turns if there's a new Philip."

"You take turns?"

"I said them! Them, not me. One, Two, and Four are insane beasts. They torture these poor copies of

Philip, and when they're done with the pitiful souls, they break them down on a quantum level just like they want to do with you. Us! I mean us."

"That's horrible."

"Exactly what I said the second I found out," said Three. "And then I escaped. That's the honest truth."

Lim ran up to them, her tiny shoes spraying sand.

"I found you!" she said, her face flushed. "Uncle says it's time to go. We'll have lunch and take you to Bennie's."

Amy stood up and brushed sand from the back of her skirt.

"Let's go," she said. "I need some benevolent women in my life."

6

On a mountain high above the Pacific, a pine forest swayed in the cold morning breeze blowing up from the ocean. An orange tabby lay on a low-hanging branch of a tree, the strong air currents blowing his fur and making the green pine needles bounce and hiss. Past the end of the branch, a steep slope of chaparral and chemise brush angled steeply and dropped more than a thousand meters to the waves booming against the black rocks of the coast.

On the ground below Sunflower, the gigantic armored tank lay on a carpet of brown needles in a strange mechanical symmetry with the orange cat, large steel paws stretched flat and head tilted back at a sharp angle to expose the tandem seats of the cockpit. To Sunflower's relief, the powerful machine was in standby mode, and silent. Given the high number of sarcastic comments directed at him, the flight computer either disliked the orange tabby more than any other cat he'd ever met, or was training for a second career as a stand-up comedian in some flop-joint bar for retired computer cores. Sunflower sighed and rested his chin on his paws.

Wood cracked from below, and he blinked his yellow eyes.

"I'm trying to take a nap, Betsy."

The brown-and-white terrier looked up from beside a higgledy-piggledy pile of twigs and small branches.

"Sorry, Sunnie! I'm making a fire. Do you wanna help?"

"No, I don't and stop asking me. There's no point to make a fire if we're trying to hide from everyone!"

Betsy tilted his furry head. "How are we going to cook our food?"

"We don't need to eat for at least another week! Those boxes of survival rations are for normal cats. Even if you could eat them, they're for emergencies and taste like wet cement on a hot summer day! Trust me, I was in Cat Scouts."

"I bet they'll taste better if we cook them."

Sunflower sighed and stared at the fuzzy line of the horizon where the ocean met the sky. "How can you go from something complex like piloting an armored military vehicle to wandering through the woods and collecting firewood like a lost kitten?"

"Kittens? I don't see any kittens. Hey! I hear something. Is that what you mean?"

A heavy and deliberate weight pressed on the pine needles at the edge of the clearing. A very large mountain lion blinked in the sun as he crept to the edge of the hollow, staring intently at Betsy and placing each paw carefully in front of him on the pine needles.

Betsy shook his furry head. "Whoa! I've never seen a kitten that big. What did his parents feed him?"

"He's not a kitten, he's a mountain lion," hissed Sunflower. "Run for the cockpit or he'll eat you!"

The mountain lion paused for a moment at Sunflower's voice coming from the trees, then continued to creep toward the small terrier.

"I hope he doesn't want to eat me, because I don't taste good at all," said Betsy. He licked his front paw. "Yuck! Tastes like dirt. Why don't you just talk to him in cat language? I'll make him a sandwich if he's hungry."

"This is Old Earth, where the size of the cat is all that matters," whispered Sunflower. "If you're not going to run, at least make a lot of noise. Maybe he'll get scared."

"Okay," said Betsy, and began to dance a jig on his back feet around the pile of wood. "Hey, doodle-ee-doo, the cat ran up a tree. Hey doodle-ee-doo, he looked what he could see. Hey, doodle-ee-doo, he saw a boat upon the sea. Hey doodle-ee-doo, it's the sailor's life for me!"

Sunflower covered his face with a paw and groaned. "I take it back. Let him eat you already!"

The mountain lion growled and jumped at Betsy, knocking over the pile of twigs and throwing survival rations around the clearing. The terrier dropped to all fours and scrambled out of the way of the fangs and huge black paws.

"Wow," said Betsy. "I don't want to be friends that much, Mister Kitten."

He dodged several swipes of the sharp claws and teeth of the mountain lion, but at last the large cat trapped the dog against a tree trunk with his powerful front legs.

"Help, Sunnie!" yelped Betsy. "He's going to eat me!"

Sunflower gathered his paws under him and prepared to jump down, when the giant armored tank jerked to life and whipped its steel tail into the side of the mountain lion with a loud thud. The large, beige-colored animal roared in pain and fled down the mountain in a spray of dry needles.

Sunflower jumped down to the base of the tree where the small dog lay motionless.

"Betsy! I'm sorry I called you an idiot. Please don't die!"

The terrier opened his brown eyes and sat up. "I was playing dead. If you don't move, they won't eat you because they think dead things are nasty."

"That doesn't work when the cat is right in front of you, moron."

"You just said you were sorry for calling me an idiot, and now you're calling me a moron?"

"Forget it. You should thank that stupid cat vehicle for saving your life. Using its tail was a nice move. I was getting ready to watch the mountain lion rip off your stinky flesh and chew on your titanium-laced bones. Talk about a horrible breakfast."

Betsy trotted over to armored cat and patted the gray metal flank. "Thanks, Wilbur!"

The steel tail of the giant, tiger-shaped vehicle thumped twice on the pine needles.

Sunflower blinked. "Wilbur?"

"That's his name. If you made friends and talked to people once in a while, you'd learn these things, Sunnie."

"You can't be friends with a machine, and I'm allergic to learning."

The orange tabby lay on the soft needles and stared for a long moment at Betsy's shambolic pile of sticks.

"This entire stupid situation is my fault," he murmured.

Betsy scrambled over to him. "Let's go find Amy and Philip! They'll want to know about the mountain lion."

Sunflower blinked. "The ship crashed in the ocean, and I can't detect any beacons or radio transmissions that aren't encrypted. We won't see Amy or Philip again."

"Where did they go?"

"Heaven."

"I thought only dogs went to heaven."

"Do you actually have a brain, or is it a pair of dried peas rattling around inside your skull? I'm not going to debate the afterlife with you. The fact is, the ship blew up, crashed in the ocean, and the only transmissions I can pick up with the radio equipment are encrypted. From here we've got a direct line of sight to where the crash happened, and would be able to receive any signals for a hundred kilometers. The only reason they aren't looking for us is because everyone in that ship is at the bottom of the sea, and dead."

"I think you're wrong," said Betsy. "I'd know if Amy or Philip were dead. I'd feel it."

"With what? The radio in your head?"

"No, with my feelings."

"Just shut up," growled Sunflower. "If any more stupid gush comes out of your snout, I'll make you feel something!"

"What about the other transmissions? That could be Amy."

Sunflower's eyes widened and he jumped up. "You're right! But not our Amy––the evil copy of Amy, the one that kidnapped my wife! The encrypted radio signals must be coming from her. She's the one who probably blew up the ship!"

"See, Sunnie? I'm not so dumb."

"Even a broken clock is right twice a day," said Sunflower. "This evil clone has a ship with a transmat, which means after we rescue Andy, we can leave Old Earth and get back to a civilized dimension."

Betsy hopped up and down. "Cool! A rescue mission!"

"The question is, how? All the *poona* bones are stacked on the side of evil Amy––she's got a starship, probably a crew of murderous pirates, and Andy. We've got the most powerful armored vehicle in the Imperial cat army, but it can't exactly jump into space and catch a starship."

"Don't worry," said Betsy. "Wilbur's the greatest! He saved us from the crash, remember?"

Sunflower nodded and stared at the giant armored cat for a long moment.

"Maybe we do have a chance," he said quietly. "But only if we trick them into coming down to us."

Betsy spun a circle, spraying pine needles over Sunflower.

"Hooray!"

The civic leaders and tourist brochures in Amy's time constantly touted Pacific Grove as "America's Last Hometown." From Amy's bouncing viewpoint in the back of a rattling truck in 1912, it looked nothing like a "last" and more like a "first." Past the green slopes of the Presidio and the rotting stench of the long wooden canneries stood a grid of proud and brightly painted Victorian houses.

The railroad station for Monterey was east of the canneries, and the line of railroad tracks kept going past the fish factories, Chinese village, and small wooden shacks full of fishery-related business to the coastal rocks of Pacific Grove and its packed arrangement of quaint houses. In 1995, the tracks had long been replaced with a wide asphalt path, just as the Chinese women in their faded brown and blue jackets would be replaced with runners in sweat pants and panting tourists in four-person, pedal-driven carts.

Amy felt like a tourist herself as she gaped at the women washing clothes outdoors, workmen hammering away at the beams of a new house, and barefoot children running in every direction along the muddy streets.

After a lunch of hot noodles and fresh red apples from the harvest fair, Lim's uncle drove his rattling truck a mile up to Pacific Grove and dropped off the girls at Lighthouse Avenue.

Not far away and up the hill on the corner of Forest and Pine loomed the Benevolent Society of Methodist Women of Pacific Grove. The whitewashed Queen Anne tower was topped with a cone-shaped roof of gray shingles and a bronze cross. A white picket fence shielded the massive wooden structure from the mud of passing horses and clattering Model T cars. The front garden was full of yellow peonies and rose bushes, the buds dead and snipped long before the cold of autumn.

Amy, Lim, and Three walked up the sloping street past three-story wooden houses of Gothic design and pastel color, grocers with fruits and vegetables on tables at the front, a bakery, a tailor and seamstress shop, and a car-repair business with a black Model T poking its nose out the wide front doors.

A man in a leather apron folded the engine cover to the side and leaned over the slowly popping, exposed motor. He glanced up at the three girls and dropped a wrench onto the engine with a loud clang as they walked up the hill. A moment later, a pair of women in ankle-length dresses and wide hats passed by with angry glares.

Amy pointed down at her pink blouse and beige skirt. "Everyone is staring at me, so I should probably find some new clothes. But you know ... these fit so well and actually saved my life. Honestly, I'd rather keep wearing them."

Lim shrugged. "Your skirt is short and above the knees, that is true. You are also not wearing stockings. The Methodists are very upset about such things."

"Above the knees?" snorted Three. "Where I'm from, only nuns wear skirts that long. In fashion terms, it's like, from the stone age."

"Nuns in your dimension probably have face tattoos and nose piercings," said Amy.

"How did you know?"

"A wild guess." Amy stopped and tugged at the hem of her wool skirt. "If I could only make it longer ..."

Amy's knees tingled where the inside liner touched her skin, and the fabric squirmed under her fingers.

Lim pointed at the hem. "It moves!"

The hem quickly dropped over Amy's knees, flowing down to the top of her borrowed boots, and split in the back, allowing her to walk freely. On the pale pink cotton of her blouse, a pattern of tiny flowers appeared, matching the blouse of a woman Amy had passed a moment before.

"That's the freakiest thing I've ever seen," said Three. "I'll take a dozen."

Amy put her hands on her waist. "Don't worry. I've got a wardrobe full of temperature-adjusting, bulletproof clothing with millions of tiny nanite bugs living in them. No, wait—it's at the bottom of the ocean."

"Probably for the best. The galactic economy would screech to a grinding halt if no one had to shop for clothes ever again."

"Miss Three is dressed as a Chinese, and that is also a problem," said Lim. "A white girl wearing clothes of a Chinese girl is very odd."

Three raised an arm and buried her face in the elbow of her jacket. The teenager hunched over and hobbled up the street like an old man, dragging one leg.

"Is this better? You can't see my face."

Lim shook her head. "It is not better. People will stare even more at this."

"I don't know," said Amy. "We can't see your face, so that's an improvement."

Three stopped and wagged a finger. "Hey! Don't be talking crap about my looks. It's your pretty face too, you know."

A truck roared along Pine Street and sprayed the girls with specks of mud. The girls shrieked and ran across the street to the white wooden castle of the Benevolent Society. On the picket fence, a sign painted with gold letters announced that they were, in fact, in the right place.

Lim pushed open the front gate. "Bennies will help you to find your family," said the Chinese girl. "They help girls in trouble."

"That's definitely me," said Three. "I'm always in trouble or making it."

Amy followed Lim through the gate. "I don't think time travel or trans-dimensional displacement is the kind of trouble she means."

"No? How about a crashed spaceship?"

"Really doubt it."

Lim tilted her head. "My English is not very good, so I do not understand what you ask. But Bennies are very nice and always help."

She led them up the stairs of the porch and knocked on a forest-green door decorated with a wreath of autumn leaves.

"There's something creepy about this place," murmured Three.

Amy spread her hands. "What? It's probably a soup kitchen for orphans. You know––Victorian London, Oliver Twist and stuff."

Three turned and pointed at the empty dirt avenue. "I don't mean the house, I mean this town. Too many trees and birds and squirrels and clouds."

"Nothing weird about that. Where you born on a space station or something?"

Three blinked. "Of course I was! What kind of question is that?"

"Oh," said Amy. "Sorry."

Footsteps thumped faintly inside the house and curtains swayed in the nearby window. A woman in her late forties opened the door, wearing a dress of dark brown serge decorated with black piping. Her red hair was streaked with gray and piled in a bun on top of her head. She smiled and wrinkles spread across her pink cheeks like rings from a pebble thrown into a pond.

"Good afternoon, Lim!" she said. "I'll fetch the box for Mrs. Foo."

The Chinese girl bowed. "Thank you, Mrs. Morgan, but I am not come for those things. There is a problem. These friends are from the sinking ship. Please, can I introduce Amy, and introduce Three."

"Teresa!" blurted Amy. "She means Teresa."

Mrs. Morgan covered her mouth. "A shipwreck? When?"

"In the night. My father took them from the water."

"You poor dears! That's why you're wearing Oriental garments."

She pulled all three of the girls inside with cobra-like speed. Before Amy or Three could protest, they found themselves wrapped in thick blankets and pushed onto a soft velvet couch. The room around them seemed ripped from a Victorian museum, with flowery wallpaper, globed lamps with velvet shades, and thick Persian rugs of deep brown. The sharp smell of wood polish hung in the air, along with the faint odors of licorice, roses, and ammonia.

Amy held a steaming cup of tea and saucer on her lap, summoned as if out of thin air by the attentive Mrs. Morgan. She shrugged the blanket off her shoulders.

"Thank you very much, but we're not cold or wet. The shipwreck happened last night, and since then Lim and her family have been helping us."

Mrs. Morgan nodded. "Yun Chow and his relatives are honest, church-going people. I shudder to think what would have happened if you girls had been saved by some of the other very un-Christian characters that inhabit that fishing village. This story of yours is very peculiar, and the first I've heard about a wreck. It wasn't the *Humboldt*, was it? The storm beached a Navy submarine, and I feared that other ships would be torn apart by that devilish wind." She clasped her hands in front of her chest. "Dear, oh dear! My nephew works on the *Humboldt*!"

Amy stared at the patterned rug below her feet. "It wasn't the *Humboldt*. It was the *White Star*."

"*White Star*? I haven't heard of that ship."

"That's not surprising. We've come a very, very long way."

"From New York, I suppose," said Mrs. Morgan. "Am I right? You speak in a sort of educated, citified way. Reminds me of my late husband, and he was from Rochester."

"That's exactly where she's from," said Three. "From that place you just said."

Mrs. Morgan turned to Three and blinked rapidly. "Pardon me for saying so, but it's very odd to meet a pair of sisters with different accents. Your sister may be from New York but you sound nothing like her."

Three cleared her throat. "We, um ... we used to live very far apart."

"Different boarding schools, I suppose. I've never heard anyone speak English like you. It sounds a bit Scottish, with a Southern accent mixed in somewhere. Are you from Tennessee?"

Three jerked up a finger. "Yes! Boy, oh boy, do I miss that place. Momma and her home-cooked squirrels. Cooked them in a pot, she did, with a brick on top so they couldn't crawl out." She jumped up from the sofa and held her ribs. "Ow! That hurt."

Amy covered her elbow with the blanket. "I apologize for my sister. She's a bit confused. It's been a shocking day for a lonely country girl like her."

Mrs. Morgan leaped forward and hugged both teenagers. "You poor girls! The horrible tragedy has overwhelmed your delicate senses. Do you have a fever? Forehead feels a bit cold. More blankets!"

She rushed out of the room.

"What exactly are we doing here?" asked Three. "That old lady is half in the bag, if you ask me."

"Half in the bag? Are you saying she's drunk?"

Three shrugged. "Or crazy?"

"Mrs. Morgan is nice," said Lim. "She does not become drunk. She is a Methodist and Methodists do not like these things."

"I agree with Lim, and I think she just wants to help," said Amy. "We don't have anything in this dimension--no ship, no place to stay, not even two pennies to rub together. If anyone needs a Methodist charity, it's a pair of stranded space travelers like us. We'll only be here long enough to get our bearings and figure out the next step. That might include going to church and making friends."

"I'll join a nunnery before that!"

"Be my guest."

"We could knock over a bank or two. A pair of flash girls like us would be rich in no time. I bet these cavemen don't even have DNA sensors and magnetic locks!"

Amy shook her head. "I gave up stealing a while ago, after ... whatever, it doesn't matter."

"You gave up after you met Philip," murmured Three. "You were smart and picked Fiji. Not me! I'm too stupid to listen to anyone and rotten to the core."

"I'm sure there's some good in you. Maybe in your big toe or the left side of your pancreas. I'll be generous--your entire pancreas."

"Funny."

Amy poked Three in the arm. "Seriously, though--keep it simple with our story. We don't want to spook Mrs. Morgan with tales of outer space and talking cats and crap."

Three pulled down the sleeves of her Chinese jacket. "I get the picture. I should also probably keep my tattoos under wraps. I bet she'd have a cow if she saw them."

"Mrs. Morgan does not have a cow," said Lim. "There is no room in the yard for a cow."

"That's not what she meant," said Amy.

Mrs. Morgan's voice boomed from the back of the house.

"Here we are. I found them at last!"

The older lady rushed into the parlor with a stack of blankets in her arms. She dropped the huge pile of colored wool at Three's feet and proceeded to wrap another layer of wool around the reluctant teenager.

"That's better," she said. "You needn't worry your pretty heads about your parents, my dears. I'm certain in the horrible commotion of the wreck and the ship, the pair of you were separated. We'll simply go down to the harbormaster and set this right."

Amy shook her head. "Our parents weren't on the ship."

"Husbands?"

Three smirked. "This really is the olden days. They still have marriage contracts?"

Amy covered Three's mouth with her hand. "No husbands or family, just a pair of sisters traveling to ... Hawai'i. We have a cousin there."

"Oh, my! The journey has turned into such hardship for you poor, lovely girls. I don't know if they receive telegraphs in Hawai'i, but I can take you to Western Union and we'll send a message wherever you like. In the meantime, I'll fix up a room and find a change of clothing for both of you. How about a hot bath? I'll start the boiler."

"Thank you for everything," said Amy. "I'm fine with my own clothes, but my sister could borrow some. The rest of our luggage and everything we had is at the bottom of the ocean."

Mrs. Morgan smiled. "Give to him who asks of you, saith the Lord. Both of you may stay here as long as it takes to sort out your arrangements. Let me air out your room. There's also the prayer meeting tonight. Such a busy day!"

A sharp knock vibrated the door.

"Busier and busier," said Mrs. Morgan. "Who could that be?"

She opened the door to a short, elderly man in a dark blue suit. Although balding, with steel-gray hair, a bristly mustache, and pince-nez glasses, he was as slender as an elf and held his black bowler hat with steady confidence.

"Mr. Woodley, how are you?" said Mrs. Morgan. "I'm afraid our afternoon stroll will have to be postponed until the morrow. Two young women from a floundered ship have just arrived, and I must attend to their needs."

Mr. Woodley's dark eyes widened and his mustache twitched. He leaned inside the sitting room to peer at the pair of girls wrapped in blankets.

"My word, Claire! Pardon me––Mrs. Morgan. The servants were gossiping this morning about the strange, awful sea creatures washing up on shore because of the storm, but I hadn't heard a jot or tittle about a wreck. It's absolutely peculiar, what with the beaching of the submarine at Port Watsonville, and now this! I hope it wasn't the *Humboldt*."

"No, thank goodness. It was a ship called the *White Star*, God save their souls."

Amy raised her voice. "Awful sea creatures? What kind?"

Woodley smiled and ducked his head. "E.G. Woodley, miss––pleasure to make your acquaintance. Please don't worry yourself about such things, servants being servants and all. They gossiped on and on about giant creatures on the beach near China Point, enough to make me wonder if the Devil himself had taken hold of their minds. According to the servants, the creatures were green and covered in scales like a crocodile, ones that roared like lions and feasted on the raw flesh of a pair of Chinese fishermen. I'm embarrassed to pass on such lurid and fantastic details in the company of ladies. I'm certain the missing men will turn up soon. A sighting of sea lions is the more Christian explanation, or I'm a monkey's uncle— pardon the expression."

"Of course," said Amy. "Thank you, Mr. Woodley."

The gentleman bowed in the doorway. "My pleasure. If I can be of any service to the young ladies or yourself, Mrs. Morgan, please do not hesitate to ask."

"Thank you, Mr. Woodley."

The older gentleman tipped his hat. "Good day, Mrs. Morgan."

"Good day, Mr. Woodley."

Amy turned to Three. "That name sounds really familiar."

Three yawned. "Woodley–schmudley. His servants got drunk and saw a dead fish, or saw a dead fish and got drunk, or saw a drunk and got drunk."

Mrs. Morgan closed the door and wagged a finger at Three. "That would be impossible my dear child. Pacific Grove is an upstanding town of Methodist values, and not a drop of that intemperate, Satanic poison is allowed."

7

Hans Weiss had managed the household of Mr. Woodley since the day the tall young man had stepped off a ship and shook the hand of the older gentleman at the end of a San Francisco pier. The blonde German had followed his employer into a sedate and unfortunately 'dry' retirement in the California Methodist community of Pacific Grove, where the discussion of a pleasurable Mosel riesling––or discussion of any wine at all––was absolutely "verboten." Fortunately, Hans and his employer Mr. Woodley shared a tendency for rebellion.

"I won't do it, Mr. Weiss!" whispered Anna.

The young maid stood in front of Hans, the afternoon light from the kitchen windows surrounding her dress and apron with a ghostly glow. She held her pale, trembling arms straight in front of her, as if she could physically block the words of the butler's suggestion.

"It's too awful," said the maid. "I won't!"

Hans sighed. He leaned over the young woman and stroked her cheek.

"My dear Anna, I simply need you to hold the lantern. I'll go first of course, and I have my pistol if anything happens. Ist Ordnung––I mean, is that acceptable for you?"

The maid took a deep breath and closed her eyes for a second. She opened them and nodded.

"Yes, Mr. Weiss."

"Good."

The butler lit a glass lantern and led Anna into the garden by the hand. He stopped at the back of the house beside the angled door of the cellar and knelt down with his ear on the whitewashed wood.

"Can you hear it, Mr. Weiss?"

The butler held a finger to his lips. "Stille, meine Schatzi."

He listened at the angled wood for a long moment, and then lifted the door with a sweep of his arm. The oiled hinges rolled smoothly to the side.

The tall butler stepped carefully down a dozen wooden steps into a cellar that smelled of damp earth, coal, and vinegar. Light from the lantern in his hand gleamed on racks of wine bottles along the wall. In the center of the hard-packed, dirt floor lay the gigantic green body of a lizard.

Scraps of stretchy red fabric clung to his arms and legs. The muscular limbs were as thick as trees but also firmly shackled to the brick columns of the house foundation by iron chains and a huge length of tarred sailing rope. The scaly green chest rose and fell slowly––a simple and natural action that made the giant lizard even more horrifying.

Anna covered her mouth. "It's still alive!"

"Hush."

The butler let go of her hand and took a small pistol from his pocket.

The lizard opened his eyes a crack, but did not move his scaly green head. He seemed to lack the small amount of energy needed to rotate his wet yellow eyes even the few centimeters needed to look at the humans. "You ... fooolsss," he hissed through jaws full of sharp, triangular teeth. "Let me go."

Hans stepped around the giant lizard, keeping his eyes and the weapon constantly pointed at the monster. He grabbed a bottle of wine, glanced at the label, and backed away.

"I cannot release you until I have a better offer," he said. "If the Smithsonian does not respond to my telegram, perhaps you will find a home with a wealthy collector." He smiled. "At the very least, I know a taxidermist."

"I hate taxes," whispered Nistra, and struggled weakly against the chains around his arms and legs. "And accountants. I'll kill all of you when I'm free."

Anna grabbed a sleeve of the butler's jacket. "Shoot it now. It's horrible!"

Hans backed slowly toward the cellar steps and pulled Anna with him. "Nein, meine Liebchen. It is worth twice as much if we keep it alive."

Nistra stared at the spider webs dangling from the wooden beams above his head as he listened to the humans shuffle back up the steps. The cellar door slammed shut, dropping him into what the disgusting monkeys considered darkness, but for the eyes of a sauropod warrior was as clear as day. After the cellar had been quiet for a short while, his ear-holes detected the scratch of tiny teeth on wood coming from a corner. Nistra silently rolled onto his belly and inched his broken body toward the sound, sliding across the dirt using his shoulders and knees.

"Cruel humans," he hissed. "They must know that rats give me gas."

On the coast a few kilometers away, three giant reptiles huddled shoulder-to-shoulder inside the black rocks of a cave just steps from the roaring surf. Multicolored scraps of fabric hung from their scaly arms and legs, and all were damp from the sea. Each of the lizards clenched his jaws angrily even as his sharp teeth chattered and his entire body shivered from the cold.

Astra pointed his chin at a silver triangle Plastra held in his claws.

"Check it again."

"I did," said Plastra. "Five seconds ago!"

"Please?"

Plastra sighed. The giant lizard pointed the triangle toward the foaming breakers of the ocean and waved it back and forth.

"Nothing."

"Did you check the battery?"

Plastra stomped the wet sand with a giant foot. "Of course I checked the battery!"

Astra groaned. "Chisna's dead and I'm never getting those ten woolongs!"

Plastra lowered the metal triangle and stared at Astra. "Nine of our friends are dead––let me repeat that, NINE––and all you care about is money? I hope the gods remember that when you return to the Egg, you whining fool."

Astra hung his giant head. "After what's happened, I don't think I believe in the Egg anymore."

"Blasphemy," said Plastra. "I'm going to pretend I didn't hear that."

George, the largest in mass and most impressively muscular of the three reptiles in the cave, opened his razor-toothed jaws and belched.

"Stop fighting," he said. "It makes me hungry."

"How can you say that?" asked Plastra. "You just ate an entire Centauran without even sharing."

"I was hungry."

Astra held up a sharp-clawed finger. "No Centauran meat for me. I hate the taste. I'll eat a slimy, stinky fish before I eat a man-monkey."

George burped again. The sauro reached inside his gigantic mouth and pulled out a brown Chinese cap covered in clear, dripping goop.

"It didn't taste like a normal Centauran," he said. "More like a stringy, free-range Centauran who really needs a bath."

"Oh, and you would know the difference?" sneered Astra. "Are you some kind of human meat expert?"

George blinked. "Yes."

"Forgive me for breaking up a lovely conversation about free-range humans," said Plastra. "But we have to find a way out of this hole Nistra has buried us in."

"More like a cave than a hole," said Astra.

"Shut up. Our fair leader Nistra is almost definitely at the bottom of the ocean right now, so we can forget about his glorious plan of taking over the spaceship."

"It's at the bottom of the ocean, too," said Astra.

Plastra said nothing, and watched the white surf crashing outside the cave. At last he nodded.

"We should wait for nightfall, when the stupid Centaurans sleep, and explore their pitiful shambles of a village. Their eyes are weak in the darkness."

"I'm not going into the water again," growled George. "I hate swimming!"

"Don't get yourself worked up," said Plastra. "I'm not planning on any more swimming for the rest of my life."

Astra spread his sharp claws. "I get it! We sneak into the Centauran village and catch a taxi back to Tau Ceti. Easy-peezey, poona-squeezey."

"You forget how backwards the countryside of Alpha Centauri can be," said Plastra. "I think we'll have to journey to the capital before we can find any kind of interplanetary flight."

George shook his brown scaly head. "But ... what if this isn't Alpha Centauri?"

"That's the dumbest thing I've ever heard you say," snorted Plastra. "You don't find Centaurans anywhere else."

"We got here really fast. I thought it took a week to get to Alpha Centauri."

Plastra rolled his eyes. "If it looks like a Centauran, smells like a Centauran, and walks like a Centauran, then we're on Alpha Centauri!"

"But it didn't taste like a Centauran."

"Shut up!"

The triangular device in Plastra's claw chirped and flashed green.

"A signal!"

He pointed the chunk of metal toward land, and it chirped louder and faster.

"A kilometer from here," whispered the lizard as he stared at the device. "Right in the middle of the human village."

George clapped his claws. "Hooray! One of my friends is not dead!"

"Not for long," said Plastra. "The vital signs are extremely low. These man-monkey animals might be preparing to feast upon him. Egg curse their black hearts!"

Astra shivered. "Who would eat a sauro?"

Plastra snapped his jaws angrily. "Deviants, criminals, and villains of the first water. Beings with no more sense of right and wrong than a television reporter. If you believe the stories, Alpha Centauri is covered with them."

George blinked. "Reporters?"

"No, you idiot! Villains who would eat the brave flesh of a brave soldier from the bravest planet in the galaxy! Once darkness falls, we must rush to help our fallen comrade." He bared his sharp teeth. "And murder every human in our path!"

George cheered and clapped his scaly palms in rhythm. "Yay! We love murder, yes we do, we love murder, how about you?"

Plastra sighed and shook his head. "Cheerleaders."

MRS. MORGAN took a pair of coins from a small velvet purse and handed them to Lim, along with a short list of items to purchase from the bakery and Bodfish Dairy.

The Chinese girl bowed. "Thank you, Mrs. Morgan. I will come back soon."

Amy stood from the sofa. "I'll go with you."

"There's no need, my dear," said Mrs. Morgan. "You've suffered a horrible calamity and should rest."

"I don't feel tired. It would be fun to walk around and look at the old buildings."

Mrs. Morgan laughed. "I'm afraid you might be disappointed in our simple village, child. We don't have any buildings in Pacific Grove that are more than thirty years old."

"Right," said Amy. "Anyway, I'd like to walk around, maybe get a bit of fresh air."

"I certainly think you've had enough fresh air for a few days, but as you wish."

"Me, too," said Three from the door of the parlor. "I want to go."

The Chinese clothes were gone, and in their place Three wore a white blouse with pale blue pinstripes and tiny pearl buttons down the front, above a dark gray skirt of heavy wool and brown pointed boots that buttoned up the side. Her pale blonde hair had been washed, brushed, and pinned at the back of her head in a bun.

Mrs. Morgan shook her head. "Such energy! If only I had that same youthful vitality. Very well––attack the town, you giggling valkyries."

Amy, Three, and Lim left the house and walked down Forest Avenue. The dirt lane passed through the commercial center of the village on a kilometer-long slope to the ocean. As they strolled closer to the ocean, the dull and regular thunder of waves on the shore increased, along with the number and variety of Victorian houses.

"Something wrong?" asked Three.

Amy shook her head. "It's this place. This is where I grew up, but it's not the same."

"Of course not! This is like the land of the cave people. I wouldn't be surprised to see some hairy ape in a tiger skin dragging a woman by her hair."

"Number one, we don't have tigers in California," said Amy. "And number two, that cave man dragging thing is probably made up."

Three cracked her knuckles in a very unladylike manner. "Made up or not, I hope someone tries it. I haven't had a good fight in weeks."

Lim glanced sideways at the pair of teenagers. "These are the strangest girls I have ever met," she murmured to herself in Chinese.

Amy pointed at a white two-story house as they walked by. "I remember this place, but everything around it is different. No electrical wires strung across the sky. No Volvos and BMWs parked along both sides of the street, without even room to walk between them."

Three nodded. "Flying cars are the worst, slamming down everywhere. Listen, just forget about it.

Once we put our plan into action, we'll be rolling in more credits than a dog has fleas."

The street descended the hill and ended in a junction with the appropriately-named Oceanview Avenue. The dirt road curved along the rocky, uneven coast, and the girls joined a steady stream of casually strolling men and women. A pair of men with cigars in their mouths raised hats to the girls as they walked by, and the smell of burning tobacco mixed with the wet, fishy smell of the sea.

"This is Lover's Point," said Amy. "I recognize the beach and the rocks on the point."

"It is called Lovers of Jesus Point," said Lim. "The Christian people liked to give it that name." The Chinese girl waved at a two-story building above the sand. "That is the bathhouse. It is very popular in the summer. The boats with glass bottoms are there on the small pier. Can you see them? My father says they are not good for fishing."

Amy pointed at a Japanese-style building made of white plaster and dark brown wood in the center of the small peninsula.

"Is that a Chinese temple? That's totally new to me."

Lim smiled. "It is Japanese and a teahouse. When it is open, you can have tea and small Japanese food."

"Weird," said Three. "Looks like an oil-change place to me."

The teenagers stopped on the street above the bathhouse, where a small beach curved west along the piled rocks like a fishhook. Each of the girls watched the waves foam onto the sand and hiss away, lost in her own thoughts and the warm fishiness of the sea breeze.

Amy shaded her eyes and stared out to sea and the gray line of clouds.

"I know you don't want to hear this," said Three. "But you have to move on. We have to move on."

"You're right––I don't want to hear that."

The railroad tracks ran along the coast, passing Lover's Point and the small wooden passenger depot, and continued through a lumberyard and wide pastures dotted with a herd of black and white cattle.

Amy and Three followed Lim to a large white rectangular building that stood at the edge of the wide grasslands. They covered their noses at the sharp smell of cow manure and the thick, fungal odor of hay.

"What's this joint?" asked Three.

Lim bowed. "Bodfish Diary. We can buy cheese and milk and butter."

"Wait––this is the where the municipal golf course is in my time," said Amy. "They should have never gotten rid of the cows. Hilarious. Imagine if some rich dude's golf ball landed in a pile of manure!"

Lim stared at Amy. "What's a golf?"

"Yeah," said Three. "Or 'manure.' You can't expect us to understand words like that."

Amy sighed. "Never mind. Let's finish the shopping."

AMY NOTICED a strange package on Mrs. Morgan's kitchen table when they returned. Tied with brown string, the bundle was about the size of small pumpkin and wrapped in coarse burlap.

Mrs. Morgan took the butter and milk from the girls, and stuffed them into the top of a waist-high wooden box. Cool white vapor floated out from the interior, and puffed away as she slammed the lacquered wooden lid.

"Is that a refrigerator?" asked Amy. "I didn't know you had those back then. I mean, now."

Mrs. Morgan smiled. "I'm not certain what you mean, dear. It's an icebox." She opened a large door at the lower front of the cabinet, and pointed at a square block of ice. "Not as fancy as what I'm sure you girls have in New York, but it works."

"Cool," said Three.

"Yes, it keeps everything very cool."

"No, I meant——"

Amy elbowed Three in the ribs. "Don't try to explain," she whispered.

The Chinese girl, Lim walked to the kitchen table and pointed at the burlap package.

"Is this a delivery? Where should I take it, Mrs. Morgan?"

The older woman smiled. "Your father came by and brought it for Amy and Teresa. Apparently, it washed up on shore, and he thought it must have come from the shipwreck."

"Really?!!"

Amy leaped at the package and unwrapped it in a flash to expose the gleaming silver cube of the transmogrifier. Apart from a coating of sand and a few scratches, the heavy cube was as featureless and shiny as before.

"A carbon converter?" said Three. "I didn't know you had one of those!"

Mrs. Morgan frowned. "Yun Chow might have been mistaken. Are you certain it belongs to you? It doesn't look like anything a young lady would have in her possessions."

"Um ... it's a lamp," said Amy, and touched the smooth top. "But I think it's broken."

Three pointed to a corner of the cube. "No, it isn't––I can see the power light blinking right there. Green means the nuclear core is stable."

Mrs. Morgan shook her head. "Teresa, my dear, I have no idea what you've just said."

Amy smiled nervously and wrapped up the transmogrifier in the burlap cloth. She stuffed the heavy package into Lim Chow's arms and pulled the Chinese girl and Three into the sitting room away from Mrs. Morgan.

"Take it as a gift," she said to the Chinese girl. "But you have to always keep it a secret, and never tell anyone about it, even your family."

Three stamped her foot. "You can't give it to her," she whispered. "In a backwards place like this, a carbon converter could make us rich!"

"Her father saved your life and mine," hissed Amy. "I want to help people for once, instead of helping myself."

"Why do I have to keep a lamp secret?" asked Lim Chow. "It is a very common thing to have."

"Because it's not a lamp," said Amy, and prodded the package in Lim's hands. "It's a ... magical box that changes whatever you put on top into a cupcake. Put something like a rock right there, and after a few seconds, it will disappear. A cupcake will come out the side over here. Never touch it when it's working, unless you want your fingers to become tiny cupcakes."

Three shook her head and walked away. "Great. Just great."

Lim Chow bowed in front of Amy. "Thank you. Please tell me, what is ... 'cupcake?'"

8

Many parsecs and dimensions ago, One had traded twelve slaves to a shady Kapetyn dealer for a pair of punishment cubes. Designed to treat the mental illnesses of cats and dogs through a combination of sensory deprivation and virtual reality projections, the large boxes were easily modified into an instrument of torture.

One stood outside the door of the punishment cube, her arms crossed and eyes fixed on a screen on the corridor wall. The image of a gray cat curled up into a ball flickered on the display.

"Traitor," One said with a sneer.

She walked a few paces down the corridor to an identical display next to another sliding door, and watched a tan and black Siamese cat squirm inside an empty metal cube, his mouth open in a terrible snarl. His eyes were shut and spittle drooled from his open jaws.

Wilson trotted up to One and twitched his furry black tail.

"Is it working?"

One shook her head. "First tell me you've caught the flying pest."

The black cat hung his furry head. "Not exactly, my Lady."

"Don't mumble! Yes or no?"

"No," whispered the cat.

"And why not?"

Wilson sat on the deck and rubbed his furry face. "The tiny thing flew into the ventilation system! We thought about pumping the gas we use to poison space weevils into the vents, but that would have killed everyone on board, it being the ventilation system and everything."

"A wise decision."

"Then, I discovered that the little flying woman had raided our supply of chocolate. I came up with a plan to trap her using candy as bait. Sadly, she had eaten every single molecule of sweets. All we had for bait was a wad of used bubble gum that Murphy found under a chair in the cafeteria. That didn't work."

One turned red and pounded a fist on the wall. "All of my chocolate?!! Do you know what that means? I'll squash the little thief like a rotten tomato!"

"Yes, my Lady," said Wilson nervously. "After that, reports of the flying pest popped up all over the ship, from the laundry room to the engine compartment. But now ..."

"Spit it out!"

"We haven't seen the flying thing or heard a peep for hours. Maybe she escaped the ship, or died. No living creature can eat that much chocolate and survive, not even an exalted goddess like yourself, my Lady."

One sighed and ran her fingers through her blonde hair to straighten it.

"Stop groveling. Why don't you reprogram one of the portable scanners to look for chemical traces of sugar? You'll find the body, whether it's alive or dead."

"Of course, my Lady! Why didn't I think of that?"

"Because you're as dumb as a bag of hammers?"

Wilson bowed. "Of course, my Lady. Silly me."

"To return to your original question," said One. "The punishment cube is functional, but the doltish cat inside isn't talking, even when confronted with his greatest fear."

Wilson glanced between One and the display screen on the wall, his long whiskers twitching.

"What fear would that be, my Lady? Freezing to death? Spiders? When he puts his hand into a bunch of goo that a moment before was his best friend's face?"

"You've been watching too many old movies," said One. "His greatest fear is working behind the counter of a Slurp 'N Derp. Of all the possible phobias, this genius MacGuffin is horror-stricken at the thought of menial employment. An intellectual powerhouse forced into serving overpriced fish sticks and salmon gum to bored cats who only stop at his repulsive gas station because it has a toilet. He's terrified at not being able to do his research––research stolen from me because of my idiotic, lazy crew. I should freeze and grind the lot of you into one enormous Slurp 'N Derp."

"Slurp 'N Derp isn't that bad," said Wilson. He licked his lips with a pink tongue. "I could go for a box of fish sticks and carton of pond juice right now, with an extra pump of tasty pond flavor!" He noticed One's steely-eyed gaze boring a hole through his head, and laughed nervously. "Of course, I was joking! It was a joke that I just made. I made it, and it was a joke. Joke! Ha, ha, ha ... Joke?"

One rolled her eyes. She pressed a button below the display with a gleaming chrome finger of her mechanical arm, and leaned close to the image of the writhing Siamese cat.

"Had enough, MacGuffin? Tell me what you know about dimensional physics, and I'll take away the pain. You'll never have to serve egg creams or wash out the nasty toilet after a dog has used it, ever again. How does that sound? If you can't say anything, just bang your head against the nearest hard surface.

Twice for yes, once for no. How about any part of your body? MacGuffin, listen to me! Gah!" One slapped the wall in frustration, and stared down at Wilson. "Stay here and watch the prisoner. If anything spews out of his disgusting mouth like, 'I give up,' or 'I surrender,' or 'Turn it off, turn it off!' then come and find me."

"If he says those things, should I turn it off, my Lady?"

"Yes!"

"What if he screams 'gurgle, gurgle, gurgle' and his head explodes? That can happen with too much time in the cube, or 'the hot box' as we like to call it. Come to think of it, too much pond juice also causes head explodation."

One leaned over the black cat and scowled. "If any 'explodation' happens to either of my prisoners, it'll be your turn in the punishment cube. Two weeks this time!"

Wilson stood on his furry hind legs and saluted. "Yes, my Lady!"

One resisted the urge to stomp back to her quarters, and simply walked away. Not because it would have been inappropriate to lose her temper in front of Wilson––she did that all the time––but because stomping across a metal deck in four-inch heels was impossibly bad for the ankles.

She wound her way through a maze of narrow corridors inside the *Hare Twist*, squeezing past large pipes, bundles of electrical wiring as thick as an elephant's trunk, and bare light bulbs swinging from the ceiling. At one point, she had to jump to the side to escape a sudden and copious spray of black liquid from a leaking pipe.

One sighed and rubbed at a tiny black spot on her blouse. "If the engine starts on that water-logged ship

of MacGuffin's, I'm moving all my furniture and research equipment there and scuttling this interstellar
garbage can. Designed by dogs means only good for
dogs."

A pair of cats in orange uniforms and black berets
stood at either side of a tall, red-painted hatch. Both
saluted as One turned the wheel-handle and stepped
inside her quarters.

Her office and bedroom were decorated in a style
which could only be described as "corporate vampire."
Heavy mahogany furniture upholstered in blood-red
velvet clashed with cubist paintings and meters upon
meters of soft black curtains on the walls. Dozens of
artificial candles wavered, their orange light fluttering
to mimic real flames. Scenes from cameras inside and
outside the ship played on large displays placed at
eye-level around the walls.

One slipped out of her high heels with an exhaust-
ed sigh, and strolled lazily across rugs made from po-
lar bear, tiger, and lion hides.

Philip sat on the couch in the bedroom, head in
his hands and sock-clad feet on a garish Tau Ceti rug
decorated with stripes and interlocking spheres. At
the sound of footsteps, he stood up.

"Thank you for the gift of clothing, Madame," said
Philip, pointing to his button-down shirt and coffee-
colored trousers. "And for rescuing me. This charity
puts me in your debt."

One smiled. Like a tigress after a satisfying meal,
she stepped slowly across the carpet and stroked the
teenager's cheek.

"So young," she murmured. "Even younger than
when I first met you."

Philip pushed away her hand. "I apologize, Madame, but I don't believe that we've met."

"Our souls have been together," said One, reaching out again to touch Philip's ear. "We have known each other forever, a pair of living forces that can be no more separated than day and night, sun and moon, asteroid miner and space weevil. I am she, and you are he."

"Excuse me?"

"I'm Amy Armstrong, and you're Philip."

"With all due respect, Madame, you're not Amy Armstrong."

One frowned. "I promise you, I am. And what is this 'Madame' business? Is it because I'm a grown woman standing in front of you, not a schoolgirl barely out of diapers? Are you afraid of the fact that I have more life, beauty, and vigor than the weedy child you call 'Amy?'"

Philip pushed her hands away and backed up as One flirtatiously touched his face and hair.

"Speaking of that matter, Mada––I mean, miss–– I would appreciate it very much if I could disembark this craft at the nearest coast, at your earliest convenience. My friends are lost at sea and I absolutely must search for them."

One sighed. "I'd like to help you, dear Philip, I really would, but I'm afraid your search would be in vain. An unknown type of explosion caused your ship to crash and sink into the ocean. I'm sure you knew that already. I sent two platoons of my best-trained swimmers, but despite our best efforts there were no survivors. This came as an utter shock to me, and now to you."

Philip's cheeks turned red. "What?!! Impossible. All they had to do was swim. Swim up! And Nick? I saved her myself, by shoving her into my pressure suit!"

"Interesting," said One. "By the way––and this is just theoretical, because the tiny woman is definitely dead––if Nick was wandering around this ship, is there something you could use to find her? Maybe a secret code word? A weakness for some kind of food that's not chocolate? Or candy of any kind?"

Philip stared at One for a moment, and then shook his head. "Pardon my rudeness, but I don't think you're being perfectly honest with me. I would know if any of my friends had perished, especially Amy. All she had to do was swim, by Jove!"

"You're exactly right; that was all she had to do," said One. "And she failed. A very pretty girl who was very bad at breathing water."

"Look here, this is no time for jokes. Do you think the death of––" Philip cleared his throat. "––of my beloved Amy is funny?"

"Absolutely not."

"Show me her body," said Philip, his voice breaking. "I won't believe a word until I see her."

"Of course."

One sat down and patted the red velvet fabric of the couch cushion.

"First take a moment and rest, child. Your face is so red you look like you're about to burst. How much do you know about me? Despite all these scars and my metal arm, I won't bite. Don't believe any rumors from the flea-bitten pirates of my crew."

Philip sat on the couch at a respectable distance. "Three said that you're evil; that you've done horrible things. Why else would she run away from you?"

"You met Three first. Is that why you believe everything from her pretty red lips? Which is more believable? The fabricated half-truths of an escaped criminal or the word of a captain of a trans-dimensional starship? In fact, I'm the commander of a fleet of starships."

"She seemed first-rate and I have no reason to believe that she was dishonest."

"A girl with that many tattoos? A young man of your upbringing must be shocked. I'm certain she was also very forward." One slid across the cushions and placed a hand on Philip's knee. "And eager."

The teenager moved to the far end of the couch. "Tattoos upon the body and unladylike behavior are signs of lower class, not a dishonest person."

One sighed and looked down at her stockinged feet. She wiggled her toes under the black silk.

"You're much wiser than I expected for such a young man. What a pity that Four is next in the rotation."

"Rotation? What does that mean?"

One stood up and smoothed her skirt. "Four is captain of another ship––the *Raw Tithes.* It's her turn to act as host for our guests. Unless, of course, you have information about the engineering of your spacecraft? Information we could exchange? Your ship is an interesting bio-metal design, one that I've never encountered. I'd be very happy if you could show me how it works. If I'm happy, you'll be happy. I guarantee it."

Philip shook his head. "To be perfectly honest, I'm not very educated in technical matters. MacGuffin and Sunflower would know more about that."

"Are those the names of cats? I'm sorry. We found several bodies floating in the water."

Philip buried his face in his hands. "If only I could have saved them! Look at me––useless and stupid. Stupid, stupid, stupid!"

One reached over and patted him on the head. "Don't say that! You seem like a very charming and smart Philip. I'm certain that you'll make Four very happy, at least for a short time."

Philip wiped his eyes. "I'd prefer to be set free on the nearest spot of land."

"In such a backwards place? This dimension has barely advanced beyond sticks and stones. For your own safety, stay with us for a few days. In that time, Four can help you search for any trace of your friends. We're using every bit of technology we have, and something will turn up eventually. Don't make any rash decisions, and let's see how things develop."

Philip sighed. "Fine."

"That's a good boy."

One swished across the animal hides and out of the bedroom. She slipped on her shoes and the hatch to the corridor slammed shut behind her, followed by a murmur of her voice.

Philip leaned back on the couch, arms behind his head. He stared at the ceiling and let out a huge sigh.

This was a spacecraft, and a very utilitarian one at that. Pipes, rectangular metal ductwork, and bundles of multicolored cables crossed the low ceiling in a haphazard jumble. Someone had attempted to cover the mess by hanging sheets of dark red cloth as a makeshift ceiling, but Philip could still see pipes and wires through gaps in the material.

"How could I be so useless?" he said to himself. "I should have given Amy the pressure suit, but then she might have drowned as I almost did. Dear, sweet Amy. You can't be dead. By Jove, I absolutely refuse to believe it!"

He sighed again, still gazing blankly at an exposed section of ductwork in the ceiling. A subtle movement caught his eye, and he stared at a square grate fixed to a steel ventilation duct by four bolts. One of the bolts began to turn counter-clockwise, so slowly that he wouldn't have noticed if he hadn't been staring directly at it. When the bolt was about to fall out of its hole, a tiny white hand emerged from the grate and grabbed it. The metal bolt slipped from the tiny fingers and plummeted down to smack onto Philip's thigh. A faint, high-pitched curse came from behind the grate. After a short pause, another bolt began to turn.

Philip stood and climbed onto the arm of the couch to get a closer look. Whatever was in the ventilation duct caught the next bolt and made it disappear, but had not calculated the effect of weight on the downward-facing, flexible steel. When the third bolt loosened completely, the grate squealed and flexed open, causing a tiny woman to scream and slide out of the ventilation duct.

Knowing something of the character of the person he had suspected was in the duct, Philip was prepared for this to happen and waited with a pillowcase spread wide, like a firefighter with an old-fashioned jumping sheet. He caught the falling woman with ease and lowered the pillowcase to the floor. As she struggled to stand free of the cloth, Philip laughed and pointed at her.

"Nick! You're alive. And ... pregnant? Not again."

The tiny blonde woman got to her feet and glared at Philip, both fists on a waist that bulged at the sides but mostly from her abdomen, as if she'd swallowed a tiny beach ball. Luckily, the red spandex minidress she wore was able to stretch. Copious streaks of dark brown sludge covered the sprite from head to toe, as if she'd been attacked by a gang of Mars bars.

"I--AM--NOT--PREGNANT!"

Philip poked the round ball of Nick's stomach. "You promised to keep yourself thin and beautiful for me, dear Nicky. How could you let this happen after you ate all of those cupcakes last week? This is just like that other fatty incident with the transmogrifier."

Nick stamped her bare foot. "I'm not fat! I just found some chocolate, okay? What's wrong with a little snack?"

"My word—it was definitely more than a 'little' snack."

"If you're going to be mean, then I'm leaving!"

Nick vibrated the dragonfly wings on her back with a loud buzz, but her feet remained planted firmly on the ground.

"Come on, come on," she said between gritted teeth.

Philip grinned. "I'm sorry for making fun of you, Nicky. You're still my favorite girl, even if you like to eat sweets a bit too much."

Nick stopped buzzing her wings. The tiny sprite slumped her shoulders and stared at her feet.

"The chocolate was good," she whispered. "And there was sooo much of it."

"Don't worry. The belly from the cupcakes disappeared after a day or so, didn't it? That's what will happen this time. You've got the metabolism of a hummingbird, along with the talent for flying, of course. I suppose around the time we've finished our tour of Four's ship—*Raw Tithes*, or whatever it's called—you'll be back to a normal weight."

Nick's eyes grew wide. The tiny woman clenched her fists and hopped up and down on the pillowcase.

"No! That's what I came to tell you—the scarface Amy and the black-haired Amy are going to kill you! I heard scarface Amy talk to the others about not hurting you too badly, because she wants to do it herself. Philip, we have to find Sunnie and Amy and Betsy and get out of here!"

"I suspected as much. Thank you, Nick, for finding me. I agree that we have to leave immediately. Have you seen Amy or the others? Are they prisoners of this mad band of murderous, trans-dimensional females?"

Nick shrugged her brown-stained shoulders. "I've been all over this stinky place, and I haven't seen anyone but you. The cats found a couple of those dumb lizard guys, all drowned and dead and stuff, but the way they flap their lips blah-blah all the time about not finding anyone but you and me, I think they haven't found anyone but you and me."

"Right," said Philip. He gently picked up the tiny sprite and placed her in his front pocket. "Plan One: we break out of this room and find a control panel, ideally a panel that gives us access to a means of transport. What transport that would be, I have absolutely no idea."

"We don't have to go anywhere," said Nick. "I've watched the scarface Amy do everything from her desk in the other room." She scratched the back of her leg. "Is there a shower in here? I feel itchy and gross."

Philip took several rapid steps out of the bedroom and into One's office. "You'll have time for all the showers in the world once we escape. Where's the control panel?"

"Have you ever been covered in chocolate and dirt and dust and a billion icky things like that? I could die from this crap!"

Philip sighed. "As you wish. Show me how to use this desk and I'll let you take a bath."

Nick leaned out of Philip's pocket and pointed at a marble paperweight on the desk. "Those two naked people hugging––turn it to the right."

Philip twisted the black marble figurine, and the glossy center of the desk rotated to reveal a bright display and a mechanical keyboard. In the center of the screen was an orange flower, the username "Real_Amy4569," and below that, an empty white rectangle with a blinking cursor.

"There you go!" said Nick. "Take me to the sink, it's my turn."

"Good show, old stick. What now?"

"Type in the password, you doink!"

"What do I use?"

"Don't look at me," said Nick. "It's probably 'catfarts411.' That's the only password I know."

Philip frowned. "I doubt that an evil transdimensional copy of Amy would use Betsy's password in any situation."

Nick crossed her chocolate-streaked arms. "Look, I'm no system hacker. I'm just a dirty sprite being held prisoner by a huge human I THOUGHT was my friend, because friends don't let friends not take a bath."

"Fine, fine."

Philip carried Nick through the bedroom into a closet-like washroom and set her in the sink. He cracked the water handle, causing the tap to drip slowly, and pushed on the dispenser to squirt a bit of soap on the side.

"Close the door!" squealed Nick.

Philip ran back to One's desk and stared at the blinking cursor.

"Password, password," he murmured. "What would she use for a password?"

Neither of Nick's suggestions worked. Philip drummed his fingers beside the keyboard, and stared at the screen.

"Bit of a smudge there," he mused, and used his sleeve to wipe a tiny mark on the display. His eyes widened. "Hold on!"

The teenager grabbed an artificial candle and held it close to the keyboard.

"The sinister Amy uses lotion on her hands," he said to himself. "And several of the letters on the keyboard are shiny with the stuff. H, I, L, P––what poppycock! I couldn't possibly make a word from those letters."

He leaned back and rubbed his chin for a moment.

"Unless ... but that's far too easy."

Philip typed his own name into the password field. The screen blinked and filled with a grid of dozens of pale yellow folders.

"Wizard! Now to find a map for this ship, and perhaps a set of secret controls. What an odd collection of boxes this evil Amy has on the screen: Personnel Hired, Personnel Fired, Personnel Spaced Out the Airlock, Personnel With Odd Names That I Can't Remember So I Call Them Dan, Spreadsheets for Punishment Cube, Funny Cat Photos, Spreadsheet for Punishing Cats Who Send Me Photos, Thermonuclear Warhead Timer (PLS DO NOT USE), Photos of Philip and Me, Draft of First Novel ..." Philip rubbed his eyes. "It all seems a bit useless. Am I missing something?" He scanned the folders again. "'Quantum Attenuation Transfuser: Information for Pre-IPO Investors.' That must be interesting."

Philip touched the folder icon, and the sparkling pancake of the Milky Way galaxy filled the screen.

"Space ... the final frontier," droned One's voice. "Or is it? What about trans-dimensional travel?"

The spiral galaxy split into a hundred, then a thousand identical Milky Ways.

"Dimensional travel ... the final frontier," continued One. "The items and precious minerals obtained through our proprietary transmat technology have given Armstrong Industries a double-digit growth rate and billions of woolongs in the past five years, but I am always looking to the future ... and to the past."

The galaxies disappeared, replaced by a montage of historical events fading in and out: the Pyramids, Julius Caesar, the Great Wall, a blonde woman in a Nazi uniform who looked like a grim-faced Marilyn Monroe.

"Imagine not only traveling across dimensions, but through time itself. Imagine the ability to create useful change in the universe, and to influence the course of history for the betterment of mankind. A rising tide lifts all boats, does it not, ladies and gentlemen?"

One appeared in the foreground, blonde hair pinned back and dressed in a well-fitted black suit and skirt, as the montage of history continued.

"With your financial support, Armstrong Industries can create a future that will last forever, from a past that is under our firm and copyrighted grasp."

The scene dissolved, and returned as a swath of airport tarmac covered in bright sunshine. A huge steampunk submarine the color of black jade sat on dozens of landing legs, stretching over two hundred meters from rounded bow to stern. A multitude of long and bulbous humps covered the dark green skin of the ship, like veins popping from the arms of a wrestler. A solid rectangle of three hundred cats and dogs stood at attention on the tarmac to the side, each wearing a black beret and colored uniform for his or her department. One stepped into the shot, wearing the same corporate black suit.

"The *Hare Twist* you see at the spaceport behind me was engineered to be a mobile laboratory in trans-chronic research, using data from my late husband's notes. I will personally take command of this project and see it to the end." One clasped her hands. "Several members of the corporate board of Armstrong Industries have become tragic victims of random home invasions––Crom rest their souls––after questioning my methods, hiring practices, and frequent use of the phrase, 'I know where you live and will send someone to stab you to death.' If they were still alive, I would say to them that I've changed, and that I've learned from my mistakes. The new board members who've pledged allegiance to the corporate values of Armstrong Industries will attest to that. As an example of my new transparency, I will give a demonstration of the quantum attenuation transfuser, and how we extract data."

The scene faded into a cramped and dark laboratory packed with display screens and white cylinders. Wires hung from the ceiling and covered the floor. At one end of the room, a silver disc in the floor was illuminated by a single beam of light. In the ceiling above the disc gleamed a circle of multi-faceted gems.

"The quantum attenuation transfuser works by breaking down the universal frequency of matter. This gives us specific data that can correlate with transmissions from the nearest Galactic Position Satellite, commonly known as SpaceBook."

A black pug with a bored look in his eyes trotted into frame and pushed a glass box containing a brown-and-white *poona* onto the silver disc. The hamster-like creature frantically jumped and scrabbled at the transparent walls of his tiny prison as the dog slunk away.

"The universal frequency has only been discovered as part of organic matter," narrated One. "This is either unfortunate or fortunate, depending upon which side of our test chamber you find yourself. In full accordance with Gliese laws, we have only experimented on *poona*, death-row criminals, and daytime talk show hosts."

Philip felt a tug at his ankle, and he lifted Nick up to the top of the desk.

"What's all this crap?" asked the tiny woman, rubbing her wet hair with a scrap of paper.

Philip shrugged. "Some sort of research."

On the display screen, the gems in the ceiling spun in rapid, concentric circles above the trapped *poona*. A moment later, a bright flash filled the room. The small animal and his glass prison had disappeared.

Nick gasped. "Whoa!"

"The living matter is transformed into super-heated plasma in a matter of nano-seconds," said One's voice. "Converting it through stages to an original quantum state. We have a recording device capable of several million frames per second, and have observed the test subject actually reversing the aging process back through what we consider 'time,' from adult infant, embryo, and egg cell. Unfortunately, my assistant borrowed the camera to film his nephew's pool party, so that footage is not available."

Philip nodded. "How interesting. Apparently she wants to make even more money by traveling through time."

Nick stopped rubbing her hair with the cloth and stared at Philip. "That's not true!"

"What do you mean?"

"I heard scarface talking about that stuff to one of the cats. She doesn't care about money. Evil scarface wants to travel back in time to find Philip."

"Me?"

"No, silly! An old person like her. Stop looking at this dumb video and find the control panel."

"How? It's still going."

"I'll do it."

The sprite hopped onto the flat screen, paused the promotional video with her foot, and swiped back to the grid of yellow folders on a blue background. She hopped around the screen, opening and closing folders by tapping them with her tiny bare feet.

"There's nothing here! It's all junk and photos."

"What about 'Ship Layout?'"

"I already know where everything is, Philly-Billy! I've been crawling around this ship forever. How do you think I got covered in so much icky dirt and cat hair?"

Philip smiled. "Steady on, old thing. I'm simply trying to help."

"There's a pair of cat fighters on the starboard side," said Nick, rubbing her fat belly and staring at the screen below her feet. "If we can open the launch tubes and unlock the controls, you can fly me away from this stupid place. That would be a change, right? I'm the one with wings. Now it's your turn to fly!"

"A cat fighter? That sounds far too small for me."

"Nah, you'll fit." Nick stared at Philip's long arms and legs. "Maybe?"

Philip sighed. "This is far too risky for my liking, but I'm afraid I haven't any other suggestions. Let's do it."

Nick stared down at the screen again. "Have to find it first." She jumped across the glowing blue display and landed on a folder with one foot, and then rapidly tapped her bare feet on a succession of commands in a drop-down menu. "Settings, View, Show Hidden Files," she murmured.

A black folder appeared in the top corner, causing the entire grid of folders to shift. A text label——'Ship Operations'——appeared below the new item.

"Awesome!" squealed Nick.

The fat-bellied sprite leapt across the glowing screen like a ballerina and landed with the ball of her right foot on the black folder. Nick tapped her feet through several options as a detailed outline of the multi-floored spacecraft appeared.

"Done. Alpha Scout is unlocked and the launch tube is open. We've got exactly sixty seconds to get to the bottom deck of the ship and launch."

Philip jumped to his feet. "But we're still inside her quarters! What about the guards?"

Nick put both hands on her waist and shook her head. "That's your problem, Philly-Billy——always complaining. Lift me up to that ventilation thingy in the other room and get your shoes on."

"I don't have any shoes."

Nick sighed. "Fifty-eight seconds."

"Sorry!"

Philip grabbed Nick and ran into the bedroom. By standing on the top of the couch, he was able to stretch his arms all the way up to the opening and shove Nick inside. The sprite disappeared and Philip heard a staccato of tiny footsteps on aluminum.

"Go to the door!" squealed Nick.

Philip ran to the entrance to One's quarters and waited, his hand on the wheel. He dared not even test the unlocking mechanism for fear of alerting the two guards outside. A sudden scream from outside the hatch. The steel vibrated from a series of violent thumps, and then Philip heard a faint tapping sound.

He spun the wheel and pulled on the heavy hatch, making it swing inside. Out in the corridor, Nick stood beside a pair of cats sprawled on the metal deck, both unconscious.

"How did you do that?"

The tiny blond woman shrugged. "I forgot I couldn't fly, and landed on the head of that one. Both of them were so scared, they ran straight into the wall and knocked themselves out. Let's go! Thirty seconds!"

Philip scooped up Nick and sprinted through the narrow corridors of the *Hare Twist,* the sprite screaming directions and waving her tiny arms. The teenager made a right turn, a left, then slid down a ladder to a lower deck, startling several cats and dogs in orange jumpsuits.

"There! Alpha!"

He jerked open a round hatch and stuck his head into a cramped, ball-shaped cockpit meant for either a large cat or a tiny dog.

"Forget this plan, Nick! It's too small for me."

The sprite windmilled her arms. "Feet first, feet first! Fifteen seconds!"

Philip sat on the deck outside the hatch. He stuck his long legs inside, pressed his feet against the clear glass above the control panel of the tiny fighter, and slid his bottom into the cramped space. As his head cleared the circular hatch, Nick jumped free of his grasp and pulled a red-painted lever inside the cockpit. A metal door whooshed behind Philip's head, taking a few hairs with it.

"My word," he grunted. "Bit of a warning next time, if you please."

The tall, dark-haired teenager found it difficult to breathe, folded in half with his head between his knees and his feet on the windscreen. If he looked up, he could see a circle of black, starry sky beyond the opening of the launch tube.

"How am I supposed ... to fly this thing ... can't even see," he wheezed.

Nick climbed onto the control panel. "Worry about that later. We've got five seconds! How do these things even fly? I only see two holes in the control panel!"

"That's it," wheezed Philip.

He jammed both index fingers into the narrow pits and felt soft buttons on the inside surface of each cylinder.

"It's not working!" fumed Nick.

"Sorry," gasped Philip. "Not ... a cat."

His raised leg accidentally brushed against a clear protective box on the right side of the cockpit and exposed a bright red button. Philip's knee depressed the button with a loud click, and a heavy, invisible force slammed against the back of his legs and threw Nick off the control panel, the engines vibrating with a deafening, high-pitched scream. The cat fighter rocketed out of the launch tube and into the night sky, spinning like an out-of-control obsidian gumball from the side of a giant flying pickle.

9

A narrow set of stairs spiraled up through the imposing white fortress of the Benevolent Society of Methodist Women, the smell of lavender and cedar oil growing stronger and stronger with each creaky wooden step, at last ending in a short hallway beneath the roof. Inside a small room at the corner, a waist-high featherbed stood in the midst of wooden chests and carefully packed boxes of clothing. The wall along the longest part of the room slanted sharply from ceiling to floor, and a multi-paned dormer window looked down upon the dirt streets of Pacific Grove and the smoky surface of the Monterey Bay.

Amy stood at the window like a statue, fists clenched at her sides and her breath fogging the glass as the fading light of dusk covered the village in shades of gray. The faint clank of pots and murmur of female voices echoed up the stairwell as Mrs. Morgan and the cook prepared dinner on the ground floor. Outside the window, a woman in a black dress hurriedly crossed the street holding a dark green umbrella with black fringe against the weak raindrops. A drizzle misted the windowpane in front of Amy's face, the droplets slowly swelling and fattening. Unable to fight gravity any longer, the water streaked down the outside of the glass and matched the tears on Amy's cheeks.

Floorboards creaked behind her, and Amy wiped her eyes with the sleeve of her blouse.

"Are you crying?" asked Three.

Amy sniffed. "I'm not crying, because that would be stupid," she said, her voice distant and hoarse. "It's just allergies."

"That would explain why your eyes are red, but not why you've been standing in the same place when I left. That must have been an hour ago. Are you mad that I took a bath first?"

Amy shook her head. "You're seriously asking me that after everything that's happened today?"

"Sorry."

Three sat on the tall featherbed and tugged her makeup case from under the sheets. She cracked open the slim black rectangle and patted the quilt next to her.

"Come over here. I'll do your face."

Amy trudged across the creaky floor and plopped onto the bed.

"What kind of girl should I be?" asked Three, as she stared into a tiny hand mirror. "Church girl? Party girl? Fake drunk girl? Psycho knife murderer from Japan?"

"None of those. Women don't wear makeup in 1912, especially good Methodist girls staying at a Methodist charity for girls in need."

Three swiped pale foundation on her forehead and cheeks with a wide brush. "That's the most depressing thing I've ever heard. I guess that's why I haven't seen anyone wearing any slap, not even lipstick. Makeup doesn't have to attract attention, you know. How about 'invisible girl?'"

Amy sat with her hands in her lap and watched the rain drip down the panes of the window.

"I've got a plan," she said quietly. "But you're not going to like it."

"Spill the beans, sister," said Three. "You want us to pretend to be boys and stowaway on a ship to the Far East? Sailors always have the best fun. Yo ho ho and a bottle of rum smashed on my head."

"No."

Three paused and waved the foundation brush above her head. "I know! We pretend to be boys and join the army! Soldiers have a great time. We'll gamble and ride horses and shoot outlaws."

Amy sighed. "No."

"We pretend to be boys and become bounty hunters who——"

"What is this about pretending to be boys?" said Amy. "I've spent enough time around my brother and his friends. They're the most annoying, smelly, and stupid creatures in the galaxy, and never leave you alone, whether it's making fun of you or asking you out on a date. Not one of them has two brain cells to rub together, so why would I pretend to be one?"

"I don't know. I thought it was a thing girls did in the old days when they wanted to get away with stuff. This is the wild west, you know. Girls aren't supposed to do anything but find a man and pop out a herd of babies."

"So what? We're not staying here."

"Where are we going, then? The magical land of fairies?"

"Look at the options. This crazy copy of both of us——the evil Amy Armstrong——is still out there. What if she didn't leave and is still looking for us?"

Three nodded. "She doesn't give up, that one. She's like a rabid *poona* in mating season. The red mist fills her eyes and she absolutely won't let go."

"That's why we surrender."

Three slapped the bed. "No way! Are you insane? There's no way I'm going back. Maybe yesterday I might have thought about it, but not now. Not after ... never mind."

"Not after what?"

Three sighed. "Forget it."

"Okay, then just listen to my plan. What if we 'pretend' to give up? It's like a Death Star situation, and one of us is Chewbacca."

"I have no idea what you just said."

"What if I contacted this evil woman and said that I'd captured you? She brings both of us onto her ship––the only transmat-capable spaceship in this dimension, now that the White Star is at the bottom of the sea––and has no idea that we're working together. I break you out of your cell and we take over."

Three nodded slowly. "You're saying we find the weapons lockers, and fight our way to the environmental controls. We could vent all the oxygen into space, but that means killing everyone on board."

"My friends are dead. I don't care about murdering a bunch of pirates."

"That's as crazy as something One would say!"

Amy shrugged. "So?"

"Okay. I guess if we had control of the ship, we could transmat until we found a civilized dimension. But why do I have to be the prisoner?"

Amy shrugged. "There's always a Han, and there's always a Chewbacca. Besides, it's my plan."

She walked downstairs to talk to Mrs. Morgan, leaving Three alone in the room. The young woman left the bed and stood at the rain-misted window, unconsciously biting the fingernails of her right hand.

"This is the worst idea ever," she whispered to herself. "Screw One and her stupid plan to trick Amy into visiting the ship. I have to keep her away from One, no matter what."

Dinner was roast chicken, carrot-and-celery stew, baked potatoes, and fluffy white rolls covered in heaps of melting butter. Four other women who were staying at the house joined Amy, Three, and Mrs. Morgan at the dining table. Luckily, none were from New York, and she was able to deflect all the questions about her and Three by talking about her recent visit to London, which wasn't a lie at all.

After the dishes were cleared away, she helped to move the dining table into the kitchen and arrange chairs around the room. A trickle of more than thirty women and men arrived at the door for the prayer meeting, the men gathering in the dining room and the women in the parlor. Two of the first guests to arrive were Mr. Woodley and his tall German butler. The older gentleman couldn't hide his romantic feelings for Mrs. Morgan––in addition to leaving a name card with the corner folded over, his eyes never left her as she greeted each new arrival.

Amy had been to Sunday school once or twice, and knew what was expected. The meeting turned into an hour-long recitation of verses and prayers while holding hands with the person on either side, one being Three and the other an elderly matron with blue-veined hands and skin as thin as tracing paper. Amy had to kick Three a few times when the teenager either became restless or fell asleep.

After the meeting ended, she dragged Three outside for a breath of fresh air but mainly to keep her from saying something strange to the group of ladies, all of whom were very interested in a pair of shipwrecked girls. A light rain fell from the night sky, and turned the streetlight on the corner into a ball of glowing white mist.

"Wow," said Three. "This is the cracker-jack life. Standing outside at night, getting drippy. Doesn't get any better than this."

"Sarcasm isn't the most attractive thing in the world, especially for a young lady," murmured Amy. "Someone told me that once."

Three shrugged. "I'll tell you one thing, that tall guy with Wheebley or whatever his name is had his eye on me. Both of us, actually. Looking us over, big time."

"Woodley's butler? So what?"

"Just thinking he could join the gang we're making ... and be my butler, if you know what I'm saying."

"You need a handler, not a butler. And we don't need a gang. Did you already forget my plan?"

"Yeah, I know. I'm just having second thoughts about the whole double-cross with One you want me to do, and going back to her crew."

The front door squealed behind them and footsteps thumped on the porch as Mr. Woodley and his butler exited the house. Upon spotting the young women, the gentlemen raised their hats.

"Good evening, ladies," said Mr. Woodley. "I wouldn't spend too much time outside."

Three pouted flirtatiously. "Because of the rain? Don't worry——we're not going to melt!"

Mr. Woodley bowed. "Not at all, Miss Theresa. I don't wish to alarm you, but a mountain lion has been seen near Pebble Beach. The army is out looking for it, even in this weather." He tipped his hat again. "Good evening!"

Three watched them walk up the street, and waved at Weiss as the tall German glanced back at her. "See what I mean? That butler totally wants to be our slave. Well, mainly MY slave, but you could have him on Thursdays."

"I hate Thursdays," said Amy quietly.

"Exactly. Wait, what?"

Amy sighed. She closed her eyes and turned her face to the sky so the tiny drops of rain could roll down her skin.

THE ARMORED CAT thumped through the gloomy dunes of Asilomar beach, its heavy, slow steps shaking the limbs of scrubby coastal redwoods and causing tiny avalanches of damp sand. A light rain whirled down from the clouds and misted the cockpit inside the mouth of the steel tiger. Through a narrow slice of glass, the head of a cat wearing a red pilot's helmet bounced left and right.

"Come on, Sunnie," whined Betsy from the back seat. "Go faster."

Sunflower tightened the strap of his helmet and stuck his paws back into the holes in the control panel.

"Do you want these backward monkeys to know we're here? Any more noise and the entire village are going to run screaming out of their caves, ready to cook us alive or something."

"Even in this rain?"

"Yes. Can you check the radar? I think we lost the soldiers."

Betsy giggled. "They looked so goofy! I want to see that again. They should be riding goats or pigs or a smarter animal, right? Horses are so silly. Anyway, it's not like they can get us while we're inside the tank." He paused. "Can they get us?"

"Of course not. But they might keep me from luring that evil Amy out of her ship. Whatever happens, we can't attract attention from the humans. As the cat warrior Colin Powell once said: 'Softly, softly, catchee monkey.'"

"That's not a cat saying, it's a dog saying," murmured Betsy. The brown-and-white terrier stared at a handful of tiny glowing balls on the holographic radar that floated above his control panel. "Those horse people are really close behind us. Are you sure we can't make friends?"

Sunflower quickly moved his paws in the control pits and halted the lumbering tank on legs. Hydraulic legs hissed and bent as Sunflower maneuvered the bulky armored vehicle down behind a nearby dune.

"Human monkeys can't see that well at night," he whispered. "So we've got that going for us. Better pray they don't find our tracks in the dog-blasted wet sand of this dog-blasted beach."

"Why are you whispering?" asked Betsy. "They can't hear us."

"Because I have a splitting migraine. There's a constant yammering and yapping coming from behind me."

"You should see a doctor. My cousin's a doctor and could fix you up, once he gets out of dog prison. He might be out already. What year is it?"

Sunflower sighed. "Please stop talking. Also, I know what your tiny brain is thinking, and don't whistle. I hate whistling even more than talking."

"Okay, Sunnie."

"No humming, either!"

"Wow, Grouchy Greg. Are you going to be this grouchy all night, Grouchy Greg?"

"Yes, until the human soldiers are gone, and until you stop calling me Grouchy Greg."

Betsy yawned and slumped his furry shoulders. He stared down at the control panel.

"Hey, Sunnie, what's an 'Overshield?' It sounds like fun."

"Don't touch that!"

A brilliant blue sphere crackled to life around the giant armored cat, illuminating the dunes like a giant searchlight from heaven. Two hundred meters to the south, a dozen cavalry soldiers in damp brown uniforms saw the flash and kicked their horses toward it.

"Uh ... my bad," whispered Betsy. "Sorry?"

"Too late for sorry! Hold onto your butt!"

Sunflower jammed his paws into the control pits and the giant steel cat leapt into the air, arcing across the night sky like a flaming ball from a Roman candle. The machine slammed its heavy legs into the dunes and sprang into the air again, jump jets flaring white and bullets from the cavalry rifles cracking past like invisible popcorn. The few rounds that hit the shield bounced harmlessly into the night with the red glow of molten lead.

"Turn that shield off so can hide again," growled Sunflower.

"I think it's stuck," said Betsy. "Computer, shut off the overshield."

"Negative," said the robotic voice of the flight computer. "Section fourteen point seven of the operating manual says that a protective Overshield (trademark) or comparable defensive screen must be deployed when receiving ballistic fire from an enemy."

"I don't believe it," growled Sunflower. "This hunk of junk hates me."

"Incorrect," said the flight computer. "I am a machine and cannot hate. I just don't like you."

The giant armored tiger curved across the sky and slammed down into a small evergreen, the explosive crash turning the tree into a shower of pink redwood splinters. The large vehicle immediately leapt into the air again, throwing Sunflower and Betsy against their harnesses.

Ahead through the narrow window, Sunflower saw a white-painted lighthouse framed against the sea, and to the right, the tree-lined grid of the human village, its gas streetlights glowing pale blue. From the map he'd studied earlier, he knew the chances for hiding or escaping the soldiers were not very good the closer they came to the village.

"This entire hive of monkeys will know we're here if we don't turn around," said the cat. "But if we do turn around, we won't get another chance to catch that evil Amy. She could leave us stranded on this monkey planet."

Betsy giggled. "You know what dogs say––sticks don't catch themselves. Whoa, Sunnie! Why are you whacking the side of your helmet and groaning like that?"

"Because I don't have a stick to throw at your face," said the cat. "Tune the radio transmitter to encrypted channel 192. We're going to send a message."

THE GIANT green pickle of the *Hare Twist* hovered a thousand meters over the dark surface of the Monterey Bay and projected an energy field that allowed light from one side to pass through to the other, turning the large spacecraft into just a smudge against the night sky. A flash of brilliant orange illuminated the side of the smudge and caused the energy field to flicker, as a tiny black dot flew from a launch tube and curved down to the ocean.

The ball bounced and curved on a wild course down to the ocean, but pulled up from the surface at the last moment as it burst through the crest of a wave. The circular pattern of engines at the rear of the ball flared brightly as it gained altitude.

"I'm going to be sick," squeaked a female voice from the back of the cramped cockpit. "Oooh ..."

"Please don't," gasped Philip.

The knees of the teenager were pushed up to his ears. His sock-covered feet were smashed against the clear windscreen of the fighter, and his hands were stretched in front of him with both index fingers stuck inside tubes in the control panel.

"Sooo ... sick."

Nick grabbed the back of Philip's shirt and climbed to his left shoulder. The tiny blonde woman coughed and spewed a stream of deep brown goo onto the front of Philip's shirt, depositing at least a pint of sweet-smelling liquid over the teenager and the inside of the cockpit.

"My word!" gasped Philip.

Nick wiped her mouth. "I'll never eat ... chocolate again."

"That makes two of us."

The sprite pointed at her belly. "Hey! I'm not fat anymore!"

"Good show," said Philip. "Please help ... I can't fly this thing much longer."

Nick jumped up to the control panel.

"How am I supposed to help you? I'm trained in minerals and gems, not cat fighters!"

"Anything ... could ... help," gasped Philip.

Nick grabbed onto the front of the control panel and stared outside.

"Pull up, pull up, pull up!"

The cucumber shape of the *Hare Twist* flashed by as the fighter barely missed the rear navigational fin of the huge ship.

"Are you trying to kill us?" asked Nick. "Head the other way. Toward land, toward land!"

"I can't see a thing! I'm folded in half, you must have noticed."

"I'll give you directions. Go left. Too much. Pull up! Down a bit. Now right. Go right! There's a big light straight ahead. Don't touch anything!"

The black ball curved and wobbled around in the star-filled sky, at last pointing itself toward a lighthouse on the coast. After all the jiggling and bouncing, every surface that hadn't previously been coated with the chocolate contents of Nick's stomach were now splattered with brown.

"Air," coughed Philip. "Need air."

"What a baby," said Nick. "You'll get air when we crash. Okay––what should we crash into? A bunch of big rocks, the mountains, or the beach? That's all I see."

"Something ... else?"

A speaker on the control panel crackled, and Betsy's voice filled the cockpit.

"Hey-yo! This is Ensign Betsy Jackson of the transport division––wait, I don't have that job anymore since I became friends with Amy and left the *Dream Tiger*. Hey, Sunnie! What's my job now?"

Nick jumped up and down on the control panel. "Betsy's not dead! Betsy's not dead!"

"I share your enthusiasm," coughed Philip, and shifted his knees away from his ears slightly. "Where's it coming from?"

The audio popped and crackled.

"Okay, starting over. Hey-yo! This is Betsy. One, two, three ... Am I talking to anyone? Scarface Amy, are you there? I don't think we should call her that, Sunnie. Maybe she's nice and wants to be friends and will give us cake and candy and chocolate. Is this even working? Ow! Stop it!"

Several thumps came from the speaker.

"I stick my head under the seat for two seconds to try and turn off this stupid overshield," said Sunflower's voice. "And you're yapping away on the transmitter?"

"Don't get mad," said Betsy. "It's not even on."

"Of course it is! I can see a green light!"

Philip wiggled his bare toes on the filthy, brown-splattered cockpit window, as he tried to keep the tiny fighter flying straight and level.

"Can you answer them?" he asked. "Are they nearby?"

"No and yes," said Nick. "I think they're somewhere close to the big light. The one rotating around? Don't know what it is, but Sunnie and Betsy are there."

"Probably a lighthouse. Give me directions and I'll point us that way."

The speakers hissed and Sunflower spoke again.

"Attention, evil scarface Amy, attention," said the cat. "I should say, copy of Amy, because we all know you're not the real Amy. She's the bravest and smartest human in the entire galaxy, and almost as good as a cat. Speaking of that, I know you have the Andy Nakamura on your ship. Surrender her and the real Amy, and you can go free. Refuse and face my wrath. That means anger, if you want to see a very angry cat. My location is thirty-six point six three three four one six by negative one-twenty-one point nine three three seven one six, but you can probably just look for the glowing blue ball near the lighthouse. Hard to miss. Amy Armstrong is my friend, and I'll be waiting for you there. Commander Sunflower of Red Squadron over and out."

"Is he trying to get killed?" asked Nick. "Scarface has a million-billion soldiers!"

"More worried about myself at the moment, actually," sniffed Philip.

Red lights flashed on the control panel and a loud, rapid beeping filled the cockpit.

"Missile lock, missile lock," said a computerized voice.

"Get us out of here!" yelled Nick.

"How?!!"

"I don't know! Move faster! Left, left! Go toward the light!"

A ferocious shockwave knocked the tiny sprite back onto Philip. Shards of red-hot metal ripped across the sky and into the cat fighter, and filled the cockpit with flame and smoke. The tiny ball fell dark and powerless toward the rotating beam of light and the black rocks of the coast.

10

The lights in the command room had been dimmed for night duty, and the normally busy and packed control stations were empty apart from three crew members. A handful of screens blinked with slow streams of data, but the majority around the walls were dead black rectangles.

One slumped in the large captain's chair in the center of the room, her scarlet high heels kicked off and lying on the floor in front of her. Steam curled from a plastic cup on the armrest, and a warm blanket covered her from chin to ankle. At the lowest edge of the blanket, her stockinged feet were spread apart lazily, the toes wiggling slowly as if she were a tired secretary at the end of the day, instead of the commander of three starships and a thousand pirates.

Her attention was split between a pair of displays on the wall. To the left flickered a subtitled video with the volume turned down. The long-haired Asian actors wore colorful silk robes and rode horses through a lush forest. The screen on the right showed an image of Four, wearing a bright yellow blouse instead of a black turtleneck, even though One kept telling her that yellow wasn't the best color for a pale complexion. Four kept her hair dyed black and cut in a short bob––a leftover of her personal life from before she had met One.

"After that, I'll tell him about my father being really mean to me," murmured Four. "About the beatings, too. Do you think that's enough? To have him fall in love with me, I mean. Boys always want to play the savior."

One frowned. Her eyes were on the Asian drama, not Four.

"We're going to throw him in the quantum trans-fuser, so why does it matter? Why do you have to play these little love games when it's your turn?"

Four pouted. "For that look on his face inside the transfuser, when he realizes he's going to die. When everything he feels is upside down and inside out."

One took a sip of her steaming drink. "It's not going to work on this Philip. He's different."

"They're all different. It's all about finding the angle."

"No. I don't think there's anything you can say, an outfit you can wear, an eyelash you can flutter that will change him. He loved that young copy of us totally and completely. You have about the same chance as changing his feelings for her as you do standing in front of a prairie fire and waving your arms."

"Maybe if I had more time ..."

"WE don't have the time. There's too much work to do." One held out her thumb and index finger, a tiny gap between the two. "I'm this close to triangulation on SpaceBook."

Four shook her head. "You know what they say about all work and no play. Wait——are you watching that stupid three-dee drama? You're not even listening to me."

One shrugged. "I can pay attention to more than one thing at a time."

Wilson galloped into the command room, tripped over the doorway, and sprawled on his furry face. The black cat scrambled to his feet and tip-toed behind the captain's chair.

"What is it?" asked One, without looking away from the two screens on the forward wall.

Wilson stood on his hind legs and bowed. "Apologies, my Lady. We've tracked the flying pest to your quarters, and I would like permission to enter and search your rooms."

Four yawned. "Too boring for me." The screen with her image snapped to black.

One sighed and took a sip from her cup. "Just do it. You don't need my permission."

Wilson rubbed his front paws nervously. "Um ... may I remind my Lady about that time with the space weevil? You said no crew member could enter your rooms after that."

Leather squeaked as One shifted in her chair. "For good reason. A platoon of cat soldiers with plasma rifles is not how you catch anything, especially a space weevil. I'm still finding burned bits of cat hair in the carpet."

Wilson smiled and flattened his ears. "Indeed, my Lady. The most recent news is that the space weevil hitched a ride to Phobos. He sent me a postcard and is doing quite well. His brother-in-law apparently found him a job in the department of agriculture."

One closed her eyes. "Please leave immediately, or you'll also be taking a dirt nap on Phobos with your new friend the space weevil."

Wilson bowed. "Yes, my Lady."

A red light flashed at one of the active stations. The beagle sitting behind it yelped and tapped rapidly on the keyboard.

"My Lady, we have a problem!"

"Keep talking."

"Someone has opened the door for Launch Tube One," said the beagle. "Alpha Scout has begun engine check and automatic startup procedures!"

One yawned without bothering to cover her mouth. "Why is this a problem? Probably just going on a scout mission. That's what scout fighters do."

"Yes, my Lady, but there's no mission scheduled. I double-checked with the flight deck!"

"Probably a bug in the system," said One. "Cancel it. Do a command override."

The beagle tapped furiously on the keyboard.

"I can't! It's a red-priority request, which means it came from you, my Lady!"

"That's not possible," said One. "I'm sitting right here. Nobody else could have——" She threw off the blanket and stood from her chair. "Yellow Alert! Lock down the ship!"

Wilson jumped to a nearby console and tapped the keys. He grabbed a nearby microphone.

"All stations yellow alert! Repeat——all stations general quarters, all stations general quarters!"

The lights in the command center changed to red and a square panel above the door flashed yellow. A low klaxon like a rapidly pealing fog horn vibrated the entire ship. After a short moment, a stream of cats and dogs galloped through the open hatch and jumped behind consoles. Displays snapped to life around the walls.

"Show me the guards outside my room," said One.

Wilson tapped the keyboard with his paws, and one of the screens switched to a camera feed of the hallway outside One's quarters. A pair of guards lay crumpled and senseless in front of the open hatch.

"Idiots!" One stomped a stockinged foot on the metal deck and immediately winced. "Ouch, ouch, ouch. Wilson——make a note to buy me a rug on your next planetfall."

"Yes, my Lady." Wilson grabbed a thin microphone nearby. "Medic to captain's quarters. Repeat, medic to captain's quarters. Two crew members unconscious with unknown injuries."

"Send a squad of soldiers to the launch tube," said One. "Do we have a feed? Show me!"

A fuzzy video appeared in the center display, showing an open hatch and Philip squeezed inside the tiny round cockpit of a cat fighter. The circular hatch slammed shut and the camera vibrated.

"Tube One is live, Tube One is live!" barked the beagle. "We have an unauthorized launch!"

The display switched to a camera outside the ship. A tiny black ball curved down to the ocean, the engines glowing orange and leaving a faint trail of vapor across the night sky.

One sat down slowly in her command chair, her shoulders slumped and mouth drawn into a tight line.

"Orders, my Lady?" asked Wilson.

"Launch Beta Scout," whispered One. "Shoot him down."

"Yes, my Lady."

A white Persian cat wearing a headset over his ears and microphone boom in front of his mouth stood from his station and saluted.

"Receiving a transmission, my Lady! Encrypted channel 192, but we have the key."

"Sounds familiar," murmured One. "Is that the channel the traitor Andy Nakamura was using?"

"Yes, my Lady."

"Let me hear it."

Static-filled audio played through a pair of speakers in One's chair.

"Okay, starting over. Hey-yo! This is Betsy. One, two, three ... Am I talking to anyone? Scarface Amy, are you there? I don't think we should call her that, Sunnie. Maybe she's nice and wants to be friends and will give us cake and candy and chocolate. Is this even working? Ow! Stop it!"

One turned and stared at the communications cat. "What in the name of Crom? Where's this signal coming from?"

"From the coast near the human village, my Lady," said the white cat. "Several kilometers from our current position."

Sunflower's voice came through the speakers.

"Attention, evil scarface Amy, attention. I should say, copy of Amy, because we all know you're not the real Amy. She's the bravest and smartest human in the entire galaxy, and almost as good as a cat. Speaking of that, I know you have the Andy Nakamura on your ship. Surrender her and the real Amy, and you can go free. Refuse and face my wrath. That means anger, if you want to see a very angry cat. My location is thirty-six point six three three four one six by negative one-twenty-one point nine three three seven one six, but you can probably just look for the glowing blue ball near the lighthouse. Hard to miss. Amy Armstrong is my friend, and I'll be waiting for you there. Commander Sunflower of Red Squadron over and out."

"I've got the location, my Lady!" said Wilson, and jabbed a black paw at his screen.

One frowned. "How many inspectors do we have left in the fleet?"

"Three," said Wilson.

"What? I had four dozen! Do you know how much those dogs charged for those flying metal monsters?"

"My Lady, the others were destroyed on Tau Ceti in the battle to recover Doctor MacGuffin."

"Beta Scout approaching missile range," said the beagle. "He is requesting permission to fire."

"Fire away," said One.

The beagle nodded. "Missile fired. Aaand ... Alpha Scout is down, and crashed on land, not the sea. Impact location is close to the human village."

One sighed and clasped her fingers together. "Send a squad of walkers to the crash location. I don't care if they turn the place into a radioactive wasteland, as long as they find Philip's body and bring it to me."

Wilson rubbed his paws rapidly. "What about the transmission, my Lady?"

The communications officer spoke up. "The background modulation sounds like a Tau Ceti design," said the white cat. "I strongly believe they are using cat military equipment, my Lady."

"Load up every transport in the fleet with combat troops," said One. "Get Two and Four on the line, and I'll tell them myself."

Wilson gasped. "Every soldier? Just to catch a pair of idiots who hijacked a radio?"

One gritted her teeth. She reached over and poked the black cat's head with a red-painted fingernail.

"Every cat and dog who can fog a mirror is going to make planetfall with plasma rifles and full combat gear, and that includes you! Turn that filthy human village into a pile of ash and glowing cinders if you have to, but bring Three and the copy back alive. If a pair of morons survived the wreck, then so can a pair of smart girls."

A SHARP PAIN jabbed Philip's cheek.

"Wake up!" sobbed Nick. "Please don't die, Phillie!"

Philip groaned and rubbed the side of his face.

"Is that you, Nick? Ugh ... I feel like someone biffed me with a hammer."

Nick tossed a metal pipe into the darkness.

"It's your imagination," she said. "Stand up!"

Philip groaned and pushed himself into a sitting position. The cat fighter lay a few meters away at the end of a long furrow of sand on the darkened beach. The ball of black metal was split open like a cracked egg, and smoke poured from the inside and streamed into the night sky. Sharp fragments of metal were scattered across the sand as far as he could see, each in their own tiny furrows or craters. A wave suddenly foamed white and crashed into the broken pieces of the cat fighter, pulling it toward the sea as if nature were trying to clean up the mess. A scatter of gun fire sounded in the night, faint enough that Philip confused it for a moment with waves striking off-shore rocks.

"Were those rifle shots?" he asked. "Even Americans wouldn't hunt at this time of night. You couldn't hit a goat tied to a fence in this darkness."

Nick leaned forward and squinted at the teenager.

"You just survived a crash and now you're talking about goats?"

"I'm talking about those rifle shots I heard."

"It's the ocean, silly!"

"I disagree. There's another one! Wait a moment––how did you pull me from the wreckage?"

Nick stamped her foot. "Don't make me hit you with that pipe again. We have to run!"

"Why?"

The tiny sprite pointed at the night sky and Philip tilted his head back.

"Polaris? The three sisters? I see nothing but the stars and the prosaic beauty of clouds swimming through the sky. What's the point?"

"Not the clouds, you silly. Look closer!"

A section of the slate-gray clouds shivered like heat waves in the desert. Philip rubbed his eyes again and stared. The shapes of three mammoth, tubular starships flickered into existence and loomed overhead, dark and menacing.

"That's scarface Amy," said Nick. "She wants you back in a bad way!"

"No! I won't have it!"

Philip climbed to his feet and ran south along the beach, the starships at his back.

"Not that way!" squealed Nick. She buzzed into the air after the teenager. "Sunflower's signal is the other direction! Don't you see the blue glowing thing? That's him!"

Philip slid to a stop in the cold sand. "What a horrid bit of business this is," he muttered to himself.

A slight movement down the beach caught his attention. He squinted and craned his neck at a jumble of tall rocks above the surf.

Nick fluttered to his shoulder. "What's wrong?"

"How queer––I thought I saw something move."

The tiny sprite giggled. "You're afraid of everything, Phillie! Remember when we watched that documentary about the cat and sauro wars? You thought giant lizards were hiding everywhere and were afraid of the dark for a week! So cute."

Three tall shadows separated from the rocks. A horrific bellow rolled over the beach, louder than the sound of the waves, and best described as the horrific scream of a leopard falling from a plane without a parachute, combined with the roar of a lion who has

unfortunately jammed his paw into an electrical out-
let. The shadows changed into three charging lizards,
their muscular legs spraying huge gouts of sand and
sharp teeth gleaming in their wide-open jaws.

"Sauros!" yelled Nick.

The sprite buzzed up the beach and away from the
attacking reptiles, with Philip huffing and puffing after her.

A ROUND fired from a .30-06 Springfield 1903 rifle
weighs eleven grams and has a muzzle velocity of 850
meters per second. The formula for kinetic energy is
$1/2\ mv2$, giving the bullet an energy of 3,973 Joules.
In layman's terms, this has the same energy as a
hockey puck traveling 450 miles per hour, or four
times the normal speed.

However, even a bullet made of diamonds and
rainbows shot from a cannon by unicorns wouldn't
have touched the overshield around the gigantic armored cat as it ran through the coastal pines and
jumped a series of high parabola over the forest. The
glowing blue sphere acted as a soapy bubble of magnetic energy and deflected the lead bullets harmlessly
into the darkness. The pursuing soldiers saw a fiery
shower of sparks as each bullet hit the shield. Mistak-
ing the sparks for successful hits, the soldiers cheered
and urged their horses faster through the trees even as
the gigantic metal tiger jumped higher and faster.

In the navigator's seat behind Sunflower, Betsy
peered at the holographic data floating over his control panel. The cockpit shook from a heavy impact and
his flight helmet slid over his eyes.

"Watch it, Sunnie!"

"You try driving this thing in the dark," said the orange tabby in the front seat. "There are trees everywhere!"

"No problem for a qualified pilot," said the flight computer.

Sunflower slapped the console. "I told you to turn that thing off!"

"But Sunnie, we need his help," said Betsy.

"Anything from the sensors?"

Betsy shook his head. "Too much static. I think it's the shield, and I can't shut it off because somebody's shooting at us."

"Safety first," said the flight computer.

"I'll give you safety," said Sunflower. "Can't turn it off because of our new friends? I'll show them."

The cockpit shuddered as the armored cat leaped into the air, brushed past a pair of narrow redwood trees, landed on all fours, and slid through the wet ferns, leaving a trail in the mud a dozen meters long. Super-heated steam blew from vents in the sides of the giant steel beast. The energy bubble around the massive vehicle colored the trees an otherworldly, fantastical shade of blue, as if the entire forest were underwater. Sunflower spun the giant machine to face the horsemen galloping from the rear.

"Don't hurt them, Sunnie," said Betsy. "Maybe they want to be friends."

"Friends don't shoot at each other."

"What about that one time? You said it was for fun."

"Different situation," said the cat. "I was the one doing the shooting."

The dozen horses of the cavalry patrol slid to a stop ten meters away, the dark brown animals shiny with sweat and blowing clouds of steamy breath in the cold night air. The soldiers pointed their rifles at the giant metal tiger.

Sunflower pressed a button. The armored cat raised its head with a deafening roar, shaking the redwood branches with a sound like a Bengal tiger that had swallowed a jet turbine. The horses bucked and reared on their hind legs, throwing half the soldiers into the ferns. This shocking development motivated each and every one of the soldiers to turn tail and run.

The forest darkened as the glowing bubble snapped off.

"Overshield deactivated," said the flight computer.

"Finally," said Sunflower. "Tell me you've found something."

"Give me a second, Sunnie," said Betsy. "Everything's covered with red jam back here."

"Red jam? Are you hurt? Betsy, talk to me! Say something!"

"Why? I was just hungry and opened a jar of raspberry jam. Clumsy me, now it's everywhere. I guess I'll have to lick it up. Yum, yum, yum, get in my tum, tum, tum."

"Are you serious? We're about to die in an apocalyptic battle with the forces of evil clone Amy, and you're licking your control panel?"

Betsy looked up, his jaws covered with red. "I can't 'not' lick it. Use your head, Sunnie!"

"If I used my head I'd be running away from a fleet of blood-thirsty dimensional pirates," said Sunflower. "Not sending out a message to get their attention!"

"Uh ... you could be right about that."

Sunflower sighed. "Please tell me that sudden beeping is a contact on the sensors."

"What? Oh, you're right! One, two, three ... I see three pickle-shaped things on the display."

"Magic pickles that learned to fly?"

"If that's true, these are the biggest pickles I've ever seen," said Betsy. "Pickles two hundred meters long and strapped to giant engines with radiation signatures. Wait––the three pickles had babies! Four, five ... six more pickles on the screen, all tiny! I wonder if they have names already."

Sunflower tapped his console with a furry paw. The holographic image in front of his nose shivered and changed to a transparent orange projection of three pickle-shaped starships. Six white dots appeared below the ships and dropped toward the surface.

"Landing craft, just like I told you," said Sunflower. "I love it when a plan comes together."

The orange tabby moved his paws in the control pits, spinning the giant armored machine in the damp redwood needles and sending it on a rocket-assisted leap through the forest. Both Sunflower and Betsy might have been thrown around the cockpit and broken a few bones from the violent acceleration, if it weren't for the safety harnesses strapping each to his seat.

"Looks like the baby pickles are coming down," said Betsy. "Do you think they want to make friends like the horse people?"

"Of course. Exactly like that."

With a crash of splintered trees, Sunflower piloted the steel tiger out of the forest and charged across sand dunes covered with thick, scrubby bushes. Ground squirrels with long, stringy tails fled for their lives across the sand, and white seagulls sprang into the sky and screamed quite a few seagull bad words at the noise.

"See that big rotating light? I'll drop you off there," said Sunflower. "That's also our meeting place if anything goes wrong."

"Nothing will go wrong, Sunnie! Everyone likes dogs and wants to be my friend."

"Right. Shove a hat on a *poona* and he'll be emperor."

"What did you say?"

"I said your fur looks nice today. Now, don't forget the plan——find a transport and get on board. Are you ready?"

"Sure!"

A low tone sounded in the cockpit.

"Warning," said the flight computer. "Multiple craft with no identifier beacons on intercept course. Gamma radiation detected. Recommend increasing speed and changing heading to ninety-four degrees."

"We're not doing that," said Sunflower. "I want them to intercept us."

"Really?" scoffed the computer. "It's your funeral."

"Yours, too, if you don't move faster, you over-engineered trash can!"

"No need to be mean about it. I've got feelings, too, you know."

Sunflower rolled his eyes. "I really doubt that."

The steel beast thumped and tore through the dunes like a steam train with Roger Bannister's legs, leaving a wide trail of broken trees and cracked branches. Sunflower pulled the controls and the armored cat slid to a stop on a trimmed lawn behind the slowly rotating light. The navigational beacon was actually a two-story house of white brick with a round tower sticking up from the roof. Inside the windows of the tower, a brilliant flash of light rotated slowly.

Sunflower pulled a lever and the jaws of the giant steel tiger split horizontally, the top half of the head folding back over the neck to reveal the twin seats of the cockpit.

The orange tabby felt a mist of rain on his whiskers, and immediately closed his eyes and inhaled a deep breath of fresh air. His feeling of peaceful calm was destroyed by Betsy climbing over the seat and shoving his doggie bottom in the cat's face.

"Hey!"

"Sorry, Sunnie!"

The brown-and-white terrier clambered over the side and dropped two meters to the sandy lawn.

"I left my helmet under my seat," he said, tail wagging.

Sunflower leaned over the side. "Thanks for that information, Captain Obvious. I'll mail it to you first thing in the——"

"Incoming fire," said the flight computer.

Sunflower chuckled. "A few little bullets won't hurt us."

"I SAID INCOMING FIRE!" screamed the flight computer.

The cockpit snapped shut with a ferocity that almost took off Sunflower's right paw, and Betsy scampered away into the darkness as if the little dog had been shot from a gun. A nano-second later, the two-story lighthouse exploded in an earth-shaking ball of flame, scattering white bricks, lumber, and glass for hundreds of yards.

Sunflower was thrown against his harness as the cockpit spun wildly and a storm of debris clanged against the steel skin. The machine stopped moving at last, but the view outside was blocked by the irregular fragments of orange clay bricks.

Sunflower pushed back his helmet. "Damage report."

"You actually think that little blast of plasma would hurt me?" chuckled the flight computer. "It wasn't even a direct hit. Oh, wait. The damage report module was damaged, eliminating my ability to report damage. This could be bad."

"That's a joke, right? I know you're just a flight computer, but that's got to be a joke."

"Battle damage is very serious."

"What are you talking about?!!"

"Let me be clear––the idea of battle damage is very serious. Apart from the damage to the damage reporting module, we're perfectly fine. One hundred percent!"

Sunflower sighed. "Blessed Saint Mittens and his three legs."

He piloted the giant beast out of a pile of bricks and wooden beams, and tromped to the smoking hole in the ground where the lighthouse had stood only a moment before.

"Can you see Betsy? Is he okay?"

"Navigator is currently hiding under a bush, point three kilometers to the east," said the flight computer. "He was outside the blast radius. Note: action required. Incoming fire."

"Turn on the overshield!"

Sunflower twisted his paws in the control pits and the steel tiger leapt into the air, side thrusters burning brightly, as a second energy blast shook the cockpit and turned night into day.

The armored cat landed on all fours in a meadow near the destroyed lighthouse. Sunflower squinted at a pair of black domes on the beach to the south. Lines of tiny figures streamed onto the pale sand from each of the transports. With a bright gleam of landing jets, two more domes skimmed over the waves and settled on the beach. The doors slammed down and even more cat and dog soldiers charged out, with a faint "hup, hup, hup" carried by the cool ocean breeze.

"Retreat is recommended," said the flight computer. "Walker radiation signatures detected."

Sunflower jammed his paws in the control pits, his furry face curled into a snarl.

"Running away isn't part of the plan!"

He turned the armored beast toward the transports and charged, zig-zagging through the dunes with great leaps that left four huge trenches in the sand when the giant machine landed. The soldiers saw him coming and fired brilliant cobalt beams of plasma from their rifles. Many of the shots of crackling energy missed but a few burned through the overshield and cut deep lines across the skin of the steel tiger. Where it was hit, the edges of the damaged steel turned bright orange.

The smells of melted plastic and heated metal tickled his nose, and Sunflower grimaced.

"Bad kitties," he growled.

He toggled off the weapon safety. At the apex of the next jump, a barrage of tiny rockets burst from pods on the back of the armored cat and curved through the night sky, almost scraping the bottom of the clouds. Like a shower of Roman candles, the miniature but highly explosive missiles rained down on the transports, blowing apart two with several dull booms and flashes of heat.

The giant steel tiger landed in the middle of the soldiers. It roared with a tremendous, sand-shivering sound and charged back and forth, batting at the astonished cats and dogs with razor claws and armored tail. Not expecting to face a military-grade Tau Ceti battle tank, hundreds of cooks, technicians, and laundry workers dropped their rifles and ran down the beach away from the gigantic, red-eyed horror. Several brigades of trained soldiers gathered in the dunes and reformed their fire teams, but Sunflower landed in the midst of each, scattering hundreds of cats and dogs in all directions. The ones still alive fled into the night.

"Damage report," said Sunflower.

"Did you forget already?" asked the flight computer. "The damage report module was damaged."

A beam of blue plasma shot from the dunes, sparking through the overshield and burning a hole through the armored cat's front leg. Sunflower clicked a toggle and fired a single missile into the darkness. A red flash and dull boom rolled over the beach.

"How many transports left?"

"Two," said the flight computer. "One is charging engines. It has now lifted off."

"What about Betsy? Did he make it?"

"The navigator is entering the last transport."

"Great. Give me emergency power on the thrusters!"

Sunflower spun the armored cat and leaped high, jump jets blazing and front claws outstretched. Although the dome-shaped transport was twenty times the size of the steel beast, it was designed for rapid, efficient delivery of supplies, not resisting an attack from Tau Ceti's finest military equipment. The armored beast plowed into the curved side of the transport, ripping with razor claws, roaring, and firing the last few missiles in the pod. The rapidly rising transport tipped sideways and curved a gentle arc over the ocean, crashing into the water with a towering white plume.

The beach became quiet, and the waves rolled up the sand and faded back the same way they had for millions of years. A few hundred cat and dog soldiers came out of hiding to search for their wounded comrades. They carried the injured animals to the last transport, and then formed a line and quick-marched to the south, where the distant thump of walkers could be heard and plasma beams turned the dark clouds orange and blue. With a crackle and fizz of retro-burners, the transport lifted off toward the three starships floating like clouds in the night sky.

Ten minutes later, a pair of red coals glowed under the waves, and the armored cat clanked out of the ocean. One of the back legs made a grinding sound and moved slower than the other three legs, forcing the machine to walk with a limp.

"I'm not designed for swimming," said the flight computer. "I shouldn't have to tell you twice."

Inside the cockpit, Sunflower rubbed his eyes. "I didn't expect to crash into the sea!"

"Crashing into a mountain would have been better?"

Sunflower guided the giant beast over the beach, the heavy paws crunching on the large number of weapons, pieces of armor, and candy bar wrappers dropped on the sand by One's frightened soldiers. He leaned forward and stared through the armored window of the cockpit.

"Looks like the survivors are moving south. I see plasma fire––what are they shooting at? We'd better finish them off."

He pressed the controls to activate a jump, but instead of leaping into the air, the giant beast simply tottered a few steps.

"What's wrong?"

"Well, pilot," said the flight computer. "I've got good   news   and   bad   news."

"Make my day and tell me you're going to self-destruct."

"Negative. The impact with the surface of the water has jostled the damage report module. It is now able to report damage."

Sunflower sighed. "The bad news?"

"Jump jets are offline. Overshield is offline. Micro-missiles are gone and offline. Land speed limited to a fast trot."

"A fast trot?"

"An overstatement. My travel speed is currently limited to the rapid jog of a pregnant duck."

Sunflower unfastened his helmet and squeezed into the back seat.

"Great. Follow those stragglers, Mrs. Duck, while I try and fix the damage."

11

Betsy dug into the sand behind a dune and kept his brown-and-white head low to the ground as the battle raged across the beach. A solid rectangle of three hundred cats and dogs in armor charged past on all fours, their paws splashing through the foaming water and the rifles on their backs shooting blue plasma fire. A terrible roar sounded in the darkness, followed by screams and thumps. The remnants of the battalion galloped back the way they had come, dropping their helmets and weapons to run even faster.

Betsy's furry ears perked up and he tried to filter the sound of explosions and plasma beams from the chest-vibrating rumble of large engines. The Jack Russell terrier gathered his legs into a crouch on the cold sand, his eyes on the glossy black dome of a transport shuttle. At the last moment, he raced down the dunes and across the beach, dodging the flaming wreckage of walkers and the bodies of cats and dogs. The little terrier scrambled up the open ramp of the transport, plopped into the nearest seat, and clicked the safety webbing around his chest. The engines kicked in hard and pushed him into the hard cushion like a melting ice cream cone.

The rest of the one hundred seats around the huge circular compartment were empty, apart from a beagle and a white Persian with scorched fur. Both animals wore olive-green combat armor on their chests and legs, but had lost their rifles. The cat wore a helmet, but it was less than functional at this point––the visor had shattered into a thousand tiny cracks, and something had scratched deep claw marks across the left side.

The white cat with the burnt fur grabbed his helmet with both paws, twisted it to the left a quarter-turn, and lifted it off his head.

"Great Holy Cheezburger," he gasped, his blue eyes wide. "What was that?"

"You should know better than me," said the beagle.

"It looked like a C-34 Battle Cat, but that's impossible! The Emperor would never sell military hardware to Centaurans. How are the man-monkeys even piloting it? Number one––they're too fat, and number two––they have brains like babies. Babies can't drive a tank! I should know––I have twelve of them at home."

"Tanks?" asked the beagle.

"No! Kittens!"

The transport tilted sharply and slowed.

"Calm down," said the beagle. "We're probably not even on Alpha Centauri. Don't believe everything you read on the message boards."

"Yeah right, genius. If we're not on Alpha Centauri, the homeworld of man-monkeys, then where are we?"

"Sitting in a transport lifting back to the *Hare Twist*." The beagle at last noticed Betsy, and raised his voice. "Hey buddy! Are you okay?"

Betsy glanced left and right. "Me?"

"Who else would I be talking to––the Emperor of Tau Ceti? Are you hurt?"

Betsy shrugged. "Not really. I scraped my leg on a stick when I ran across the beach, so if you guys have a bandage, that would be great!"

The beagle and cat glanced at each other.

"What's your name and unit number?" asked the cat.

"Betsy. I'm with Blue Squadron. That's a good answer, right? Do you guys have any marshmallows? I'm starving to death."

"There's no Blue Squadron," said the beagle. "I've never met this guy or heard of him. He's a spy!" He jumped up and stuck his front paws under the seat. "Where's my pistol? I think it fell between the seat cushions."

The white cat shook his head and gave Betsy a friendly wave. "Nah, you're just paranoid. I think I met him at a party last week. That's right––Terry's friend. Must have been hit by a blast or something. Shell-shocked. His little brain is probably *somon* pudding right now." The cat lowered his voice. "Honestly, with these little dogs you really can't tell."

"If you say so," murmured the beagle. "Hey, buddy! You don't look so good. Check into the medical bay once we're back on the *Hare Twist*."

The white cat shrugged. "In other words––see the doc after we dock."

Betsy waved a paw. "Super-duper, new friends of mine!"

PHILIP SPRINTED up the beach, the fear of being torn apart by a pack of sauropods motivating the dark-haired teenager to run faster than he ever had in his life.

A high-pitched whine grew in volume overhead, but Philip dared not look up for fear of stumbling and being ripped to shreds by the reptiles at his heels. He held up a hand against the sudden gust of wind that blew sand and sea foam into his eyes. The gust was strong enough that Nick grabbed onto Philip's shirt at his shoulder and held on tightly with her tiny fists.

The hurricane of sand and water grew stronger, forcing Philip to stop running and cover his face with both arms. A pair of huge black domes with glowing flat undersides settled onto the sand only meters away from the teenager, the spindly landing legs bending to adjust for the angle of the beach. Doors opened and ramps slammed down at the front of both transports. Bright red beams flashed across the sand, and a pair of giant, two-legged monsters clanked outside and stomped down the ramps, each step shaking the earth like miniature earthquakes.

"The other way!" shrieked Nick. "Go back!"

"Too late," whispered Philip.

The tall things ran forward like a pair of steam trains on legs and surrounded Philip and Nick with mechanical clanks and sighs. Up close and without the lights blinding him, Philip realized they were machines, not beasts.

Five meters tall and mostly leg, the walkers were shaped like giant cannon balls with the knees-backward legs of a flamingo. Broad stripes of black, green, and brown were splashed across the dull metal skin. Weapon racks on each side of the large ball held a cluster of long cannons and sharp-nosed missiles, and facing Philip were a pair of triangular windows that glowed red in a manner that oddly resembled the eyes of a jack-o-lantern. Below the two windows were stenciled a series of numbers in a military style. In contrast, a mouth was painted on both machines with bloody, dripping fangs, and this made their appearance even scarier.

The walker directly in front of Philip thumped a few steps closer and with a whir of gears, pointed its weapons down at the teenager and Nick. After a pause, a static hiss came from a speaker on the front of the machine.

"That's not it," said a deep, electronically-modified male voice. "What about this button? How am I supposed to yell at them if they can't hear me yell at them?!!"

Philip raised a hand. "I can hear you."

"Terry, it's working," said the giant walker behind Philip.

"What? I guess that WAS the right button." The speaker in the first walker cleared his throat. "Get on the ground! Arms above your head!"

Philip promptly flattened himself on the sand.

Nick twisted and pulled his shirt collar. "Don't give up, Phillie," she whispered. "Run for it!"

A fierce growl and the rumble of galloping reptile legs floated on the fishy ocean breeze to Philip's ears.

"Soon," he whispered.

The walker behind Philip clanked as it turned to face the long beach to the south. It spoke with a syn-thetically-modulated female voice.

"Lieutenant––five contacts approaching rapidly from heading one-four-four."

"Nothing to worry about," said the first walker. "Just more Centaurans on animal transports. What did you call them?"

"These aren't horses, Lieutenant. The contacts are two-legged, not four."

A third walker strode into the darkness toward the sounds, his red searchlights swinging left and right across the beach. The lights stopped abruptly.

"Sauros!" screamed the pilot.

Metal clanged and shrieked. With a bright bang, the tall machine disappeared and showered Philip and the other walkers with blackened bits of metal. A horrible roar came from the darkness, loud enough to drown out the crashing waves.

"Weapons hot!" yelled the Lieutenant. "Pattern Three! Pattern Three!"

Philip looked back and saw a giant brown sauro in the center of the smoking wreckage, a sharp-toothed grin on his face and the leg of a walker in each fist.

"Fight!" he roared. "Fight! Fight! Fight!"

Missiles flared toward the lizard and blue plasma hissed across the beach as the platoon of walkers leapt into action, spreading into a loose formation and firing at the giant lizard, who––if anyone had been polite enough to ask––was called George. George tossed one of the steel legs at a walker and knocked it into the dunes with a burst of fire and sparks. The sauro gripped the other leg with both claws, and used it to block the plasma beams and swipe away the missiles like a frenzied home-run hitter. He jumped at the central ball of the nearest walker and ripped it apart with a terrible howl as three other sauros joined the battle, each leaping with unnatural speed and slashing at the machines with impossible strength.

"Run!" yelled Nick.

Philip didn't need to be reminded twice. He scrambled to his feet and sprinted into the darkness.

SUNFLOWER CLIMBED into the pilot's seat and slipped the helmet over his furry orange head.

"I think I fixed it. Sent power for the shield into the leg motivators."

"Multiple contacts on our current heading," said the flight computer.

"Is that the rest of those pirates that work for evil Amy? I'll make short work of them."

"Yes ... and no," said the flight computer.

Sunflower peered through the armored glass between the upper and lower jaws of the tiger-shaped tank.

The entire coast south of the demolished lighthouse was lit up like a fleet of dog freighters full of illegal fireworks that crashed into each other over a volcano. Green and blue plasma beams streaked across the dunes and the dull thump of explosions turned the sand orange. Columns of smoke that smelled of burning plastic boiled into the sky, thick and oily—— definitely not from a brush fire. The scattered shadows of cats and dogs ran back and forth against the flames, and a tall, two-legged machine toppled over in pieces. With a flash of engines, a transport lifted off and skimmed the white surf, the crazy fireworks of the battlefield shining across its glossy black dome.

Sunflower rubbed his eyes and stared at the battle. "Blessed Saint Mittens and his three legs. Any idea what's going on?"

"Radiation coming from military-grade vehicles and weaponry," said the flight computer. "From the radio broadcasts, the pilots are cats and they're losing badly. Very, very badly."

"How can you tell?"

"Lots of screaming and calling on Saint Fluffy," said the flight computer.

Sunflower squinted at the darkness. "Something's coming!"

He stuck his front paws into the pits of the control panel and lowered the giant armored cat into a crouch.

Dark, four-legged figures rushed across the dunes at top speed toward Sunflower, but instead of attacking, the mob of two hundred cats and dogs ran past and continued toward the lights of the human village. The terrified animals were covered in blood and sand, and were missing weapons or parts of their combat armor. Their eyes were open so wide that Sunflower could see the whites even through the faceplates of their helmets.

"Well, that's different," he said. "They just ran past us."

"Contact approaching," said the flight computer. "A bipedal organic."

"Probably what the idiots are running from," said Sunflower. "Nothing we can't handle, right? I'm sitting in the most powerful tank the glorious Tau Ceti Empire has ever produced. There's nothing I can't rip apart with these claws!"

Sunflower grinned and clicked his paws inside the control pits, causing the armored cat's steel tail to twitch back and forth.

"Get ready to be shredded, you devil dogs," he cackled. His eyes grew wide. "What the——?!!"

Sunflower pulled the cockpit release lever. The head of the steel tiger split horizontally and swung back, letting in the cool night air. Sunflower unbuckled his safety harness and stood on his hind legs.

"Philip! You fizz-brained sack of monkey meat!"

The teenager had stopped at the sight of the giant shape in the darkness and turned to flee in another direction when Sunflower's voice rang out. He spun and sprinted back toward the armored tank.

"Sunflower! I thought you were dead!"

Nick buzzed out of the darkness. "He probably should be! I bet he's been naughty and bad."

The orange cat shook his head in disbelief. "I don't understand. The ship sank into the ocean and I thought everyone drowned. We looked for you!"

"Who's 'we?'" asked Philip. "And where did you get this giant thing?"

"It was down in the cargo hold of the ship. Betsy and I were sitting inside, and the next thing we knew, the ship exploded and sank."

Nick clapped her hands. "Betsy's alive, I told you! Where is he?"

"They've probably caught him already," said Sunflower. "He's on a secret mission to get inside evil Amy's ship."

Philip rubbed his forehead. "What about Amy? Have you seen her?"

"No. It's just been me and Betsy."

"That message you sent was a great idea," said Philip. "Nick and I would've never found you without that."

The ground vibrated and a walker sprinted past, its tall metal legs throwing sand high into the air as it ran away from the beach. A series of guttural roars came from the darkness.

Sunflower shook his furry head. "I could swear that sounds like——"

"Sauros!" yelled Philip and Nick, and bolted past the armored cat.

Sunflower fell back into his seat and snapped the cockpit shut. He jammed his paws into the control pits and spun the steel beast with a violent crackle of underbrush and hiss of hydraulics.

"Three biologicals approaching," said the flight computer. "From the sound signature, the probability of the contacts being adult sauropods is ninety-seven percent. Probability of survival in combat against three adult sauropods with no overshield and empty missile pods is zero point six percent."

"I know that!" growled Sunflower, with fangs bared. "Why do you think we're running away? Send all power to the leg motivators."

He drove the steel beast as fast as it could go toward the glow coming from the human village.

As the rapid thump of the walker and Sunflower's armored cat faded away, an unnatural silence returned to the coastal dunes. Black-crowned herons gripped branches in the pine trees and stayed silent, coyotes watched the night carefully and kept their bellies to the sand, and fluttering moths folded their wings and waited. Even the low-hanging clouds seemed to slow down with anticipation.

A manzanita bush crackled and burst apart with an explosion of red branches. The giant brown sauro George shoved his way through the bush and stopped in a patch of pink-flowering ice plants. A pair of shorter but still very muscular lizards jumped through the bushes on either side of the giant. One held a triangular device in his claws.

George looked at Plastra. "Do you think they think we're following them?"

Plastra stared down at the tracker. "Why would they think a silly thing like that?"

"Because if I was them, I would think that I was following me. Wait––if I was chasing me, I would think I was them. Wait––"

"Shut up, George." Astra pointed at the lights of the human village. "We're following Nistra's signal, and they're running away from us in the same direction. It's just a coincidence."

George shook his head. "What's a coing-ka-dink?"

"A coincidence is two idiots that aren't related," said Astra. "Your father and mother, for example."

George grabbed the smaller sauro around the neck with both claws.

"My mother is a saint!" he snarled. "You take that back!"

Plastra smacked George on the shoulder, his yellow eyes wide. "Wait—what if they're the ones keeping our dear brother prisoner? They're running back to finish him off for good!"

George dropped Astra and charged toward the village, his muscular legs churning up and down like pistons.

"Stay alive, buddy!" he roared. "We're coming for ya!"

WITHOUT TELEVISION, video games, or holographic gladiator matches, the people of 1912 went to bed much earlier than Amy expected.

Three flung her nightgown onto the bed. "I'm not wearing this freaky outfit. I'd rather sleep naked!"

Mrs. Morgan had given the teenagers identical long-sleeved gowns of white cotton. The garments buttoned high on the neck and the bottom hem reached all the way to the floor. Amy had already changed into her gown, and brushed her blonde hair in front of a small oval mirror on the wall.

"Absolutely not," she said. "I'm not sharing a featherbed with anyone naked. Also, you promised to try and fit in with everyone else."

"I did? I don't remember that."

Amy stopped brushing and turned to stare at Three. The older teenager shrugged.

"Okay, okay. Don't give me those sad kitten eyes. Hey! Let's do each other's braids. We're sisters, after all."

Amy returned to the mirror and hair-brushing. "How quaint. Dimensional copies pretending to be twins."

"No twins here, babe. You're much better looking. I've taken too many elbows to the face to be beautiful. See this nose? Broken twice."

Amy squinted at Three. "I can't tell. Your nose looks fine to me."

"Robotic surgeons do wonders. Just don't ask them about the weather."

"Why not?"

Three shrugged. "Bug in their programming. They go berserk and start killing."

The girls took turns parting each other's hair and plaiting the blonde strands into two braids. When both were done, they admired each other's work in the mirror.

"Twins," said Amy with a faint smile. "Sort of."

Three pumped her fist. "Yeah! We're gonna to take over the universe!"

Amy blew out the lantern, pulled the round bed-warmer from under the quilt, and slid under the warm covers of the featherbed with Three.

"Good night. Sleep tight."

Three rolled onto her side to face Amy. "Hey, kid," she murmured. "I need to tell you something about me and the other copies."

Amy closed her eyes. "I'm too tired," she whispered. "Wait until morning."

"Fine."

Amy took a deep breath and let it out slowly, trying to imagine sunshine and a warm country meadow. The house was deathly quiet in the way that only pre-electronic houses could be, with no refrigerator, central heating, or computer systems to hum, beep, or whir. Amy listened to Three's breathing as it slowed and became whisper-quiet.

Something cracked outside the window. Amy opened her eyes and sat up in bed.

"What was that?"

"Fireworks," said Three softly. "Or a firing squad."

"A firing squad? After dark?"

"Fireworks," murmured Three.

A distant boom rattled the window. An unknown number of horses galloped down the street, their hooves beating the dirt with a rapid clip-clop.

"That's no firework," said Amy.

She climbed over Three and crept barefoot to the window. A dull thud shook the glass panes and the wooden planks of the bedroom floor.

"Something's happening and I can't see anything," she said, and grabbed her leather boots. "I'm going outside."

Three groaned. "Come on, it's just a cannon or a mining accident or something stupid."

"I don't think so. You can stay here if you want."

Three tossed off the covers and shoved boots onto her feet. "No, I can't. I'd fall asleep, you'd come back and wake me up, I'd pace the floors until dawn with no sleep and pull out my hair, then jump off a bridge because who wants to live without hair?"

Mrs. Morgan and the handful of other women staying at the Benevolent Society were gathered on the porch. All had been staring at the light show in the west, and turned when Amy opened the door.

"My dear children, I hope you weren't disturbed," said Mrs. Morgan. "The Army has decided to try out their new cannons, apparently."

"That's what we reckon is the case," said another woman in a nightgown. "Or a ship off the coast has caught fire. It's a calamity either way, no bones about it. Will all this noise, none of the cows will give milk in the morning."

Amy followed Three down the steps to the garden, where the older teenager pointed to the sky.

"Plasma rifles," she whispered. "Look! Blue streaks against the clouds, definitely plasma. Sounds like it too, if you listen hard enough."

The clouds glowed orange from a series of rapid explosions, and several of the women on the porch screamed.

"Lord save them," said a female guest. "Think of the brave young men!"

Mrs. Morgan held up a hand. "Ladies, please. The Presidio is on the hill behind us. It must be an artillery drill."

Three turned to Amy and lowered her voice. "It's not artillery, it's micro-missiles. I've heard that fizz-shriek enough times." She held up a finger. "Wait––that's impossible. One doesn't have anything that uses micro-missiles. I wonder if Four bought some military hardware from the cats and never told me."

The lights of a Model T flashed by as it rattled at high speed toward the blue and orange glow in the sky.

"It sounds like whatever it is, it doesn't belong in 1912," whispered Amy. "That evil Amy Armstrong that you call 'One' could be there. This is our chance to face her."

Three stared at Amy. "She's not alone––she has three ships! *Wits Hater*, *Raw Tithes*, and *Hare Twist*, all packed with cats and dogs and each meaner than the next. You see those plasma bursts and explosions? These cotton nightgowns are about as good as butterfly wings when it comes to deflecting military weapons."

"I didn't say I wanted to fight."

The residents of Pine Avenue stood on their porches along the street watching the show. Eventually the blue and orange flashes stopped and the rumble of explosions faded away, and most of the citizens snuffed their oil lanterns and returned to bed.

"Something's wrong," said Three.

"Who won?" Amy asked. "Who was even fighting?"

"Don't you hear it? The screaming, the horrible grinding. It sounds like a robot with his hand caught in a blender."

Amy shrugged. "That's how a Model T sounds backing up."

"Be serious!"

"I am. Look for yourself."

The black Model T that had driven toward the lighthouse a moment earlier appeared under the glow of a distant streetlight, reversing up Pine as fast as possible and surrounded by fleeing villagers like a horde of lawyers around a recent lottery winner. The frantic crowd overtook the car and dashed by Amy and Three with expressions of horror and shock on their faces.

"Flee!"

"Monsters ... monsters!"

An ancient man in red flannel pajamas tottered up the street, his long white beard swaying down to his waist.

"It's the end," he moaned. "The end, I tell you. Run for your lives!"

Mrs. Morgan pushed the other women back inside and waved at Amy and Three.

"Girls, come back inside! Hurry!"

"Much appreciated, Mrs. Morgan," said Three. "But if it really is the end of the world, I want a front row seat."

The red-haired woman stared at Three for a second with her mouth open in shock, and then closed the door. The drapes at the front window parted and she stood there, mouth moving silently as she spoke to the women behind her.

"You should be nicer," said Amy. "Especially to someone that gave us dinner and a place to sleep."

Three crossed her arms and pouted. "I thought I was being nice. I really DO want a front-row seat."

The crowd of villagers in their pajamas ran past Amy and Three and continued up the street, the women holding up the skirts of their nightgowns as they ran and the men jogging along, urging the ladies faster.

The Model T was never designed to move rapidly in reverse gear, a fact which brought many colorful curses from the driver. At last he jumped out of the car and ran after the crowd, leaving the automobile to putter harmlessly in the middle of the street without a driver.

Amy squinted. "Is that a cat? That's a cat wearing a helmet!"

A gray tabby shot out of the darkness with an olive-green helmet bouncing on his furry head and brown armor plates jiggling on his back. He sprinted by with a spray of gravel and dust and continued up Pine Avenue. A strange thunder grew in the darkness beyond the last streetlight, and a mob of over a hundred cats and dogs rushed by the two girls, some wearing armor and most covered in sand and blood. A few carried plasma rifles on their backs, but none gave more than a desperate, wide-eyed glance at the two girls as they galloped past the white gate of the Benevolent Society.

Three pointed at the tails of the animals as they fled into the night. "Those are One's soldiers! And that was a brigade from Two's ship!"

"If she sent them after us, they're not doing a great job," said Amy.

Rapid, loud thumps shook the earth and caused the rosebushes to sway. Amy and Three hid behind the white fence as a steel monstrosity five meters tall bounded out of the darkness and hurtled past in the direction of the fleeing cats and dogs. A pair of dangerous-looking cannon barrels bracketed the large steel sphere above the legs. Irregular green and black horizontal stripes covered every inch of the ball-shaped body and chicken-bent legs. Like the frightened cats in front of it, the machine kept its glowing triangular window-eyes fixed straight ahead, and never turned them left or right.

"You don't see that every day," said Amy.

Three scratched the back of her leg under the cotton gown. "What? It's a walker from *Wits Hater*, but the pilot barely looked at us. Why would she risk sending walkers to find us? The maintenance on those things is murder!"

Amy stood from behind the fence and watched the walker thump away down the street. "The bigger question is ... what's it running from?"

Three pulled Amy back down. "Watch out!"

The damp grass below Amy's fingers shook violently, and she would have fallen into a rosebush if Three hadn't caught her. With a hiss of hydraulics and click of oiled steel, something large and even heavier than the walker passed by. Through the wooden slats of the fence, Amy glimpsed an armored tail and a leg of gray metal.

"That's Sunflower!"

She jumped to her feet and ran after the limping steel tiger.

"Wait!" hissed Three.

"It's Sunflower's cat-tank from Tau Ceti, I know it!" Amy yelled over her shoulder as she ran.

"Amy?"

A voice from behind called her name, but it wasn't Three. Amy slid to a stop on the packed dirt and spun around.

Philip stood under the light of a streetlamp, his shirt and trousers ripped and covered with dark brown stains that looked suspiciously like chocolate. He stared at Amy, his eyes wide and mouth gaping.

"Amy!"

She ran to him faster than she knew she could run, and hugged him tighter than she had thought she ever wanted to hug anything. The cloth of his shirt was rough on her cheek and smelled of sand and the sea, but mostly chocolate and throw-up.

"I thought you were dead," she sobbed. Her eyes were wet with tears and she kissed him hard on the mouth.

Philip pressed his rough cheek against hers. "I thought the same! Oh, dearest Amy. One lied to me and said that you had drowned!"

Three walked up to the pair, a hand on her hip. "Hello, sailor. Got a kiss for me?"

Philip glanced at her. "No time for idle chit-chat. Quick, follow Sunflower!"

Nick buzzed out of the darkness. "Run, you silly billies! Oh——hello, Amy. You're not dead. That's super great!"

Amy wiped her eyes on a sleeve. "Thanks, Nick. It's good to see you, too."

A terrifying roar split the night, followed by a stream of snarls and growls.

"Run!" shouted Philip.

The teenager grabbed Amy's hand and led the girls in a flat-out sprint after the armored cat.

12

One screamed and punched a hole through the communications console with her metal arm. She ripped the nearest display off the wall and threw it across the room, where it exploded in a shower of sparks.

"Why can't you animals do anything right?!!"

Wilson peeked around the side of One's leather chair. The command center was normally full of navigators, weapons specialists, and communication officers, but now the room was empty apart from the black cat and One.

"It was a Tau Ceti battle tank, my Lady! We never expected to fight a tank on such a backwater planet, not to mention three male sauropods."

One flung a high-heeled shoe. It missed the cat and bounced under a console station with a dull clang.

"That's what I pay you for––to expect the unexpected!"

She collapsed into her chair with a sigh, and kicked off her remaining shoe.

"How many transports made it back?"

"A transport of ours and one from the *Wits Hater*, your worship."

"The troops on the surface? How many are left?"

"One hundred and ninety-seven, plus a walker. We finally made contact with a couple of brigade officers. They stopped the retreat and are reforming inside the human settlement."

One combed her short blonde hair back into place with her fingers. She took a deep breath and let it out slowly. Her facial scar faded back to a pink vertical slash down her cheek.

"Send the transports back to the surface. Grab Philip, Three, and the copy and bring them to me."

Wilson gulped hard. "Many apologies, your beautifulness, but the transports need at least an hour to finish refueling and repair the damage, not to mention that we haven't any soldiers left to do the grabbing."

The cat spoke slower and slower as he watched One's face and her scar flush red again.

"Damn your eyes!" she shouted. "I'll do it myself!"

One jumped down to the helmsman's position below the wall of viewscreens and squeezed into a seat designed for a beagle, or at best, a large cat. She slammed her fists on buttons and cranked levers with the wide-eyed madness of an ocelot cornered by a gang of taxidermy students.

"If you want something done right," she fumed. "You have to do it yourself."

Wilson grabbed an armrest with his front paws as the deck pitched down sharply. Pencils and dusty pieces of somon candy clattered across the floor, and a plastic collector's cup from Phobos FunTime City bounced against his legs.

"My Lady, please stop! This is crazy!"

One stared at a black-and-white video feed above her head that displayed a bird's-eye view of Pacific Grove. The darkness of night and the leafy tops of the trees along the streets hid much of the view. One tapped a button to activate the heat-sensitive camera, and the video zoomed down to a pair of teenage girls in nightgowns. Both were holding hands with a young man and running as fast as they could along a dirt lane.

One clenched her teeth. "Crazy or not, I'm finishing this."

***

AMY, THREE, AND PHILIP sprinted up the hard-packed dirt of Pine Avenue and away from the growling sauropods. Nick followed, the wings of the tiny sprite buzzing in the cold night air.

Most of the villagers had disappeared inside their houses and blown out their lanterns. Philip ran up to a number of front doors and banged on them but the frightened people only stared at him from the windows and pulled the curtains closed even tighter. The three sauropods had slowed their pursuit and stayed in the shadows behind the teenagers, but that made the giants even more menacing. The ferocious lizard-men roared now and then, but mostly chatted and laughed to each other as they walked, like hunters following a wounded animal.

Sunflower and his massive steel tiger had disappeared into the night, leaving deep paw-prints in the packed earth. A faint clank and hiss sounded in the darkness, but nothing moved under the blue light of the gas-powered street lamps.

Amy cupped her hands around her mouth. "Sunflower! Where are you?"

"Chasing those other cats and dogs, I wager," said Philip. "How the devil did he manage to get away from us?"

Three wiped her forehead with the back of her hand. "Great, just when we need help. I don't know if you've heard anything about sauros, but they're big and green and will rip into us like a spicy chicken dinner."

Philip grabbed the hands of both Amy and Three.

"I'm not giving up. Nick, go find Sunflower!"

The tiny blonde woman nodded and shot into the darkness, her dragonfly wings droning like the overworked engine of a miniature lawnmower.

Amy ran with Philip and Three for another hundred meters. Without warning, she pulled the other two to a stop.

"Wait a sec ... I recognize this place. This is where I live!"

Philip squinted at her. "Pardon me, dearest, but you must be mistaken."

"He's right," said Three. "You came from 1995 or whatever, not the boring olden days of cave people."

Amy stamped her foot. "No! I mean, this is my neighborhood. There's old Mr. Whitehead's house, that red place is where Hassini lives, and across the street is Ellen's house."

Three shrugged. "So? Where's your house?"

Amy pointed to the mansion on the north side of the street. A pile of red-painted gables, peaked dormers, and steep, redwood-shingled roofs were combined with a four-story crimson tower, shaped like a wooden rocket bolted onto the side of the large house.

"Cool story," said Three. "You know we're about to be eaten alive, right?"

Philip glanced nervously at the sauropods behind them. The lizards had linked arms and were dancing a happy jig up the center of the empty street. Somewhere in the small village, church bells began to clang.

Philip pulled the girls forward. "Run for the door! Be quick about it!"

The three teens ran across the dew-covered lawn toward the front porch. Halfway up the steps, the large walnut front door opened and Mr. Woodley leapt out, a green dressing gown over his pajamas and a pointed nightcap over his gray hair.

"Amy? Theresa? What are you doing outside? Come, come!"

The older man waved the teenagers up the porch and into the mansion. He slammed shut the heavy wooden slab and secured it with a dozen brass locks and chains.

"Everything's gone mad," stammered Woodley. "Cats and dogs running in the streets! Ungodly machines shaking the earth! It's the end of days!"

Philip peeked through a curtain. "Indeed."

"Stay away from the windows, young man," whispered Woodley. "The horsemen of the apocalypse will see you!"

"It was a giant metal cat, not a horse," said Three.

"Three!" hissed Amy. "I mean––Theresa!"

Philip shut the curtains and turned to Woodley. "I'm very sorry, but my friend Nick is still out there."

Hans Weiss strode in from the kitchen wearing a blue silk dressing gown.

"You won't see that friend tonight if he's smart," said the tall butler. "He'll be hiding in a cellar somewhere."

From the doorway to the kitchen, the young maid Anna peeked at the assembled company. A cotton gown and yellow robe hung from her thin shoulders, and a simple cap trimmed in lace covered her hair.

"Is it safe?" she whispered.

"Not yet, dear," said Hans.

Woodley cleared his throat and glared at the tall servant.

Hans bowed his head. "I mean––Miss Anna."

Three wandered into the parlor, her boots thudding quietly on the soft blue carpet. She stared in wonder at the array of lacquered furniture, paintings, and treasures locked in cabinets behind glass.

"This is your house, Amy? You never told me you were rich."

"I'm not. This place belongs to Mr. Woodley." Amy's eyes widened. She spun around and jabbed a finger at the older man. "You're E.G. Woodley!"

Woodley tilted his head slightly. "I certainly hope so, young lady. I was this morning and I hope nothing has changed." He turned to the butler. "Hans, fetch the gun and my pistol and be quick about it!"

"Already have done, sir."

The butler handed a long, double-barreled shotgun to his employer and lifted a black .38 revolver from a pocket of his dressing gown.

Philip held Amy's hand. "Is this truly your house, dear? Something has upset you."

"This IS the address where I grew up, but it's not the right house. We lived in a four-bedroom ranch. This is E.G. Woodley's house, the one that burnt down in 1912."

Mr. Woodley cracked open the barrel of the shotgun. Hans gave him a pair of red-jacketed shells and the older man shoved both into the open breech of the gun.

"This is indeed my house, young lady, and this is the year of our Lord nineteen hundred and twelve. As you can plainly see, a fire has not occurred and the ceiling of my stately manor continues to cover all of our heads."

"Amy, it doesn't matter," said Three. "It burnt down in your dimension, not this one!"

Philip peeked through the curtain. "Hush! We have guests."

The white-painted planks of the front porch creaked and splintered under the movement of something extremely heavy. Murmurs and menacing giggles rattled the windows.

Woodley lifted the shotgun. "To the ready, Hans!"

"En guarde!" shouted the butler.

The two men leapt into the entrance hall and pointed their weapons at the front door. Amy, Three, and Anna took cover behind a sofa in the parlor.

"Why can't I have a weapon?" growled Three. "You could cut off my hands and I'd still be a better shot than these bozos."

"Because they're scared of you," whispered Amy. "It's the madness in your eyes."

"Madness is hiding behind this couch and waiting for a stupid sauro to eat me."

Deep whispers came from outside the front door. The faint sounds ended with four careful knocks.

"Hello, there," said a gruff male voice. "Is anyone home?"

"This is dumb," said a deeper voice. "Let me in, Plastra, so I can murder everyone!"

"You catch flies with honey, not blood," said the first.

"Have you ever seen a dead body, Plastra? Flies everywhere!"

"Point taken." A heavy thud shook the door. "Open up! We just want to talk."

"That's a shocker," said Three. "I always thought sauros were the 'kill first, ask questions later' kind of guys."

Scrunched up behind the sofa next to them, Anna wrapped her arms around her knees and shivered. "Horrible things. Please don't let them in!"

"Don't worry, Anna," Mr. Woodley said over his shoulder. "Hans and I will protect you from harm."

Three rolled her eyes. "Yeah, but who's going to protect you?"

"Stop it," said Amy. "The sauros will eat them first. That gives us a chance to run."

"Good point."

Woodley waved Philip to the door. "Boy! Open the door and see what these men want."

"Pardon me, sir, but they aren't men."

"Enough of your lip! Hans and I can handle these ruffians. Open it."

Amy stood up from behind the sofa. "Philip, no!"

The dark-haired teen held up a hand. "Not to worry, Amy. Please stay there."

Woodley and his butler pointed their weapons at the door as Philip approached. The teenager turned all the latches, unclasped the locking chains, and pulled open the heavy wooden slab. Huge, shadowy beasts darkened the porch outside.

"Yes?" Philip asked with a raspy voice, and cleared his throat. "Good evening."

"I don't know if it's good or not," growled a deep voice. "But it's going to be very, very bad for everyone if you don't give us our friend."

"Your friend? Who, may I ask, is that?"

"Don't play stupid," growled the voice. "George is here and he's got enough stupid for the entire planet."

"They killed him already!" growled another voice. "Murder everyone! Slice open their bellies!"

"Shut up," said the first voice. "Listen carefully, monkey boy. Hand over Nistra and we'll all go away. Probably not quietly or peacefully, but we'll go away. You'll live to see another day, bounce little monkey babies on your knee, and tell scary stories about what happened. On the other claw, if you chopped up our friend and baked him into a sauro pie, then you should kneel down and pray to the monkey gods, because we will definitely kill you."

"Hey, Plastra––let's turn THEM into pie!" shouted another deep voice.

"Shut up," said the sauro. "I hate pie. Now, what's your decision, monkey boy? Our comrade, or a painful death?"

"Wait a moment," said Philip. "Is the friend you're looking for called Nistra?"

"Of course!"

"I thought he drowned in the crash. But to be honest, I have no clue where he is. If you're working for One, why do you care about Nistra?"

"We're not working for anyone," sneered Plastra. "Hand him over and we'll take it from there! The tracker says he's at this location."

"What's all the growling?" asked Mr. Woodley. "Tell us what's happening, boy."

Philip turned to Woodley and Hans.

"Pardon me, sir, but these ... gentlemen say that a friend of theirs is inside your house, and they'd like to speak with him. His name is Nistra."

Woodley frowned. "I don't know anyone by that name. Is it Greek? In any case, the man is certainly not in this house. We've no guests in the house apart from the two girls behind me. Isn't that so, Hans?"

The butler swallowed hard. "Yes, sir. I mean ... no, sir!"

Woodley waved the end of his shotgun at the door. "Bid them good night, and fasten the locks."

"Certainly."

Philip closed the door and began to fasten the dozen brass locks along the frame.

"Nistra," whispered Amy. "Why are they asking about him?"

Three shrugged. "Maybe the dumb lizard survived the crash. You did, and you're as tough as a wet noodle."

"Thanks. But why do they think he's here?"

An ear-splitting roar shook the walls and cracked all the panes of glass at the front of the house. Philip jumped away from the door as a heavy weight smashed against the other side. The carved walnut burst apart and flew across the foyer, scattering chunks of broken wood and splinters everywhere.

Two huge reptiles pushed through the leftover pieces of the door and sauntered into the house—— towering, scaly beasts with arms like tree trunks, claws as sharp as knives, and wide, alligator-like jaws full of pointed teeth. Naked apart from scraps of clothing, their dark green armored skin was smeared with blood and sand and the occasional tuft of cat fur.

Hans pointed the shaking muzzle of his pistol at the monsters. "Mein Gott in Himmel," he whispered.

Mr. Woodley jerked the shotgun to his shoulder. "Fire!"

Amy covered her ears as a deafening boom shook the house and a cloud of evil-smelling smoke boiled to the ceiling. When it cleared, the sauros stood in the same place.

The pair of giant lizards glanced at each other and giggled.

"What was that?" asked Plastra.

"For killing flies, I think," said Astra. "Or scratching an itch."

The sauros marched forward into the room, forcing Philip, Woodley, and Hans into the parlor. The three quickly lined up shoulder-to-shoulder in front of the sofa to protect the girls. The lizards followed them into the parlor, splintering the doorframe as their wide shoulders squeezed through and cracking the lacquered floor under the weight of their clawed feet.

"Give us a challenge," said Astra. "Don't you monkeys have real weapons?"

The window in the parlor exploded with a huge crash of wood and glass, and a brown sauro much larger than the other two tumbled onto the carpet inside. He stood and shook off the glass shards with a horrific snarl that made Anna scream.

"It's murder time!" he bellowed.

Plastra tossed a broken part of the window frame at George's head. "Shut up, you idiot! Can't you use the door like a civilized person?"

The giant brown monster blinked. "Uh ... sorry. I got excited."

A stream of books and lamps flew across the room as Three began to fling anything and everything at the invaders.

"Aim for the eyes," she yelled. "They hate that!"

Amy grabbed her arm. "Stop! If One sent them down here, they won't hurt us."

Plastra sneered a mouthful of sharp teeth. "No one sent us here, monkey girl. Nistra snuck us onto a stupid starship to take it over, but the useless, monkey-made thing blew up and sank, so here we all are. Case closed!" A triangular device in the sauro's claw beeped loudly. "My tracker's going wild, so I know he's not dead. Bring me Nistra!"

A pot clattered onto the floor of the kitchen, and the group of sauros charged toward the sound.

The back door was open to the garden and a cool night breeze flowed inside. A wide trail of mud led from the door to a large scaly hump in the center of the kitchen, wheezing and gasping his way across the tiles. Nistra pulled himself forward claw by claw, covered in dust, cobwebs, and rodent hair.

"Rats," he hissed weakly. "Rats ... rats ... rats ..."

Mr. Woodley dropped his shotgun and pulled his nightcap down around his ears. "What the devil is that?!!"

"Oh, no," whispered Hans. He ran to Anna and hugged her tight.

Plastra knelt and touched the wounded sauro with a scaly claw. He stood and looked around at the other two reptiles.

"Take care of Nistra," he growled.

George grabbed Plastra's arm. "No! He's not that sick. We can help him!"

"I don't mean the 'kill him' definition of 'take care of him,' you thick-yolked egg-eater. I want you to clean him up and treat his injuries."

"Oh," said George. "Sorry."

With glistening yellow eyes, Plastra turned to face the humans.

"Time for me to take care of the monkeys."

George grabbed his arm again. "No! We don't have enough medicine!"

"Idiot! This time it's the other way! I'm going to kill them."

"Oh. Sorry."

Plastra grinned jaws full of sharp, pointed teeth at the humans.

"Try to run. Or don't. It doesn't matter. I'm smarter, faster, stronger, and tougher than any Centauran on this stupid monkey planet."

"This isn't Alpha Centauri," said Three.

"Yeah, it's Earth, you moron," said Amy. "Who's stupid now?"

Plastra shrugged and raised his claws. "Who wants to die first? So many choices."

Philip raised his fists and stood in front of Amy and Three. "Don't touch them or you'll regret it, you monster."

George looked up from bandaging Nistra on the kitchen floor. "Save me a leg!"

"Breast for me," yelled Astra. "Wait––do we have any mustard?"

Amy crossed her arms. "Gross. Hey, um, there's somebody at the door. Can't you hear that? Might be tastier than us monkeys."

Everyone, including the sauros, stared at the open doorway to the porch, where something clattered like a woodpecker who'd drank too much coffee.

Plastra stared at Amy and Three and nodded. "Yes, you pack of Centaurans are very skinny and lean. I'm going to see if there's a fat little moggie outside. Trust me––if this is a trick, I'll make summer sausage out of everyone. And yes, I still remember the recipe."

The sauro thumped through the house to the broken remains of the front door and stuck his head into the night air.

"Sounds like a tap-dancing *poona* out here. Show yourself! Who's there?"

"Your worst nightmare!" squealed Nick's high-pitched voice.

The tiny sprite flew at the eyes of the giant reptile, punching and kicking with all her might, and somersaulting away from his grasping claws.

"A sprite! Egg curse its black heart. I can't see—someone find the sprite spray! Do you know what happens if we don't kill it? The little buggers get in the walls and lay a thousand eggs a week!"

"That's an old sauro's tale," shouted Astra. "They lay eggs in candy."

"Shut up and help me!"

The two other sauros rushed into the parlor and grabbed and jumped at the tiny blonde woman flying around Plastra. After a few seconds, George caught her in both claws. He had enough time for a satisfied giggle before Amy cracked him in the back of the head with an iron poker, and Nick buzzed free.

The brown giant turned to Amy. "You'll pay for that," he growled. "Wait––what's happening? I'm getting the shakes!"

"Not enough Vitamin P in your diet," said Astra. "I keep saying it, but you don't listen."

A constant vibration rolled through the house and knocked paintings and lamps to the floor. George fell onto the blue carpet and held his belly with both claws.

"The shakes!" he screamed.

"You idiot," said Plastra. "It's not the shakes. We all feel it."

Amy spread her arms and steadied herself against a wall. "You're both idiots. This is California and it's an earthquake!"

A roar came from outside the house, a sound like a really, really angry jet engine with fangs.

Philip pulled Amy and Three back behind the sofa. "Get down!"

The wall of the parlor blew apart in a tornado of bricks and splintered lumber. A giant armored cat charged into the house slashing and hammering at the sauropods with its titanium claws, a huge steel tiger stuck inside a tiny wooden cage and using every bit of its body to smash it to pieces in a cloud of broken plaster and snapped wooden beams.

Amy ducked as the armored tail smashed through the wall above her head, covering her in dust. A line of glass shone red between the open jaws of the tiger, and she glimpsed an orange tabby in a pilot's helmet.

"Sunflower!"

The giant machine smacked Astra through the front window of the house like a cat playing with a yarn ball, and dodged George's dangerous claws by leaping straight up through the ceiling, creating a gaping hole and almost bringing that side of the house down on the heads of Amy, Philip, and Three.

"Run!" screamed Three.

The teenagers climbed through the large hole in the wall Sunflower's armored tank had made, and dashed across the lawn followed by Woodley, Hans, and Anna.

The group stood on the street and watched the red mansion shiver and crack from the loud battle between Sunflower and the giant lizards. Clouds of dust and broken furniture flew from the already-smashed windows as the sauros and the steel machine moved around the ground floor. One of the brick chimneys tumbled down from the fourth floor, a sight which caused Mr. Woodley to kneel down and pray.

Hans touched the shoulder of his employer. "I'm certain insurance will cover the damages, sir."

Woodley shook his head. "No one will believe me," he whispered.

Nick buzzed down and landed on Philip's shoulder. She pointed at the house.

"That's Sunflower! I found him."

Amy smiled. "Thank you, Nick. You're the best."

"Of course! Anything for you guys."

Inside the house, Plastra rode the armored cat like a horse and clawed at the armor on its back. "Return to the Egg, you fur-covered cat monster!"

Astra watched the combat between Sunflower and the other two sauros from a not-so safe distance of ten meters.

"Where did a cat tank come from and who the seven suns is he?"

"I'm your worst nightmare!" yelled Sunflower through the speakers.

"Awful," sneered Plastra. "Worst. Line. Ever."

A desperate, claw-and-tooth battle between an armored Tau Ceti tank and three adult sauropods is not something you see every day, so it was natural that neither Amy, Three, Philip, or Nick noticed the approaching starship in the night sky.

NO MATTER what the sweaty hucksters on late-night holovids say or the recruiters in front of the astrogation schools tell you––flying a spaceship is hard. Rocket science hard.

One was no spring chicken when it came to navigation, and she had more hours in the pilot's seat than other captains, but she was also a woman with a ferocious, homicidal jealousy simmering beneath the surface.

Despite Wilson's terrified warnings, One brought *Hare Twist* in too hot for a proper landing. Unlike a hoverski or a Centauran snow sled, an interstellar starship shaped like a knobby green space pickle with a length of two hundred and twelve meters has little wiggle room when it comes to landing. A less impatient pilot would have circled the area, cleared the landing zone visually, and engaged the hoverjets for a slow descent. One was not that pilot, and kept the forward turbines at half-speed while engaging the hoverjets at the last second in order to come in low and fast. She smashed through six houses.

The first was a house of God, technically. The square white steeple of the First Methodist Church of Pacific Grove exploded in splinters from the impact with the huge green bow of the *Hare Twist*. The roof of Chester Brown's stately Queen Anne-style mansion was next, scraped off by the curved keel of the ship, which plowed successively through the upper floor of two houses, completely obliterated the next two dwellings, and plowed straight through the center of E.G. Woodley's iconic, red-painted mansion, most of which was thrown a kilometer into the fields east of Pacific Grove. The remains of the roof and wood beams tumbled into the back garden of Mrs. Phineas Egglestein's property next door, quite upsetting her cat and putting it off milk for three days.

Apart from the aforementioned feline, no villagers were harmed in the reckless landing that One carved through the village. Even though it was far past their bedtime, all of the residents of the crushed houses had scrambled out of their houses and run to E.G. Woodley's mansion to watch the fight between the gigantic metal tiger and the horrific lizards.

The slap of air from the starships crash landing had knocked the teenagers off their feet, and Three helped Amy and Philip stand up.

"Great green-eyed goblins!" she yelled. "That woman's crazy!"

Amy rubbed a scraped elbow. "You're telling me?"

Nick buzzed up to the group and waved her tiny arms. "Sunflower's in trouble! Help!"

The teenagers ran after the flying sprite to Mrs. Egglestein's back garden. The bodies of two sauros lay unmoving, twisted around splintered lumber and broken begonias. Nearby, the armored steel cat lay on its side, covered in bricks and redwood beams and boiling with black, oily smoke. The head and right forepaw jerked weakly and made a grinding sound. A steady, high-pitched beep came from under the pile of rubble.

Nick landed on the head and banged her fist on the scratched, blackened metal.

"Sunflower! Say something, you dumb cat!"

Amy climbed up the pile and pushed at a huge wooden post on top of the armored cat. Philip joined her and helped to roll the heavy beam to the side.

Three waved at the teenagers from a safe distance. "Hello? We can't waste any time! One just crashed her ship through a house not ten meters from the two of you—do you know what she'll do to us?"

"Sunflower tried to save us," shouted Amy. "I'm not leaving him!"

"Bravo," said Philip, as he bent over and pushed away a pile of bricks. "That's the Amy I love. By the way, what exactly are we doing? I'm not overjoyed at the thought of being re-captured."

"It's a military vehicle, right? I'm looking for the emergency release!"

Amy's fingers brushed across a seam in the neck of the giant armored cat. She used the hem of her nightgown to wipe off a coating of dust around a red-and-white striped circle.

"Found it!"

She lifted the protective cover and twisted a small handle inside.

Philip pulled her back as explosive bolts fired with a loud crack, sending the top half of the steel beast's head flying off. As the armored cat was lying sideways, the heavy titanium cover flew through the wall of Mrs. Egglestein's house and landed in her drawing room.

Sunflower lay limp and unmoving in the pilot's seat, hanging sideways in his straps and still wearing his helmet.

"You stupid cat," hissed Amy. "Wake up!"

The orange tabby didn't move, even after Philip unbuckled him from the straps and pulled him out of the cockpit to cradle the cat like a baby. Amy unfastened his helmet and Sunflower twitched in Philip's arms. He coughed and a trickle of bright blue liquid dripped from his mouth.

"Never ... take me alive," he mumbled. "Pig-faced ... son of a ... monkey."

"There's the Sunflower we love," said Amy. "Good to see nothing's changed."

The ground shook and bricks tumbled down the pile. A giant, two-legged walker thumped out of the darkness and pointed two large, dangerous-looking cannons down at Amy, Philip, and Three. A dozen cats and dogs in combat armor surrounded the teenagers and pointed plasma rifles at them.

"Don't move one molecule!" shouted a beagle wearing a helmet and green chest armor. "We've got you."

"Time to leave?" squeaked Nick.

"Time for 'Plan B,'" said Amy, and held up her hands. "How about it, Three?"

Three reached for Amy's hair and untied the blonde braids.

"You should wear a ponytail if you're going to pretend to be me," she whispered. "Make sure to walk like a boy and spit when you talk. Also, don't let anyone see your arms or legs."

"Why not?" asked Amy.

"Because I've got tattoos and you don't!"

"We're both covered in white plaster. It's not going to matter."

"Just keep them covered."

Three fluffed out Amy's hair, pulled the blonde strands into a rakish ponytail on the left side of Amy's head, and then squeezed both arms around Philip's waist.

"Steady on, there," said Philip.

"She's pretending to be me," whispered Amy. "Trust us."

Three fluttered her eyelashes and gazed at Philip with big kitten eyes.

"Pardon me, you handsome, strong man, but could you help a confused little girl who's down on her luck? How about a kiss?"

"I don't sound like that!" hissed Amy.

More church bells began to peal, adding to the collection ringing through the night. A rapid clang like some kind of alarm started up down the hill closer to Lighthouse Avenue, and Amy heard men shouting and horses galloping through the dirt lanes. The mob of villagers along the street grew even larger as everyone in town ran to get a look at the massive green pickle of a starship that had plowed through Mr. Woodley's house. On the same side of the ship as the crowd, loud, sizzling cracks shot into the night sky like out-of-control fireworks and sent the villagers fleeing into the dark, including Hans, Anna, and E.G. Woodley.

A middle-aged woman in a gray skirt and jacket walked around the mountain of fresh earth and wood at the bow of the ship, gracefully navigating the broken furniture, lumber, and fallen brickwork in spiky black heels. Her blonde, shoulder-length hair was streaked with white, a color that matched her smoke-colored outfit. A pink scar slashed down the left side of her face from forehead to chin. The fingers of her right hand gleamed silver in the faint light from the street lamps and held a bulbous black pistol.

The woman stopped in front of the teenagers, and a grim smile spread across her scarred face.

"Well, well, well. What do we have here?"

Amy crossed her arms and spit on the ground. "Screw off, I'm not going back! Take these kids if you want, but touch me and there's going to be a fight."

One shook her head at Amy. "There's no need for such a performance, dear. I know you're not Three—— she has a tiny butterfly inked on the side of her neck."

"Blast it," said Three. "Forgot about that one. Oh, well."

One turned the pistol on Three. "'Oh, well' is an appropriate description of the past few days. Everyone knows how badly you've failed your mission. You were supposed to trick the copy into coming with us, and instead caused one of the worst cock-ups I've ever seen! You spent your time making friends and playing on the beach, while I have to crash-land through this stupid human village just to stop both of you from running away. You've let me down far too many times, Three. In the past I've forgiven you of worse mistakes, but now ... your fate will be the same as the others."

Three stamped her foot. "What? No! Two and Four won't stand for this. We had an agreement!"

One waved the pistol back at the ship. "Take them to the brig. Also, put that flying pest in a jar some-where."

Beside her, the black cat Wilson cleared his throat and bowed from the waist.

"We no longer have a brig, my Lady. After the punishment cubes were installed, you turned the brig into a sauna."

One nodded. "That's right, I forgot about that. Throw them into the sauna!"

"No!" squealed Nick, and grabbed her head. "My hair will go flat!"

"You monster," whispered Amy.

One smiled sweetly. "It's better than the brig. That place was nasty––mold and space weevils everywhere."

The cat and dog soldiers prodded Amy, Three, Philip, and Nick over the bricks and remains of Woodley's house, and around the curving bow of the badly-landed ship to the circular hatch of an airlock.

"This isn't the way it's supposed to happen," said Amy.

Three sniffed. "You think?"

Philip walked behind the two girls and carried the limp Sunflower in his arms like a baby. "This might be the time for me to say something pithy, like 'keep a stiff upper lip, dear' or 'don't give up the ship.' Unfortunately, I haven't a clue what to do. All of our friends are wounded or captured."

Sunflower coughed in Philip's arms. The orange cat opened his eyes a slit.

"No," he whispered. "There is another."

13

After the transport docked with the *Hare Twist*, Betsy headed toward the medical bay like the beagle had said, but once he was out of sight of the crew he scampered through the corridors looking for any floor plans or signs of where a prisoner might be kept.

"Where's the jail?" he asked the rear end of a German Shepherd that was sticking out from a square ventilation hole in the bulkhead.

"The what?" asked a hollow voice.

"The jail?" asked Betsy. "You know, the place with bars on the windows and free holo-TV?"

The German Shepherd backed up from the ventilation opening and pushed his grease-covered goggles up on his head to stare at Betsy. A battered wrench was strapped to one paw.

"Are you pulling my leg? Terry put you up to this, didn't he?" The dog spun around and stared down the corridor. "Terry! I know he's hiding somewhere. This is one of his jokes."

"It's no joke," said Betsy, wagging his tail. "One of my friends is in the jail."

The German Shepherd blinked. "Did you hit your head or something? I think you mean the punishment cubes." He stepped closer and lowered his voice. "Don't ask about the punishment cubes unless you want to end up there."

Betsy nodded his furry head. "I do, I do!"

"Quiet! It's true; you terriers really do have small brains. Go down the corridor that way, climb the first ramp on your left, and you can't miss it. You'll probably hear the screams before that."

Betsy trotted away. "Thanks, buddy!"

"I'm not your buddy and we never had this conversation."

Betsy spun around. "What, buddy?"

"Never mind."

The German Shepherd sighed and climbed back inside the ventilation duct.

Betsy shrugged his furry shoulders and trotted along the cramped corridor in the direction the German Shepherd had pointed.

Laughter and loud cheers startled the little dog. He poked his head into an open doorway and saw a dozen cats and dogs in a room decorated with balloons and party streamers. The animals wore cone-shaped, red paper hats on their heads and held drinks with the 'manos' bracelets around their front paws.

"Hurrah!"

A calico cat raised a glass full of green liquid and a goldfish.

"Here's to the next fifteen minutes!" she shouted.

Furry paws came from behind and pushed Betsy into the room.

"There you are," said the beagle from the transport.

"Guess he wasn't shell-shocked after all," said the white Persian with the scorched fur. "He found the most important room on the ship."

"Hey, buddies," said Betsy. "What's going on?"

The calico cat lowered a paper hat onto Betsy's head and snapped the rubber band under his chin.

"It's a fifteen-minute party," she said. "Cheers! Wait——someone get this dog a drink!"

"What's a fifteen-minute party?"

"Good gravy! Back to the medical bay with you," said the white Persian.

The calico cat giggled. "We're celebrating not dying, silly! Most crew members who get sent on a planetfall mission only last fifteen minutes, but we made it back!"

"Oh, no! Do they get killed or something?"

The cats and dogs in the room burst into laughter.

"Killed?" asked the calico, wiping tears from her eyes. "Bless your little heart. No, they just run away."

The beagle nodded. "The Lady is a ferocious boss. I'd bolt for the hills myself if it weren't for my student loans. Take my advice––don't go to astrogation school."

"Cool story," said Betsy. "I gotta visit the jail. Catch you later!"

The white Persian watched the terrier saunter out of the party room, and shook his head. "Brain damage, mates!"

Out in the corridor, a pair of cats in grease-stained orange coveralls saw Betsy and blocked his way. One of the cats pointed at the little dog and murmured in the other cat's ear. Without warning, the entire corridor vibrated and filled with a loud thrum. The lights in the ceiling turned red and the deck tilted down sharply, causing the cats to tumble and slide away, trying and failing to grab the metal floor with their claws.

Luckily, Betsy was wearing both of his "manos" on his front legs and could snap them out. He grabbed the edge of a doorframe next to the ramp and hung on tight. As the ship leveled out to a more horizontal angle, the terrier scrambled up the sloping ramp to the next deck.

He paused in the corridor above as a Yorkshire wearing a communications headset galloped past. The gray dog jumped through a hatch and slammed it shut with a bang.

"Weird," murmured Betsy, and looked at the ceiling. "What's with the red lights and the noise? Sounds like the engines. What if they're on fire? That would be really bad, so I need to move fast!"

Following the German Shepherd's directions, he scampered down the narrow, cable-lined hallway past a pair of strange doors, each decorated with the crudely-painted image of a cat's head, its tongue sticking out and an "X" over each eye.

Betsy skidded to a stop and backed up. "Fun One" and "Fun Two" were scrawled over the doors respectively, and a tiny display was mounted to the right of each door at normal-dog height, or waist-height for a human.

Betsy stood on his hind legs and brushed his paw over the first display. A video feed glowed to life on the screen and showed a Siamese cat standing behind the counter of a fast-food restaurant. He wore a brown apron around his neck and a white cap that was too large over his ears. The cat's jaw hung slack and his eyes held the dull, unmoving stare of someone who had either taken too many sleeping pills, watched the entirety of "Three's Company" in one sitting, or watched the entirety of "Three's Company" in one sitting and needed sleeping pills to numb the pain.

"Welcome to Pwason King, how may I help you?" droned the cat on the screen. "Our special today is fresh-caught kribich. Would you like milk dipping sauce, poona dipping sauce, or red dipping sauce? Please do not ask what is in the red sauce. I do not know."

"That looks like Doctor MacGuffin," said Betsy. "He's not dead!"

He tapped through the controls on the screen, shut down the mental broadcast, and slapped a button. The door swished open and the little terrier poked his head inside the punishment cube. The glassy walls of the tiny room still glowed with bright energy and fuzzy shapes glided under the surface, like the shadows of whales under the sea. The crumpled heap of brown and tan fur that was once the Siamese cat Cynthia MacGuffin lay shivering in a corner with his eyes squeezed shut.

Betsy prodded the cat with a paw. "Wakey, wakey!"

MacGuffin hissed and jerked violently with his eyes still closed.

"No refunds!" he screamed, and batted the air with his paws. "It's been seven days! No refunds after seven days, even with a receipt!"

"A what?" asked Betsy. "I didn't buy anything, I swear."

MacGuffin cracked open the yellow slits of his eyes and stared up at Betsy.

"No refunds after seven days," he rasped. "Unless you're the regional manager. Are you the regional manager?"

Betsy blinked for a moment. "Yes."

MacGuffin jumped straight up like a possessed cat and saluted with a paw to his forehead. "Ja vo, mein Kommandant! What are your orders?"

"Uh ... I order you to come with me!"

The Siamese cat opened his yellow eyes wide. "That's impossible! Who would clean the Slurpee machine? And I have to serve the customers. They need me!"

"I don't see any customers," said Betsy. "Unless they're really small and you sat on them."

MacGuffin grabbed his bottom with both paws and raced in a circle around Betsy. "Oh, no!" he shrieked. "I've killed the customers! What will I do, what will I do?" He stopped and jabbed a paw into Betsy's chest. "You! Regional manager. Get me out of here! Let's steal a hovership and flee to Amber. We'll change our names to Lois and Tina!"

"Great! Let's go, Lois. Follow me."

MacGuffin trailed after Betsy and walked out of the punishment cube. "Are you insane? You're Lois, and I'm Tina."

The metal deck vibrated from a deafening rumble and a violent impact that slammed both animals into the cables along the corridor wall. The ceiling lights flashed and a klaxon began to moan from a lower deck.

Betsy pulled MacGuffin up from the floor.

"Holy Tardar Sauce," groaned the cat, holding his head with both paws. "What happened?"

"We're going to steal a hovership and run away," said Betsy. "My name's Lois and you're Tina."

"What are you talking about?"

Betsy shrugged. "Okay, you can be Lois, I'm not picky. It's a little bit silly because you said just a second ago that you wanted to be Tina."

"I'm Doctor Cynthia MacGuffin, you idiot!"

"But you just said––"

MacGuffin curved his back and stretched his front paws. "I was suffering from a leftover effect of the punishment cube. I guess you're here to rescue me from that horrible copy of Amy Armstrong. If that's the case, lead the way."

Betsy wagged his tail. "Sure! But there was something I was supposed to do ... something really important."

MacGuffin rolled his eyes. "More important than saving my life?"

"Oh! I know!"

Betsy scrambled to the second punishment cube and stood on his hind legs. The video screen for "Fun Two" showed a gray cat kneeling beside a cage on the edge of a cliff. Trapped behind the rusty bars of the cage was an orange tabby that looked very much like Sunflower.

Betsy tapped through the screens and deactivated the punishment cube. The terrier jumped through the now-open doorway and barked at the small gray cat sprawled inside.

"I'm Betsy Jackson! I'm here to rescue you."

"Betsy ... who?" asked the cat in a weak voice, her eyes still shut.

"I'm Sunflower's friend and I'm here to save you!"

The cat opened her green eyes wide. "Sunflower? You know my husband? Where is he?"

"Come on!"

Betsy pulled the gray cat Andy Nakamura out of the punishment cube. He helped her to stand on all four feet, and she blinked at the Siamese cat waiting outside.

"That's not Sunflower."

"Of course not. That's Tina––I mean, that's Doctor MacGuffin."

MacGuffin raised a paw. "Felicitations."

Andy shook her head abruptly, as if she were trying to fling away cobwebs.

"Let's go," she said. "Take me to your ship."

"I don't have a ship," said Betsy.

"This isn't much of a rescue. How are we supposed to escape?"

Betsy hung his furry head. "I didn't think that far."

Andy sighed and covered her face with her gray paws. She jerked them away and stared at the deck below her feet. "The ship isn't moving. Why isn't the ship moving? That means we're in deep space or we've landed somewhere."

"We may have crashed, actually," said MacGuffin. "There was a bit of a bang and I hit my head. You wouldn't have noticed because you were still in that horrible room."

Andy paced back and forth, the end of her gray tail twitching rapidly. "What I've noticed is you two have no idea what you're doing." She growled and bared her teeth. "We need to get to engineering, and fast. Follow me!"

The gray cat sprinted down the corridor like furry lightning, and Betsy and MacGuffin ran after her as fast as they could.

AMY PUSHED Three against the wall of the sauna and held her there with both arms.

"You tricked me! The escape pod, pretending to be my friend ... it was all a bunch of lies. A bunch of stupid lies to get me here!"

Philip pulled her away and stood between the girls. "Amy, this won't help. Please calm down."

"I don't care if it doesn't help, and telling someone to calm down doesn't make them calm down, it just makes them madder! We're about to be evaporated by my evil, dimension-hopping twin, and it's all her fault. Am I the only one who remembers how the escape pod exploded and almost killed all of us?"

Sunflower lay in a corner with his eyes shut, slumped against the lacquered slats of the sauna wall. A bruise covered one eye and his fur was smeared with blue blood.

"Please," murmured the orange tabby. "The yelling ..."

"Sorry," said Amy. "I get upset when I've been stabbed in the back."

Three held up her hands. "Okay, okay, okay. I lied about some stuff at first, and yeah, my pod exploded. But trust me––I had no idea that One was crazy enough to plant a bomb. I don't want to die. I'm just like the rest of you!"

"Hard to believe," said Amy. "Even harder when you say, 'trust me.' "

Three bowed her head and stared down at the lacquered maple planks of the sauna. "When I first met you, I thought I could trick you into coming with me somewhere and One could pick us up. But the crash and that little swim in the ocean put things in perspective. I've seen her do some awful things ..." Three shook her head. "I thought I had a deal with One to help her catch all of these copies, but she was just using me. After those fishermen rescued us, I decided to run away for real. I honestly wanted to help you and be your friend. No, it's true! I really wanted the two of us to roll around the Old West, kicking butt and raising hell. I wanted to tell you about everything last night, before all of this happened."

Amy crossed her arms and turned away. She began pacing the wooden floor of the small room.

Philip sat on a wooden bench next to a metal birdcage. "A convincing outburst, Three, which does us as much good as a tinker's cuss. Friends or enemies, traitors or comrades––we're all trapped." He patted the top of the birdcage. "One isn't going to permit another escape, especially after what happened with Nick and myself."

Inside the cage, the tiny sprite stretched out on a pillow and rubbed her flat belly.

"I ate all of her chocolate! She probably hates me forever."

Amy sat on the bench next to Philip and held his hand.

"How did the two of you survive the crash?"

Philip shrugged. "I put on another pressure suit and went back inside the sinking ship. I found Nick and stuffed her inside the suit, but I suppose the helmet didn't seal properly or something like that. It filled with water and I passed out. When I came to my senses, I found myself in One's bedroom on the *Hare Twist*. Apparently, her crew pulled us from the wreckage. She was quite pleasant during our first talk, but shortly after that, Nick found me and told me the truth."

"Truth about what?"

"That One lied when she claimed to be searching for you, and about keeping me alive longer than a few days. I was going to be nothing more than a plaything for Two, something that I'd rather not think about now that I'm a prisoner again. Once I discovered these startling facts, Nick and I stole a fighter and landed as close as we could to a radio signal from Sunflower."

"Landed?" squeaked Nick. "Ha!"

Amy glanced at the orange tabby in the corner.

"Sunflower was broadcasting something? Why?"

"Until he comes out of his daze, I have no idea. It certainly attracted our attention, and the attention of One and her murderous soldiers."

Nick jumped from her pillow and shook the tiny bars of her cage.

"It's from a cat story!" she squealed. "A nursery rhyme about a kitten tricking a dog and making him jump into a lake. I bet that was Sunflower's plan."

Three snorted. "Nursery rhymes––are you serious? One is going to zap me, Amy, and Philip to death and kick the rest of you out an airlock. She's very efficient that way."

Philip let go of Amy's hand and stood up.

"Now look here––what the blazes are you talking about? The woman may be mad as a hatter, but she's not going to harm anyone apart from me. I'm the one with torture and death hanging over his head."

Amy patted the wooden bench. "Philip––please sit. You don't know the entire story."

"Enlighten me."

Three shrugged and leaned against the wooden wall of the sauna. "Short version or long?"

"Short for now, please. Ask me again after we survive being hung from the proverbial yardarms."

"One believes she can travel back in time by destroying the Amy Armstrongs from other dimensions," said Three. She pointed at the center of her chest, and then to Amy. "Right now, that means the two of us."

"My word," said Philip. "But ... I thought time travel was impossible."

"It is," said Amy. "Somehow she found a way, and has some kind of crazy machine. She doesn't just want to kill us, she wants to turn us into energy with this thing."

"We won't be the first," said Three. "She's had lots of practice."

Philip thought for a moment, and then held up a finger. "Are you talking about the quantum attenuation transfuser?"

"How do you know about that?" asked Three.

"I read a few articles on her computer before Nick and I escaped. She was researching trans-dimensional travel with her husband, apparently, and that's why this ship––the *Hare Twist*–– was constructed in the first place."

Three sat on the bench. "Whatever she was in the past, One is a power-hungry monster now. She murdered her husband––don't ask––and wants to go back in time to before he was dead. She's got this maniacal theory in her head that if she turns enough copies of Amy Armstrong into quantum data, she can make it happen. I was just along for the ride, honestly. Never thought she'd figure it out."

"Enough copies," murmured Philip. "You said she's had practice. How many Amy Armstrongs have you murdered so far?"

Three leaned forward with her elbows on her knees and stared at the floor. "I don't know."

Amy walked across the room and stood in front of her.

"How many?"

"Hundreds," whispered Three, still staring at the floor. "I stopped counting. I didn't like thinking about it."

Philip sighed and rubbed his chin. "A better question is, how many more does she need to finish this foul research?"

"Only a few," said Three. "She kept saying the end was near."

***

ONE STORMED into the circular control room of the *Hare Twist* with a pale face. She threw her jacket at the command chair and paced the small open space behind it, absent-mindedly rubbing the fabric of her white silk blouse with the fingers of her human left hand. Her other arm hung stiffly at her side, the chrome fingers reflecting the crimson light from the ceiling. As she paced, uniformed cats and dogs dashed into the room, saluted One, and strapped into control stations. The trickle of frantic personnel ended after a minute, but half the seats were still empty.

The black cat Wilson nervously waited next to One's chair, and ended her walking trance by clearing his throat. One jabbed a red-painted fingernail down at her first officer.

"Idiot! You're always making noise when I'm trying to think!"

Wilson bowed. "Apologies, My Lady, but the crew are back on board and we've sealed the airlocks."

One grabbed an armrest and settled in her chair. "Lift off immediately."

Wilson waved at the beagle sitting at the pilot's station. The dog jammed a red knob forward and pulled back on a small wheel, causing the deck to vibrate and pitch up at a slight angle.

"Any word from engineering?"

"We're cleared for atmospheric travel only," said Wilson. "It's going to take a few weeks to inspect the damage to the lower decks and clear them for vacuum travel."

"Could we depressurize those areas and still leave the planet?"

Wilson nodded. "A partial loss of pressure would be fine, but most of the cargo would have to be moved to the upper decks. We're short of space as it is."

"Run it by Terry, anyway. Status on survivor beacons?"

"We've detected a few dozen along the coast. Another platoon must have survived the battle and somehow got separated."

"Well? Are you doing anything about it?"

"Soon, my Lady. The only transport we have left is being inspected for damage."

One drummed her fingers on the armrest. "Stop inspections and send it down for those soldiers. I can't afford to lose any more crew." She twisted around to the white cat at the communications station. "Open a channel to *Wits Hater*."

The middle-aged face of Two appeared on the central screen.

"*Wits Hater* actual. What do you need?"

"That silver ship you hauled out of the ocean——is it ready to fly?"

Two shook her head. "Repair teams flushed the water and cleaned out the dead fish, but can't get the engines re-started. Nothing wrong with them, just won't start. We've been sitting up here in the mountains just staring at it. Even the jumper cables we rigged aren't working."

One waved a hand. "Fine, fine, I get the point. Call me if anything changes."

She pressed a button on her armrest and the screen went dark.

"Incoming message from *Raw Tithes*," said the communications cat.

"Go ahead," said One.

The black-haired Four appeared on the central screen wearing a black turtleneck. Cats and dogs in crew uniforms ran through the control room behind her.

"We caught a couple of sauropods down in that human village," she said. "One of them is huge-- never saw them grow that big. He was running through the streets, carrying the other lizard on his back. Beat up pretty bad, that second one. Took all of my thorazine to make the big one stop fighting and go to sleep. We don't have anywhere to keep them, so I'm wondering what to do."

One rubbed her fingers together. "Why in the five sons would you bother to keep them? I don't have a room strong enough to hold sauropods, either. Kick those green-skinned plasma bombs out the nearest airlock and pray to Crom that you don't see them again."

"How about the crashed ship? That's probably where they came from. Maybe they can tell us how to start the engines."

One hooted with laughter. "You want to interrogate a sauropod? You might as well strip naked and cover yourself in teriyaki sauce, because they'll eat you alive."

"That's not going to happen. I'll just ask a few questions."

"Well, it's your funeral."

Four grinned. "Isn't it always?"

The copy of Amy with a short black bob disappeared from the central display. The view changed to a video feed of the ocean from a thousand feet up, pale gray and glistening in the moonlight.

One rubbed the human fingers of her left hand over the chrome, mechanical bones of her right in a circular motion and stared at the screen for a long moment, a moment that would have been much longer if a Yorkshire terrier in green overalls hadn't bolted into the command room, tripped over his own four feet, and tumbled head-over-tail into a weapons station with a huge bang. The gray dog scrambled to his feet and whispered in Wilson's ear, causing the yellow eyes of One's second-in-command to grow as large as two fifty-woolong coins.

One drummed her fingers and watched Wilson. The black cat grabbed his tail with his front paws and fidgeted with it as he stared down at the metal deck.

"Well?" asked One. "Are you going to tell me what's happened, or should I wait for it to be printed in the ship's newsletter?"

Wilson gulped. "I, ah … apologies, my Lady. It's just that …"

One leaned forward. "Don't tell me something ridiculous has happened like my two prisoners being freed from their punishment cubes. News like that would send me on a catacidal rampage starting with the black cat in front of me."

Wilson bowed. "Of course, my Lady. It was nothing silly like that! It was the exact opposite of two escaped prisoners. Uh, which would be …"

"The opposite would be finding lots and lots of chocolate to replace everything eaten by that flying pest."

Wilson jumped up and pointed a paw at One.

"Yes! That's what happened. Two prisoners have NOT escaped, and we've found a chocolate. Your chocolate."

"Fantastic. Where is it?"

Wilson glanced left and right. "Where is it, where is it … oh! It's down in the human village. They like chocolate. It's down there, and they have it. Definitely. Lots of it, and definitely."

One leaned back in her chair and sighed. "Wilson, you idiot. Of course they have chocolate, but it's far too dangerous to send anyone down to get it."

"Of course, my Lady."

"How long until sunrise?"

Wilson scrambled to a nearby station and stared at the display. "Two hours, sixteen minutes."

"Prepare the quantum attenuation chamber for three subjects."

"For immediate testing?"

One looked down at the metal fingers of her hand, spread out on her lap.

"No. For two hours and sixteen minutes from now."

14

The feather-like clouds above the Santa Lucia mountains brightened into shades of scarlet and orange as morning approached. The colors slashed across the deep blue sky like strokes from a giant brush and contrasted sharply with the dry yellow mountains and colorless ocean. The *Hare Twist* hovered three hundred meters above the waves and would have excellent views of the sunrise.

One had the prisoners chained at wrist and paw. She led the way to the port observation room, where she ordered them to face the floor-to-ceiling windows as the pilot turned the ship to the south. A dozen cat and dog soldiers stood behind Amy, Philip, Three, Sunflower, and Nick, the barrels of their plasma rifles pointed at the captives.

Amy stared at Monterey and Pacific Grove on the coast. A faint haze of smoke hung over the two villages as the cannery smokestacks warmed and kitchen maids lit fires to prepare the morning breakfast.

"What's the point?" she asked. "I'm not even from here. Why would I want to see it?"

"A last sunrise for the condemned," murmured Philip next to her.

One walked to the window in front of the captives and rubbed at a speck of dirt on the glass. "I don't really know why I want to make such a dramatic spectacle of this. I suppose for some moments in life, there are no words."

Three groaned. "Shut up and kill us already."

One turned to the captives and calmly folded her hands behind her back.

"You have every right to think of me as an inhuman monster, but not a cruel one. The procedure for transforming your bodies into super-heated plasma is painless, and you'll feel nothing. Capturing you has cost the lives of hundreds of crew members and millions of woolongs in damaged equipment, but I do this for science, not for any revenge."

"I didn't ask you to chase after us!" said Amy. "Those dead cats and dogs are your fault."

Philip nodded. "Good show, Amy. Like any megalomaniac, she's trying to shift the blame to us. There's no excuse possible that will wipe clean your slate of monstrous behavior, whether that excuse is science, religion, or the good of the country. Why can't you take responsibility for your actions?"

One turned to stare at the scarlet glow behind the mountains. "Great discoveries require great sacrifice. I don't have to explain myself."

"But your actions betray you. Bringing us here at sunrise could only be because you wanted to explain yourself."

"We know the real truth," said Amy. "You want to see your husband again."

One flushed and her scar turned red. She jabbed a finger at Three.

"You shouldn't have told them!"

The teenager shrugged. "What are you going to do——kill me?"

"You had a choice. You've always had choices, Three——to do as I asked, to kill or not kill, to run away when you got bored. But you didn't, you stayed with my crew and are just as responsible as I am for the deaths of those dimensional copies. I suppose getting rid of you is my way of erasing that debt."

"It's just like Philip said," growled Amy. "You're trying to feel better about killing us!"

SPACEBOOK AWAKENS 225

She took a step toward One, but soldiers grabbed her chained arms and pulled her back.

"You're right about Three having a choice," Amy continued. "But she's not like you. Whatever happened in the past, she decided to help me. We became friends, and it wasn't just because we had to survive. Don't make the mistake of thinking everyone sees the world like you do."

"Another feature of megalomania," said Philip.

One smiled grimly. "A megalomaniac sees herself at the center of everything, even when she's not. In our case, we ARE the center of everything. Think about the fact that Amy Armstrong and Philip Marlborough are the only true constants through every dimension in the universe. The pattern of our molecules is a code for understanding time itself!"

Three rolled her eyes. "Here we go again ..."

"All of those things can be true and you can still be crazy," said Amy. "One fact doesn't cancel out the other."

"You're missing the point by focusing on me," said One. "We're all the same––you're Amy Armstrong, she's Amy Armstrong, and I'm Amy Armstrong. Each and every one of us is smart, talented, and mischievous, and will do whatever it takes to get what she wants. Look at the people chained next to you that you call 'friends.' Amy Armstrong dropped into their lives like a plasma bomb and they've been picking up the pieces ever since. If you think I'm a villain, then you should look in the mirror."

"I haven't killed anyone!"

"This is ridiculous," said Philip. "Do as you will, but stop needling us to death."

One stepped in front of the teenager and touched his shoulder. "It doesn't have to be death for you, dear

Philip. Travel the universe with me. Forget these people and save your life."

Philip shoved her hand away with his elbow. "I'd rather die."

One smiled. "Would you? Turn that latch below the window and pull up on the bar. Both you and your precious Amy can leap to your deaths into the sea. It's impossible to survive a fall at this height. Isn't that the meaning of true love——dying together?"

Philip grimaced. "I'd rather you jump, Madame."

Amy grabbed Philip's hand and glared at One.

"You wouldn't know anything about true love, would you? Only someone who's dead inside would say things like that."

The older twin of Amy turned to stare at the first gleam of sunshine behind the eastern mountains. She took a deep breath and let it out slowly.

"You might be right about that, Amy Armstrong."

The heavily-armed cat and dog soldiers marched the prisoners out of the observation room, down one deck and toward the center of the ship. They stopped the group at a thick metal hatch covered in red-and-white warning stripes and labeled in the center with the large block letters "Q.A.T." Someone had scrawled a question mark in black marker after the letters.

One pointed at the door. "Wilson——have that graffiti cleaned up."

"At once, my Lady!"

The black cat licked a paw and jumped at the scrawled question mark to wipe it away. This was silly for several reasons, mainly because he couldn't jump that high.

"You imbecile," said One. "I didn't mean right now. Seriously, if you hadn't been abandoned in a junk yard as a kitten, I'd track down your entire family and have them killed for stupidity."

Wilson bowed. "Thank you for bringing up memories of my painful and lonely childhood, Your Beautifulness."

One shielded her fingers from view as she entered a code into a keypad next to the door. Unseen gears clicked and spun inside the wall. The floor shook as the metal hatch rumbled to the side and revealed a small compartment with another hatch in the opposite wall.

"Everyone inside," said One. "Move! Not the troops––wait in the corridor."

The soldiers pushed Amy and her friends through the door, and One and Wilson stepped behind them into the small, closet-like room. The black cat pressed a red button and the hatch whisked shut.

One pulled a glossy black pistol from her pocket and waved it at the prisoners. "Take off the restraints."

"I wouldn't do that," growled Three. "I'll claw your eyes out."

One held up the pistol. "That's why I have this. The machinery in the next room generates strong magnetic forces. For the benefit of your tiny brains, that means all iron-based metals have to be left outside. That includes your disgusting flying pest."

Nick banged on the bars of the birdcage with her tiny fists. "What? I'm not made out of metal."

"No, but the cage is, and I'm not letting you out."

"You'll pay for this, you monster! Sprites never forget."

As Wilson removed the chrome handcuffs around the wrists of each of the human prisoners, One kicked the birdcage with a high-heeled shoe and laughed. "I have punishments prepared especially for you, my little fairy devil. Anyone who eats a year's supply of chocolate deserves something special. Those treats were worth a queen's ransom in space. Do you like brownies?"

"I love them!"

"Good. You'll be the special ingredient."

Philip gasped. "You wouldn't dare!"

He set the limp Sunflower on the floor and stepped toward One. She aimed the pistol at his forehead and the teenager backed away with his hands up.

"Even if you take this weapon from me, there are a dozen crew members outside with rifles. All are very upset about the recent death of their friends. All of which was your fault."

Amy knelt beside the birdcage and touched Nick's tiny hand through the bars.

"Don't give up, Nick," she whispered. "Whatever happens to me or Philip, keep fighting."

Nick folded her dragonfly wings and crumpled to the floor of the cage, sobbing.

"Take off your shoes," One said to Amy and Three. "Definitely metal in those old things."

"Cats don't wear shoes," murmured Sunflower. The orange tabby raised his head from the floor, his eyes closed. "Dummy."

"We'll find out who's a dummy when I have you stuffed and mounted in my office. Wilson, stay here and guard the cat and the flying pest."

The black cat bowed. "My Lady."

One pressed a button next to the interior hatch and the door whisked to the side. She waved the pistol at the three teenagers and prodded them forward.

The large room inside was packed wall-to-wall with blocky white equipment and tall glass cylinders filled with blue liquid that bubbled like giant lava lamps. It seemed more appropriate for testing Pop-Tarts than real science, or where a very anti-bacterial seventies deejay could write his memoirs. At the far end of the room, a beam of light illuminated a silver disc on the floor. Concentric circles of multi-faceted gems gleamed in the ceiling directly above the disc, so clear and bright that it hurt to look at them.

One kept her pistol aimed at the backs of the three captives and stepped over the spaghetti tangle of cables on the floor to a keyboard and display bolted to an island of five white cylinders. She glanced through a few pages of data on the screen and tapped the keys for a moment.

"Very good. All systems in order. Now––who's first?"

The hatch opened and Wilson stuck his black furry head inside.

"My Lady––"

"What is it, you brainless fleabag?"

"Two and Four desperately wish to talk to you, my Lady. Both *Wits Hater* and *Raw Twist* have lifted off from their landing areas and are approaching our position at high speed."

One sighed. "What's twisted their panties now?"

"I don't know, my Lady," said Wilson. "Everyone knows that Four doesn't wear them, so how could she––"

The cat ducked as a high-heeled shoe banged off the hatch.

"Get out, you fish-flavored moron! Tell them a story or share recipes or something. I'm busy!"

Wilson disappeared and the hatch shut with an oily click.

One stepped out of her other high heel and stood on the cables in her nylon-clad feet. She pointed the pistol back at the teenagers.

"As I was saying——who's first?"

Philip stepped in front of Amy. "Whatever villainous torture you have planned, take me. Leave Amy and Three alone."

Amy grabbed his arm. "Philip!"

One shrugged. "Tempting, I suppose, but the entire point of this overly dramatic production is to study the universal frequency data from dimensional copies. I can't get the data without those two."

"You've found others before. You can find others in the future."

"There's no guarantee. Why should I give up two birds in the hand for any number hiding in the transdimensional bushes?"

"Because these young ladies are precious to me," said Philip quietly. "Especially Amy."

Amy hugged him around the waist. "Forget it. She wants to make us beg, and that's what you're doing, Philip."

Three crossed her arms and glared at One. "Unbelievable. I spend years slaving on your pirate ship and this is the thanks I get. Get this over with, and quick."

"My crew may all be pirates, but any one of the mangy dullards are better than you," said One. "How many times did they save your skin? How many times did they find you in a corner of Phobos Station, completely drunk off the cheapest dog beer? You wouldn't remember any of that. You're a self-centered, destructive child with no point to your life, and I should have done this a long time ago."

Three turned red and stared at the floor. "Yeah ... well, you ..."

Amy put an arm around Three. "At least she knows she made mistakes. At least she tried to do something at the end, unlike you. You don't care about anything but this pig-headed goal of traveling into the past to save your husband."

"Who was murdered," said Three. "By you."

"What's going to happen when you save him?" asked Amy, raising her voice. "Do you actually think he'll be happy that you killed hundreds of innocent people to get back to him? You can't be that stupid. There's a little voice in your head that you try to squash, just like you squash everything, a little voice asking you over and over: 'Am I the same person? Can he see me under the scars and the metal arm?'"

Three smirked and pointed at One. "You're doing all this for nothing. He's going to reject you."

"And everything you stand for," said Philip.

One shook her head and chuckled. "Wow! This has been fun. Honestly, it has. The other dimensional copies mostly whined for their lives or yelled at me. It's very interesting to have my life analyzed by a bunch of giggling teenagers, but it doesn't change any-thing one bit. All of my energy since the tragedy has been driving me toward this research, and I'm not about to be driven off course by your noodle-headed logic." She waved the pistol at Amy. "You first. Step on the platform. Move! I can de-res a dead body if I have to."

Amy hugged Philip and kissed him.

"I love you," she said.

"I love you, too," he whispered. "Let me go first."

She shook her head. "I don't want to see you die."

Amy pushed Philip away and walked over to the illuminated silver disc. She stood in the center of the light, hands clenched at her side to keep them from shaking, and glared at One.

"Do it."

One shrugged and tapped a long series of keys. The hum from the equipment grew to a high-pitched whine. The multiple circles of gems above Amy's head began to spin and gleam through the spectrum, covering Amy's blonde hair in a pattern of rapidly-changing colors.

"NO!" screamed Three.

In a flash, she leapt across the room and pushed Amy off the silver disc. A blinding beam of light struck Three in the back, and the room filled with the smell of lavender and burning cotton.

"Well, well," murmured One, typing at the control panel with one hand while keeping the pistol aimed at Philip with the other. "This should be interesting."

Three lay sprawled across the disc on her stomach, grimacing in pain and breathing fast. Curls of smoke rose from the burnt edges of a large hole in the back of her nightgown. Below the hole, the skin of her shoulder blade was as white as chalk.

"No! What have you done to her?!!" shouted Philip.

"She did it to herself," said One. "I didn't make her jump. From the data, it seems she caught a partial de-res. This should be very interesting to watch. Normally the subject is sent back through time to an original quantum state in a process that takes nanoseconds. This will be different."

Amy knelt beside Three and touched the teenager's head.

"That was stupid," she said. "Why did you do that?"

"Can't breathe," gasped Three. "Sit ... me up."

Amy turned the young woman over and helped her into a sitting position, supporting her with an arm behind her back.

"Thank ... you," gasped Three.

"Something's wrong," said Amy. "You're getting smaller. Your neck tattoo is gone!"

Three had changed from a seventeen-year-old version of Amy to a skinny pre-teen in a matter of seconds, her chest shrinking, hips and shoulders narrowing, and body mass disappearing. The curls and highlights in her hair vanished as it straightened and returned to the same blonde shade as Amy's.

"Her body is experiencing a reverse quantum event," said One in a bored tone. "Don't worry, the end result will be the same."

Three pulled up the sleeve of her nightgown and held out her right arm to Amy. As both watched, the tattoo of a purple orchid disappeared from her pale skin.

"Age ... eight," gasped Three, with a higher-pitched voice.

Amy wiped tears from her eyes and hugged the shrinking girl tight.

"I'm sorry," she said. "I messed up everything, and I'm sorry."

The tiny hand of a five-year-old touched Amy's cheek.

"Don't cry," said Three. "Happy ... to be ... your friend."

Amy held her off the cold floor as the girl shrank down to a chubby toddler with pink cheeks and golden hair. The nightgown slipped away and Amy held a gurgling, blue-eyed infant in her lap.

"It stopped," she said, and stared at One. "She stopped shrinking."

One jiggled the pistol at Philip. The teenager ran his hands through his hair and paced back and forth, eyes wild and looking as if he wanted to burst.

"No moving, dear Philip, or I might get nervous." She glanced at the display. "Very interesting. The quantum attenuator seems to have reduced Three to the age of a month-old infant. This has incredible possibilities for the beauty industry."

The hatch whisked open and Wilson stuck his furry head inside.

"My Lady, it's very urgent! Code red situation!"

One bent down and threw her other shoe at the cat.

"Shut that door!"

Amy took the empty cotton nightgown and wrapped up baby Three, then stood up with the infant in her arms. Amy kissed the baby's soft cheek and Three giggled and tried to grab her hair.

"Stand on the platform with the child," said One. "I'll do both of you at once this time."

"Leave them alone!" shouted Philip. "This is unbearable."

The deck vibrated and a loud rumble came from somewhere in the ship.

"Sounds like you've got a little problem," said Amy. "Don't you want to take a break? Maybe find out what's going on?"

"That's exactly my plan after I've dealt with the pair of you," said One. She aimed the pistol at Amy. "Get on the platform or I'll shoot the baby."

Amy held baby Three tight to her chest and stepped onto the silver disc with the infant. As the hum of machinery grew in volume and the circles of gems began to spin, casting colors over her and the baby, Philip dropped to his knees and covered his face with both hands. The smell of lavender became stronger.

"Don't worry, Philip," shouted Amy. "I——"

Unbearable heat and pain flashed through her body, and with a crackling burst of light everything in the universe disappeared.

15

After Amy and baby Three vanished, a booming crash shook everything in the room and the deck jerked up and down.

One picked herself up from the floor and aimed the pistol at Philip. She stared at the display screen and sighed.

"Blast and double blast."

Philip laughed bitterly. "What? Shocked that everything is falling to pieces, and you're about to get your comeuppance?"

One shook her head. "Not quite. The data I gathered from your two girlfriends is still not enough. I could have sworn those were the last copies I needed to find the location of SpaceBook."

The out-of-focus side of Wilson's face appeared on the display. Cats and dogs were running back and forth in the background, and a low-pitched klaxon sounded.

"That doesn't matter, just override the video," he said to someone off-camera. "I have to talk to her." The black cat looked up. "Oh! My Lady, you must come forward at once!"

"Just tell me what's wrong, you dolt."

"*Wits Hater* and *Hare Twist* are firing at us! They said something about you killing Three."

"There's no way they could have known about that," said One. "But it doesn't matter. Deploy countermeasures and raise the magnetic shields. Neither one of those idiots have missiles that can break through my shields. I designed it that way."

The screen filled briefly with static as another rumble shook the deck.

"Shields and weapons are down," gasped Wilson. "I can't talk to Engineering at all, and the hatches have been blocked from the inside! We're flying at top speed and barely staying alive."

"Why didn't you tell me this before?"

The black cat blinked at her. "Um ... I tried."

"Hail them. Patch it to this console."

A few seconds later, the screen split into the faces of two women: a blonde in her thirties, and a young woman with her hair cut in a short black bob.

"Where's Three?" asked Two, the one with the bob. "Put her on screen!"

"Stop firing at my ship and give me time to find the little scamp," said One. "All of this damage is going to come out of your profits, you know. It's not good for a working relationship."

"There is no relationship," said Four, the older blonde. "Stop playing this game. We know what you did to her."

One held up her hands. "Gossip and lies. Girls, girls––let's calm down. Can't we talk about this without lobbing high explosives at my very, very expensive starship?"

Four leaned close to the camera and sneered. "Someone in your very, very expensive starship sent us an unencrypted video feed of the quantum attenuator chamber. We saw everything, and saw you kill her! Did you know that Three was the closest thing I had to a sister?"

One shrugged. "Oops?"

"The pact is broken," said Two. "Say your prayers to Crom, you she-devil. It doesn't matter. I doubt you even believed in him in the first place."

A violent crash like a sudden earthquake broke the display and sent equipment flying through the room, including the control panel which fell on top of One. Philip felt weightless for a second, and then crashed back to the deck. He scrambled on hands and knees to the hatch, opened it, and squeezed through. Inside the small preparation room, Nick's bird cage rolled around and banged on the walls as the decks pitched left and right. Inside the cage, the tiny sprite held on to the bars with all her might.

Sunflower raised his head weakly from the floor. "Hail ... the conquering hero ..."

Philip stepped over the cat. He cracked open the hatch to the corridor and carefully peeked through the gap.

"Don't do that," said Sunflower. "Pirates ... everywhere."

The sprite shook the bars of her cage. "Get me out of here, you fuzzball!"

Sunflower held up a paw. "Does this look like a can opener?"

"The hallway is empty and the ship is under attack," said Philip, and pushed the hatch open.

"Under attack?" squealed Nick. "From who?"

"It doesn't matter. Let's go."

He ripped off the door to Nick's cage and she buzzed into the air.

"Thanks, Philly!"

"What about Amy?" asked Sunflower. "She take ... a powder break?"

Philip shook his head. "She's gone."

Sunflower blinked. "Gone to the litter box?"

"She's dead," said Philip, crouching through the narrow doorway into the corridor. "And so is Three." He leaned down and took a plasma rifle from the deck. "I'll probably join them before the day is out, but

I'll be damned if I don't take a few of the beasts with me. How about you?"

Sunflower's yellow eyes grew wide and his lower lip trembled. The orange tabby scrambled to his feet, jumped into the corridor, and grabbed a plasma rifle. He stood on his hind legs and pulled back the slide mechanism of the rifle, loading an energy round into the chamber with a loud click.

"Nobody kills my friends without my permission!" he roared. "Time to rock and roll!"

The orange tabby screamed a high-pitched battle cry and charged down the corridor, firing his plasma rifle wildly. This could have been an epic display of cat bravery, if there had been anyone to shoot back, or anyone at all.

Sunflower ran the length of the corridor, opened a pressure hatch, charged down another empty corridor, opened another pressure hatch, and kept running forward, firing his plasma rifle and screaming.

"Die, you motherless pigs! Die!"

A featureless metal bulkhead stopped his progress. The only possible exit was a round hatch in the floor, which the orange cat began to pound on with the butt of his plasma rifle.

"Open up, you cowards!"

Philip ran up to Sunflower, with Nick buzzing over his shoulder.

"The one time in my life when I go mad with rage and want to kill something, and there's nobody around," said the dark-haired teenager. "Astonishing."

"Sunflower scared them away!" said Nick.

"They're below us," said Sunflower. He set his rifle on the floor and tugged at the wheel of the hatch. "Can't you hear them? There's a magnificent battle going on below our feet and we're missing it!"

"I'll take your word for it," said Philip. "Your hearing is better than mine."

"Help me! I don't have my manos bracelets."

Philip turned the wheel and pulled up on the hatch. As it cracked open, the corridor echoed with the 'hissing-bee' sound of plasma rounds being fired and the loud clang as they struck metal. The smell of ozone and burning hair also swirled up from the opening.

Nick buzzed down and leaned over the edge. "Who are they shooting at? Each other?"

"Who cares?" snarled Sunflower. "Eat plasma, you dirty rats! Yaaaa!"

The cat grabbed his rifle and jumped through the hole in the floor.

Philip slung the strap of his rifle over his head and slid down the ladder to the next deck.

"For queen and country!" yelled the teenager.

The corridor was thick with smoke and the blinding, blue-green flashes of automatic plasma fire. Bodies of cats and dogs were scattered along the floor, some wearing helmets and chest armor. The ones who were still alive had their backs to Philip and Sunflower, and fired their weapons down the corridor at an overturned metal cabinet, now blackened and half-melted from plasma rounds. Behind the makeshift barricade, a couple of hidden cats or dogs lifted their weapons sideways and fired back blindly at One's soldiers.

These same soldiers found themselves under attack from the rear, as Sunflower and Philip unloaded a full clip of plasma shells at their backs. In a matter of seconds, the soldiers dropped their weapons and fled into side corridors, leaving the smoke-filled passage empty.

A furry gray paw lifted a plasma pistol over the barricade. A green bolt of energy cracked from the weapon and sizzled between Sunflower's ears, forcing him to dive to the floor.

The orange cat laughed and grabbed another plasma clip from the belt of a dead Pomeranian.

"Ha! Missed me, you cross-eyed son of a *poona!*"

A gray cat peeked over the barricade. "Sunnie?"

Sunflower's yellow eyes grew wide.

"Andy!"

He slung his rifle onto his back and sprinted over the bodies in the corridor and leaped over the barricade to hug the gray cat.

"I thought I'd never see you again," she said. "Never!"

"Is it really you?" Sunflower stared at her. "Is it really Andy Nakamura?"

"Of course! Don't you know your own wife?"

"I do, I do!" Sunflower glanced at Betsy. "Hey there, Betsy." He did a double-take. "Betsy!"

The brown and white terrier barked. "Hi, Sunnie!"

Sunflower shook Betsy's paw. "You did it! I thought you'd die in the first ten seconds, but you actually did it."

Betsy lifted a plasma rifle. "Sure, but Andy and MacGuffin are the smart ones. They're the ones who figured out the hard stuff with the engines and the power."

The Siamese cat poked his head out from underneath an engineering panel.

"What? An elementary problem. These matter turbines are ancient technology."

A dull boom shook the walls and floor, and a transformer blew inside the ceiling, showering sparks on their heads. Loud klaxons began to wail.

Philip climbed over the barricade, followed by the buzzing sprite Nick.

"I don't wish to break up the quaint reunion with Betsy and Doctor MacGuffin, but this ship is falling apart. Find us a transport or a flying vehicle!"

The Siamese cat MacGuffin shook his head. "Impossible. The last transport was sent to the surface and the cat fighters are gone. Deployed against the other two ships, most likely."

Philip slumped his shoulders. "So be it. I have nothing to live for, anyway."

"What?" asked Andy Nakamura. "Why would you say that?"

Betsy grabbed a fresh plasma clip from the floor and jammed it into his rifle.

"Doc, you said you had an escape plan. Or was I dreaming? I could have been dreaming. I do that a lot."

"You were not dreaming," said the cat, typing fiercely at the keyboard of the engineering station. "We have temporary control of many systems of this vessel, and I have pre-programmed the thrusters to take us close to shore. At a low altitude, we can leap into the sea without any harm. Apart from getting wet, of course--a fate worse than death for some cats." He stared at the group. "Several of you need a bath, so I consider a dip in the ocean to be a benefit."

Andy grabbed a leg of Philip's trousers. "Why did you say you have nothing to live for?"

"Yeah," said Betsy, wagging his tail. "Also, where's Amy?"

"She's dead," said Philip, his voice breaking. "Both her and Three."

"Three?" asked Andy. The eyes of the gray cat grew round. "Not that awful machine on B Deck!" She leaped at MacGuffin and slapped his furry chest with her paws. "You said you cut the power!"

MacGuffin cringed from her blows. "I said that I tried, not that I was successful. There's a difference, especially when plasma rounds are zinging over my head!"

The floor bounced and swayed from a thunderous boom. A handful of large metal panels fell from the ceiling and clanged onto the deck.

Sunflower grabbed Andy's paw. "My wife and I found each other after two years, Doc, so I don't want to go to the big litter box in the sky just yet. Get us out of here, mister super-genius big brain!"

MacGuffin tapped the console and a three-dimensional outline of the Hare Twist appeared on the display, flashing with angry patches of red.

"We need an exit from the ship," said the cat. "The closest undamaged portal is located inside the starboard observation room."

Philip leaped over the barricade. "I know where that is. Follow me!"

"Wait!" said MacGuffin, and hastily searched through a cabinet on the wall. "The smoke in the ship has reached asphyxiation levels. Take these."

He tossed clear oxygen masks connected to bright orange canisters to each of the group, who snapped the masks around their faces.

"What about me?" squealed Nick. "I don't want to die."

Philip opened a flap of his shirt pocket.

"I'll share mine," he said. "Ride inside here."

"Cool!"

The group charged out of the engineering section and into clouds of oily black smoke. Philip took the lead, holding a plasma rifle in one hand and guiding himself along the corridor with the other.

As they stumbled over the pitching and rolling floor of the stricken ship, eyes stinging and tearing up from the poisonous smoke, no crew members appeared to challenge them with anything even as dangerous as a wet fork.

"The crew must have already fled in escape pods," shouted MacGuffin.

A sudden lightness of being caused Philip to drop his rifle. Everyone grabbed onto bundles of cables on the wall or door openings as the ship's deck angled down sharply and the loud hum of the nearby engines became a deafening roar. A hurricane of air rushed through the corridor and whisked away the deadly smoke.

Gravity returned as the ship slowed. Philip untangled himself from the cables on the wall and pointed at a hatch down the corridor.

"There it is! Starboard Observation."

He spun the metal wheel and pulled open the door. The dark-haired teenager stepped back, mouth open and oxygen mask falling from his fingers.

A gale of howling wind shuddered and whirled through the burned, twisted remains of the room. A powerful force had ripped away the floor-to-ceiling windows and left only fragments of bent metal where the vertical frames had been bolted. The ends of loose wires and cables whipped around in the powerful air current, which clawed at the broken edges of the deck, ceiling, and insulation and continued to rip away pieces in a blackened stream of dust and debris outside the ship.

Philip pointed at the distant smudge of land outside the broken window. The coast was simply a line of brown on the horizon.

"We're too high!" he shouted. "And too far!"

MacGuffin pushed by Philip into the room. "What? I set the flight computer for fifty feet!"

Betsy, Sunflower, and Andy Nakamura joined him.

"We can't jump from this high!" yelled Sunflower. "We're at least a thousand meters above the ocean!"

"Tell me something I don't know!" shouted MacGuffin, against the roaring air current.

Andy shielded her eyes from the wind and looked around the room. "We need a command console! I can hack into the system!"

"Why does Philip have his hands up?" asked Betsy.

Philip walked slowly into the damaged observation room, his hands at eye level and palms empty. One shuffled behind him, dripping blood from her fingers and holding a pistol at the teenager's back.

"Drop those weapons," she screamed.

The shreds of her jacket and skirt were covered in soot, with patches of deep red soaked through in a dozen places. She held the pistol with the silver fingers of her right hand, using it every few seconds to wipe away the blood that dripped from her scalp into her left eye. One's human left arm was jammed inside her jacket, like she was a wounded female Napoleon on the battlefield.

MacGuffin, Sunflower, and Andy dropped their plasma rifles and pistols. One's assistant, Wilson, appeared from behind her and tossed the weapons into the wind tunnel of the broken window, where they tumbled into the sea far, far below.

One stared wide-eyed at the cat. "Why did you do that, you idiot? Those cost me thousands of woolongs on the black market!"

Wilson glanced left and right nervously. "I, um ... you've lost millions of woolongs already from the damage to the ship. What's a few thousand?"

"Brainless fish-face! You're going to the punishment cube as soon as it's fixed!"

Wilson frowned. The cat opened his mouth to say something, but changed his mind and simply bowed his head.

"Of course, Your Prettifulness."

Philip lined up with his friends. The group faced One and turned their backs to the blue sky.

"You've lost," Philip shouted over the roar of air. "Your ship is damaged. Leave us alone and you'll never see us again."

"Damaged!" screamed One, her face scarlet. "My ship has been blasted to pieces because of your stupid girlfriend! But you'll be happy to hear that my weapons and defenses are working now." She wiped the trickle of blood from her eye. "That won't bring back my research. You destroyed everything that I worked for!"

Philip pointed a finger at her. "You destroyed everything I love!"

"So what? Find a new girlfriend. I could have given you ten more exactly like her. The dimensions are full of them."

"There was nobody like Amy," shouted Sunflower. "Nobody!"

"Right," barked Betsy. "She was the best!"

Philip backed slowly toward the edge of the damaged room, the fierce air current whipping his brown hair around his head. He glanced at the ocean sparkling in the morning sun, far, far below.

"What are you doing?" shouted One. "You can't survive that jump. You can't kill yourself before I kill you!"

Philip took Nick out of his pocket and carefully set her on the deck.

"Farewell, my friends!"

He placed both hands over his heart and fell backwards into the open sky.

"No!" squealed Nick.

Betsy leaped forward and grabbed the tiny woman in his jaws before she could follow Philip over the edge.

"Why did he do that? Why?" sobbed Nick.

"Mmph phrbdn nmmm," mumbled Betsy with the sprite in his mouth.

Sunflower turned to Andy Nakamura. "Shall we?"

She hugged him tearfully and nodded. The two cats ran to the edge and leaped over the side.

"Sunflower!" yelled Betsy, opening his mouth.

Nick buzzed toward the edge. Shocked by the multiple suicides, MacGuffin made a clumsy grab for her and slipped. Both the Siamese cat and the sprite tumbled into the open sky.

Wilson sprinted up to the edge, the strong air current blowing through his black fur.

"Stop it!" he shouted. "Stop it, all of you. This is madness!"

Betsy looked down at the ocean, and then turned back to One and the black cat.

"There's my ride!" he shouted. "See ya, suckers!"

The brown-and-white terrier leaped off, his little legs flailing and tail wagging.

One screamed and tossed her blood-covered pistol after the dog. "Just great! I'm not going to have anyone to torture!"

Wilson crawled to the edge and looked down, searching for any sign of those who had jumped. He turned to One, stood on his hind legs, and saluted with his right paw to his furry black forehead.

"You won't even have me!" he shouted. "I quit!"

One watched the black cat tumble backwards into the strong air current and fall out of sight. She sighed and turned to leave, but a movement in the clear blue sky forced her to stop and stare in wide-eyed horror at a rapidly-approaching shape.

"No!"

The maroon and gray prow of the *Wits Hater* rammed into the observation deck and drove through its sister ship with the sound of a locomotive hitting another locomotive and both falling down an elevator shaft of the Sears Tower. A series of huge explosions ripped through both ships. The pieces fell a thousand meters into the ocean, smoking and burning like a massive, slow-motion fireworks display that had gone horribly, horribly wrong.

16

The light burned Amy from the top of her blonde head to the tips of her toes.

She floated through a dream of waves breaking on a beach. Faces floated above the spray: Three, Philip, Sunflower, her stepmother Lucia.

Amy opened her eyes to a cloudless blue sky and the soft murmuring sounds of a baby. She lay at the bottom of a crater of sand, the curved sides as smooth and shiny as a glass bowl. Baby Three lay wrapped in her old nightgown next to Amy, sucking on her fist and looking around with bright blue eyes.

"Mum mum," she said, and waved at Amy. "Mummumum."

Amy smiled and kissed the baby on the cheek. "You're a cute little monster, but I'm definitely not your mommy."

She hugged the baby to her chest. As she stood up, the glassy surface of the crater shattered under her boots like thin sugar candy. The sand poured through, and Amy pumped her legs to climb out of the crater before the walls could collapse.

The clear blue waves of a tropical ocean foamed and hissed away from her feet on a beach of white sand that spread left and right as far as she could see. A breeze whirled her hair from behind, full of the humid, earthy smells of plants and wet earth. Amy turned and saw a thick forest of palm trees towering over the beach, heavy with clumps of green coconuts. Behind the jungle, the sheer cliffs of a mountain rose hundreds of meters into the sky. Palm trees and scrubby bushes clung to the black volcanic rock, their leaves spread to catch every scrap of sunshine, and thick vines looped and slithered up the cliffs and across the vertical rock at impossible angles.

"So ... heaven is Hawai'i?" murmured Amy. "That's impossible——even God can't afford to buy property there."

"Mumum," said baby Three.

"Exactly. I'm just going to assume that we're both alive and castaways on this island. Do you think I dreamed all that stuff about talking cats and traveling through dimensions? Maybe I went on a three-hour tour and the boat sank. Nah, that's too corny and also I'm not wet. Maybe I was trying to get a tan and fell asleep on the beach."

"Mumum."

Amy looked down at her cotton nightgown covered with mud, redwood splinters, and streaks of orange brick dust. The lace hem had ripped off, and the loose threads floated lazily over her sand-covered boots.

"Sunbathing in this outfit? It's easier to believe in talking cats. I'd also never take a baby sunbathing. I may not be your mommy, but I know that much about babies."

A gleam at the top of the mountain caught her attention. Amy used a hand to shade her eyes from the hot sun and walked further down the beach with baby Three to get a better look.

"Is that a radio tower? That means people are here. I don't know if I should be happy or sad."

"Mumum," said baby Three.

Amy spotted a narrow trail that rose above the jungle, cut across the mountain, and led to the summit. She walked a kilometer down the beach to a muddy trail through the leafy green vegetation, frightening a large yellow bird that cawed like a crow and flew away. A pair of bamboo poles covered in strange symbols stood on either side of the opening to the jungle, the black paint faded from the sun and rain. Every twenty meters identical poles lined the trail hacked through the thick bushes. Birds woke from afternoon naps and cackled down at Amy as she followed the muddy path, swatting with her free hand at buzzing clouds of blue-green flies that tried to land on baby Three's face. After fifteen minutes of walking the path met the base of the mountain, where crude steps had been chipped out of the black, volcanic rock.

Amy sighed and looked at the sleeping baby in her arms.

"Godspeed, Amy Armstrong," she murmured. "We're going to be murdered at the top and eaten by cannibals, or murdered at the top and eaten by crazy alien robots. Either way, something bad is going to happen."

She climbed the steps carefully with the baby, stepping over vines, fallen rocks, and jumbled wreaths of stick and mud that were probably nests for the handful of white birds circling overhead. The path gradually rose above the humid cloud of birdcalls and buzzing insects that was the jungle, and into a cool breeze that smelled of clouds and the ocean.

When she reached the halfway point up the side of the mountain, Amy stopped to take a break. She shaded her eyes and scanned the sky and the endless blue ocean.

"I don't see any other land," she said. "I guess I'll have to call this place Gilligan's Island. So what if it's not original? Yes, baby, you should get used to me talking to myself. I'll be Ginger and you can be Mary Ann. You're a tomboy, not a movie star."

Baby Three squirmed and began to cry.

"Sorry! You can be Ginger."

The infant continued to cry, no matter what Amy did. She gave up trying and continued to climb up the dangerous steps with the baby.

At last a pair of massive wooden pillars marked the summit and the end of the path. Painted red, ten meters tall, and as wide as a man's shoulders, the large posts were linked at the top by a square beam, also painted red. An angled line of black symbols coiled around each pillar, rising like a scroll from the bottom to the top.

Amy passed between the pillars and walked over the orange-brown bricks of a small plaza. Round concrete bunkers covered in leafy vines framed the plaza on the left and right. Directly ahead, an aluminum antenna soared into the sky from the roof of a much wider concrete bunker––this was the "radio tower" she'd seen from the beach. Around the edges of the plaza, tropical flowers sprouted from dozens of wooden planter boxes. A hand trowel lay beside a box full of pink blooms with hexagonal petals, and a straw broom leaned in a concrete doorway.

"At least these cannibals like gardening," said Amy. "Well, let's go meet them. With all the noise you're making, I'm sure they're already breaking out the spices and heating the water. Do I want to be boiled to death or barbecued? Choices, choices."

Amy walked toward the wide bunker that supported the radio tower. A pair of windows stood on either side of a green metal door decorated with a wreath of vines and white flowers.

She was within arms-reach of the door when it clanked and squealed open on rusty hinges. A young woman stepped out. She wore a silky white gown, a garland of purple flowers in her long blonde hair, and was the spitting image of a twenty-something Amy Armstrong.

The woman clapped her hands and hopped up and down on her bare feet. "Ooo, a baby! I haven't seen a baby in years!"

Amy wrapped both arms around baby Three and backed away.

"Another copy of me? Stay back––I won't let you hurt us!"

The young woman held up her hands. "Don't be scared! I came here the same way as you."

"You're not working for One or her flunkies?"

"Who do you mean? I help the Keeper with his hobbies and stuff, but that's not really like working for him. We're married and it's a partnership. Do you understand these things? Do you have marriage in your dimension?"

"Of course we do!"

The young woman lowered her hands. "Sorry. I meet so many girls from other dimensions. Some of them don't even understand basic things from my culture."

"So many girls? What are you talking about?"

Baby Three coughed and wailed again, and her screams echoed across the plaza. A door opened in one of the smaller bunkers. A pale girl stuck her head out and sprinted toward Amy and the girl in the white dress, her bare feet slapping the bricks. Her blonde hair was split into braids and curled on top of her head, and she wore a short dress of sheer blue material that whipped around her bare arms and legs. This new, skinny arrival was another identical copy of Amy, only a few years younger.

She dashed up to them in her bare feet and stared at Three.

"A baby!" she squealed, and danced in a circle. "Baby! Baby! Baby!"

Baby Three stared at the newcomer for a moment, and then started to scream even louder.

"There's something wrong with her," said the twenty-something Amy.

The Amy in the blue dress pouted. "No, there's not! She's a perfect little cutie pie."

Amy shrugged. "I'm not going to argue with either of you, because that would be like arguing with myself and that's the point when I've actually lost my marbles. If I think about it too hard, I have to admit I probably went crazy a long time ago, way before One shot us with that death ray."

"You're not crazy––that's how everyone comes here," said the skinny copy. "I think she's just hungry. I'll get some coconut milk."

She ran back across the plaza.

"I can feel a question on your lips," said the twenty-something copy. "I am Blanca. The other girl is Lannie."

"I'm Amy."

Blanca smiled. "Of course you are. All of us are Amy Armstrong. If you decide to stay with us you'll have to take a new name. All of that is up to you, of course."

"I'm getting a very creepy vibe from this place," said Amy. "You're not going to chain me in the basement or chop me into little pieces, are you?"

Blanca laughed. "No, no, no! You're a funny one. I hope you decide to stay, because I think we'd be great friends."

A door slammed. Lannie sprinted across the plaza, the skirt of her blue dress flapping over her bare legs and a large coconut in both hands.

"Baby food!"

Amy switched the crying Three to her other arm. "How's she supposed to eat that?"

"All right, all right," said the young girl Lannie. "Keep your raspberries in your pockets."

"I have no idea what that means."

Lannie shrugged. The girl took a thin silver tube from a pocket in her dress, held it on the brick plaza with her toes, and rammed the coconut down onto the tube. Liquid seeped from the end of the tube and dribbled a small, dark patch onto the bricks. Lannie turned the coconut over and held the end of the tube over Baby Three's face. After a few drops fell inside her mouth, the infant stopped crying and began to suck on the tube.

"I guess babies are smarter than I thought," said Amy. "Now we've solved that problem, can someone please in the name of Captain Crunch tell me where I am?"

Blanca smiled and curtseyed, spreading the filmy white fabric of her skirt with both hands as she bowed.

"Welcome to Fiji, the island paradise."

"We're on Earth? That's great! I always wanted to visit the South Pacific."

"Not that Fiji," said Lannie. "Fiji is the name of this planet."

"Great," said Amy, and let out a deep sigh. "Are we even in the Milky Way galaxy?"

Blanca nodded. "Yes, and on the same spiral arm as Earth, just closer to the galactic center."

"Okay," said Amy. "I'm going to ask a question that has probably never been asked in the history of the English language. If I'm not dead or dreaming this, how did I and my dimensional copies end up on this planet?"

Blanca giggled. "That's actually a very common question around here."

"Everyone asks that," said Lannie. "Even me! I think baby needs a burp."

"A what? How do I do that?"

"Hold her up to your shoulder and lean back a little--that's it--and pat her on the back."

Amy followed Lannie's instructions and Baby Three let out a series of tiny burps.

"Mumum," she said.

Blanca clapped her hands. "She's so cute!"

"Can someone please answer my question?" asked Amy.

Blanca touched the baby's tiny fingers. "The Keeper should be back from fishing soon. He likes to explain these things himself."

Lannie flipped the skirt of her blue dress up and down like a fan. "Keeper, shmeeper," said the girl. "It's just Philip."

BABY THREE became fussy after her meal of coconut water. A horrifying smell coming from the nightgown in which the infant was wrapped forced the two young women to create a makeshift diaper from a bath towel. After a bit of rocking, the baby fell asleep in a box padded with old clothes.

Amy wandered through one of the concrete bunkers with Blanca, as the young woman talked a steady stream about her flower collection, the types of migratory birds that visited the island, and the household uses for lava rock. The bunker coiled down into the mountain like an underground skyscraper, each level warmed by the earth, given light by a circular shaft open to the sky, and watered by spring-fed pipes in the walls.

All of the rooms curved around the open, atrium-like shaft in the center. Blanca led Amy to a curved concrete barrier topped by a railing and pointed over the edge.

"It just keeps on going," she said. "I'm too scared to go past the sixth level. There's no point, anyway—we have everything we need on the first two floors."

Amy leaned over the railing and stared into a circle of deep, pitch-black nothing. The light that streamed from the round hole in the roof of the bunker faded out of existence forty meters down, below the seventh floor. A trickle of water rolled out of the level below her and plummeted into the darkness, spreading out into a misty rain as it fell. Amy listened for the smack of drops hitting the bottom, and heard nothing but the moan of a breeze from outside the bunker.

"Creepy," whispered Amy. "What's down there?"

"Nothing important. Just Keeper—I mean, Philip—stuff. He takes a trip to the lower levels every few days."

"Fishing?"

Blanca giggled. "Oh, no! He does that on the other side of the island, sometimes in his boat."

"So what exactly is this place?"

"I showed you. It's where I live with Philip and Lannie."

"Not THIS place." Amy spread her arms. "This PLACE."

"You mean the island," said Blanca. "I like to think of it as an airship station."

"A what?"

"Sorry. You probably don't have airships where you come from. Let's see ... it's like an old-timey port with boats and everything. People are coming and going all the time, but very few stay. There are lots of things to do, but I can understand why they leave. If she didn't have me to talk to, Lannie would have left, too."

"But how did any of us get here?"

"I'll let Philip talk about that. It's not a big secret or anything, it's just that he's much better at explaining things. I'm not good at science––I barely passed theoretical astrophysics in elementary school."

Amy watched the water cascade into the abyss below.

"Theoretical astrophysics in elementary school," she said. "Wow."

"I know; it's embarrassing," said Blanca. "But don't bring it up with Lannie. She came from a dimension where they didn't even have it in school! Like, ever."

"Shocking," said Amy.

They climbed a flight of steps out of the bunker and into the sunshine. For lunch, Lannie and Blanca prepared a spicy soup made from roots and green vegetables, and served it with chunks of flaky-crusted bread. All three sat around a sunlit table next to a window open to the plaza, eating while a warm breeze gently pushed up the curtains. The smells of the loamy, humid jungle and heated bricks of the plaza mixed with the spicy fragrance of the soup.

Lannie couldn't take her eyes off Baby Three, who was still sleeping in her box on the floor.

"Such a pretty baby," said the skinny girl. "You must be proud."

Amy almost choked on her soup, but managed to hold up a finger. "Whoa, there. Number one: she's a friend, not my baby. Number two: I popped out of thin air onto this island after thinking I was going to be disintegrated by an evil copy of myself. Being proud is the last thing on my mind!"

"Sorry," said Lannie. "We never see babies here, just other Amy Armstrongs."

"Sometimes other Philips, too, but mostly just us," said Blanca.

Amy shrugged. "I don't even know if she's a real baby. She could be a tiny little human."

Lannie glanced sideways at Blanca, and then leaned toward Amy. "You know what babies are, don't you? Tiny little humans."

"Of course I know that!"

Lannie's eyes widened and she covered her mouth with a hand.

"Oh no," she whispered to Blanca. "I bet she doesn't know where babies come from. Her dimension is probably really strict!"

"I'm not telling her," whispered Blanca, hiding her mouth. "It's too embarrassing. Tell her they come from the Moon or something. She won't know the difference."

Amy sighed. "You two are ridiculous. I can hear everything you're saying."

The faint scrape of footsteps came from the plaza, and Lannie jumped up from the table.

"It's Philip!" she squealed.

Both she and Blanca dropped their spoons and sprinted through the doorway to the plaza like children hearing the ice cream truck. Amy followed at a pace more leisurely than light speed. She stepped onto the warm brick to see the young women with their arms wrapped around a tall man holding a net bag of large silver fish in one hand and a fishing pole in the other.

He must have been two or three times the age of Amy's Philip, with long gray hair pulled into a pony-tail and a gray beard shot through with streaks of white. His faded white shirt and shorts exposed bare arms and legs as tanned and brown as a field worker, with lean, stringy muscles moving below the skin. He laughed at something from one of the girls, and white teeth flashed in his bearded, tanned face. This old-man version of the love of Amy's life raised a hand and waved at her.

"Amy!" he shouted. "Welcome to Fiji!"

The voice gave Amy chills––throaty and rough like chopped wood, but still Philip's voice and with Philip's upper class English accent. She walked across the plaza toward him, not understanding why her knees were wobbly and her face so hot. Her hands shook so she tried to hide it by cracking her knuckles and then rubbing the side of her neck. At last she decided to hold them behind her back.

"How's it going, Phil?" she asked.

The young women clinging to Philip stepped away, and he bowed gracefully to Amy with a hand on his chest.

"It's a pleasure to meet you, Miss Armstrong."

Amy bent over with her hands on her knees, and let out a huge sigh. "Wow! What a relief! I thought you were Philip for a second there, and were going to say you've been waiting thirty years for me to show up, with a big speech about true love and crap."

Blanca and Lannie giggled, and Philip burst out laughing.

"That would be quite amusing," he said, after he recovered. "Especially since I'm married to the stunningly beautiful Miss Blanca here." He hugged the older version of Amy tight around the waist. "Ever since the day I laid eyes on her, I knew we were meant to be together."

"We all look the same," said Amy. "How is that even a thing?"

Philip held a finger to his lips. "Hush! Don't stir the soup if you're not going to eat it."

"What? You people keep saying things I've never heard before!"

Philip shrugged. "It's a common saying where I'm from. In any case, I'm certain you've many questions to ask such as: how did you arrive here, what is this place, and where are the Jaffa Cakes? The first two questions will be answered shortly as I clean my catch, and to the last question level four is packed floor to ceiling with boxes of them. Apparently, Jaffa Cakes will outlive us all. The unknowable riddle: why do cats like Jaffa Cakes?"

"Maybe they didn't like them," said Blanca. "That's why there are so many boxes left."

A baby's cry came from the open window of the bunker.

"She woke up!" yelled Lannie, and sprinted across the plaza.

"What the devil is that sound?" asked Philip. "A wounded animal?"

Blanca poked him in the ribs. "It's a baby, silly. Don't you know anything?"

"Yeah," said Amy. "Don't they have babies on your planet? Um, to be clear, this is a planet, right? I just got here; it could be a holographic space station run by blobs of alien goo for all I know."

Philip frowned. "It is a planet, and yes, I'm familiar with the human growth cycle. Unfortunately, I haven't seen or heard an infant since I arrived on this island. It's an absolute impossibility. How could a child survive the journey?"

Lannie walked out of the bunker, holding Baby Three at her shoulder and patting the infant on the back.

"She's not an impossibility," said the skinny girl. "Unless you mean impossibly cute!"

"I guess she survived the same way I did," said Amy. "An evil copy of me––of us––caused my ship to crash. She caught up to us after a few days and shot me and a copy named Three with her quantum attenuator thingamajig death ray or whatever, and I woke up on the beach."

Philip nodded. "The same story has happened to most who arrive on this island, including Blanca." He turned to the young woman. "Where is this 'Three' she mentioned? Is she hiding in the jungle?"

Amy pointed to the infant in Lannie's arms. "She's right here––the baby is Three. I was supposed to die first, but she pushed me out of the way and got hit by the beam."

Philip held up a finger. "Wait—don't say a word! She then regressed temporally down to an infantile state. That's remarkable—a partial attenuation. I knew this could happen, but to see the results with my own eyes ..." He held his hand out to the baby, and she grabbed his thumb in her tiny pink fingers. "So many variables in play: the previous age of the subject, the energy source powering the quantum transfuser, the length of exposure. Some of this I can guess, but I'm afraid the test would be impossible to recreate."

Amy took the baby from Lannie. "We're not test subjects. I knew this was some kind of freaky mad scientist place. The only way you're doing experiments on me and the baby is after we jump off the mountain and drown ourselves."

Philip laughed. "No, no. I was just talking to myself. I'm awfully sorry if I caused any alarm. Neither you nor the baby will have to do anything you find uncomfortable." He bowed from the waist. "You are my guests."

Amy patted Baby Three on the back. "Tell me what happened to the other 'guests' before I decide what's uncomfortable or not."

"Of course. Allow me to clean these fish as we talk. Lannie, boil the water. Blanca, please bring the knives and gutting table."

"This is getting worse by the minute," said Amy. "Point a knife at me and I'll kick you where it really hurts."

Philip spread his arms. "We haven't an icebox on this island, and I mustn't let my catch go to waste. There's an abundance of salt for preserving food, but no cooling."

In several short trips, Blanca carried out a bucket, a roll of canvas, and a low wooden table, the top of which was heavy marked and crossed with deep cuts. She set everything next to the bunker under the red flowers of a bougainvillea, and unrolled the canvas to reveal a half-dozen knives of various lengths and thickness.

Philip kissed her on the cheek. "Thank you, dear."

He sat in front of the low table, placed a large fish on the cutting surface, and sliced open the silver belly with one of the knives.

"Blanca and Lannie are friendly and intelligent young women," he said. "However, I'm certain any explanation they've provided about this place has confused you."

"They haven't explained much at all, apart from Blanca being your wife, your hobbies of fishing and spending time underground, and the fact that a stream of Amy Armstrongs have been going through this place like Grand Central Station."

"I don't understand that metaphor, but I assume you mean that the island has seen heavy traffic from copies of Amy Armstrong," said Philip. "That's absolutely true. They arrive on the beach as you did, and leave in much the same way. Lannie and Blanca came here like you, of course, but chose to stay with me."

Amy shook her head. "Why?"

Philip scooped the guts from the fish and dumped them into the bucket. With a crunch of the knife, he chopped off the head and placed it to the side.

"Allow me to answer a more important question: are you dead? Are you stuck in a queer sort of afterlife with a strange old man? The answer is no, and no. The copy that sent you here goes by a few names, but you most likely know her as 'One.' She believes that her research into quantum attenuation will allow her to travel back to a point in the past before she shot and killed her husband, the Philip of that dimension, and she has been sending Amy Armstrongs and Philip Marlboroughs to this island for the past five years. Each time she sends someone through the transfuser, she thinks she's killing that person, but believes the sacrifice is worthwhile because she's getting closer to the day she feels brave enough to step inside and use it on herself."

"You figured all of that out without even meeting her? That's good."

Philip smiled and ran a scaling knife along the side of the fish. "I've talked with exactly two-hundred and forty-three Amy Armstrongs. The woman called One seems to unload some of her guilt by telling the victims everything before she puts them through the quantum process."

"She told me it's almost done. The research, I mean. She'll probably go on killing people, anyway. Is it true? Can she really travel back in time?"

"Absolutely," said Philip. "She could do it now. In fact, she could have done it before she fell down the dark hole of sending dimensional copies through the quantum attenuator. She could have used the machine on herself and arrived on the beach in the same manner as you and the baby."

"Here's a stupid question––why hasn't she?"

Philip shrugged. "She doesn't trust anyone, doesn't trust the data, and certainly doesn't trust herself enough to take the chance. She's afraid, and in the end that fear will destroy her." He pointed the knife at the wooden gate across the plaza. "Of course I could be wrong, and she could appear at the top of those steps in the next two seconds. Anything's possible."

"Not anything. A giant eggplant isn't going to fall out of the sky filled with candy and rainbows."

"The probability of that happening is indeed rather low," said Philip, and grinned. "You have quite the sense of humor, Miss Amy Armstrong."

Amy paced back and forth with Baby Three in her arms. "What would she do when she got here? Get married to you and go fishing? Just to be clear, you're not the Philip that she thought was cheating on her?"

"Absolutely not. In my dimension, I never met an Amy Armstrong. I've made up for that during my time on this island, however, and I've had the good fortune of knowing many."

"And burying them underground after you murdered them, right? I don't see any of these two-hundred forty-three you're talking about."

Philip laughed. "You're absolutely a charm! I've never harmed a hair on their heads. If Blanca and Lannie haven't explained, this place is a transitional area, a sort of way station along the quantum highway. The Amy Armstrongs and Philip Marlboroughs that arrive here can choose to return to their own dimension, or travel wherever in time or space they choose. Most return to their own dimension, but others, understandably because of war or lack of family, choose somewhere nicer like Zeta Five. Do you have amusement parks in your dimension? Imagine the most fantastic amusement park you've ever seen, but covering an entire planet."

Amy stared up at the soaring antenna. "Any time or place they want? But how? I don't see any spaceships or rockets. Do they climb that thing and jump into fairyland? Click their heels and wish for home?"

Philip placed another fish on the table. "The quantum machinery is all underground. Think of this as less of an island and more of a tiny mouthpiece for a musical instrument the size of a planet. An artificial world, designed to harmonize with universal ley lines and therefore magnify the signals coming from SpaceBook Prime."

"Ah ha! I knew it. Can we go there?"

Philip shrugged. "SpaceBook Prime is a dead world, populated solely by automatons and robotic machinery, following instructions from long-dead masters. That's why the galactic SpaceBook signal is rotten with strange advertisements for products that don't exist. If I could discover how to remove those without interrupting the SpaceBook tracking signal, then I would have done so many years ago."

"So this planet was made by these people, the ones that built SpaceBook?"

"Cats, not people," said Philip. "The few facts that I know for certain are that they were very powerful, but for some reason teleported their entire civilization into the past. Who knows? Maybe they were bored. Cats are like that. Whatever the case, they're long dead now. Only the machinery of SpaceBook exists, constantly providing the satellites scattered throughout the spiral arm with a stream of useless, smutty advertising."

"Speaking of smutty, why are you still here? You can go anywhere you like in time or space."

"True," said Philip, crunching his knife through the tail of a fish. "But who would act as the Keeper? Someone has to help the confused people who arrive on the beach. In my dimension, I was the lead scientist for a transdimensional space-folding project. When it came to the first test, I sent myself through the portal and landed here. It was quite a shock, but you've seen that yourself. An elderly couple you might know called Amy and Philip were the Keepers at that time. Instead of returning to my dimension, I decided to stay and help."

"My Philip is still in trouble," said Amy. "What are we waiting for? Send me back right now!"

"Good things happen to those who wait, dear Amy," said Philip. "Might I point out that it's time travel? You won't arrive any later, whenever you happen to leave."

17

Philip cleaned the rest of the fish and scraped off the scales, and then Blanca and Lannie brought out a wooden bucket and a bag of salt. Lannie covered the bottom of the bucket with salt, Blanca packed a layer of fish, and Lannie added more salt. The layering of fish and salt continued until all the fish were in the bucket. Blanca then poured half a gallon of boiling, salty water over the fish, and Lannie covered the top with a circular wooden lid. The girl placed a heavy rock on top of the lid and pushed it down.

"What's with the rock?" asked Amy. "The fish aren't going to jump out. They already died and went to fish heaven."

Lannie smiled and wiped her forehead with the back of her hand. "It keeps the meat under the salty water. It will be good for weeks this way."

Philip stepped out from the bunker in patched overalls that had probably been safety orange a long, long time ago, but had faded to pale yellow. A belt full of leather pouches and clinking metal tools circled his waist,. He wore sturdy boots on his feet and carried another pair on top of a bundle of green cloth.

"Take these," he said. "They'll protect you on the journey down."

Amy shrugged. "Thanks, but green's not really my color. I'm getting used to the barefoot life."

Philip pointed to the handle of a large sword strapped to his back.

"Spiders and sometimes worse things breed in the lower levels," he said. "They'll bite through that flimsy dress, whatever color it may be."

Amy grabbed the boots and overalls. "I love green! It's the best."

She gave Baby Three to Lannie and wore the protective suit over her nightgown by jamming her legs and the long skirt inside, and slipped her feet into the boots. Blanca and Lannie stood quietly and watched as she zipped up the front. Amy sensed that the young women were waiting to say goodbye.

"I wish you could have stayed," said Blanca, and wiped away a tear. "We just met, but I feel like I'm losing a friend."

She hugged Amy and kissed her on both cheeks.

"I know," said Amy. "But don't feel so bad––you're living in a tropical paradise."

She took Baby Three from Lannie. The young girl kissed the baby on the cheek and hugged them both.

"I'm never this sad when other Amys leave," she whispered. "I think it's because of your cute little baby. Please stay! I promise we'll have so much fun everyday. And we'll finally have enough players for whist!"

"I don't know what that is, but I'm sorry. I have to try and help my friends."

Lannie nodded and stepped back.

"Ladies, enjoy yourselves for the next few hours," said Philip. He kissed both of the young women on the cheek and walked away, the tools rattling on his belt. "Don't forget your chores for today."

Amy waved. "Bye! Have a nice life."

"Mumum," said Baby Three, causing Lannie and Blanca to burst into tears.

Amy followed Philip into the bunker and down the concrete stairs to the next level, her arms tight around Three and eyes on the deep atrium in the center. Each set of stairs was on the opposite side of the circle, so they had to walk halfway around the level to descend to the next floor. The tools on Philip's belt jingled softly with every step he took, but otherwise there was little sound. The cold silence of the underground chamber made the faintest of sounds louder, including Amy's breathing.

"You told Blanca and Lannie that you'd be gone for hours," she said. "How far down this rabbit hole are you taking me?"

"The entire planetoid is a gigantic machine," said Philip. "I mentioned that earlier, or at least I believe I did. Old age curses the mind as well as the body."

"Right," said Amy. "The island is some kind of mouthpiece for a gigantic instrument. So we're walking down to level twenty? That's not too bad."

Philip shook his head. "Much, much further. Level eighty-eight."

THE LIGHT from the wide hole in the sky dimmed as they walked lower. At the tenth floor, Philip took a metal rod from his belt and twisted the end. The entire cylinder glowed bright blue and illuminated the stained concrete floor.

"Please take this. I need my hands free.'"

Amy took the rod from Philip. The light glowed red through her fingers.

"Wow," she said. "Tell me you made this from coconuts and I'll lose my freaking mind."

"Great Scott, why would you think it's made from a coconut? This is one of the last remaining fragments of technology from the cats that built this planet. Almost all of it has crumbled to dust."

"You mean the ancient space cats that are actually from the future but went to the past?"

"I sense a joking tone in your question, but yes—— that is correct. Please walk faster. We have many levels below us."

Amy held up the glowing rod and followed Philip around the circular level and down the next set of steps. The trickle of water she'd seen on the top level had spread into a mist as it fell. The tiny droplets whirled over the balcony and created tiny droplets on her green coveralls.   Amy glanced down into the endless hole and wished she had a penny.

"If these cats were so smart, how come they didn't invent elevators?"

"That's a good question," said Philip. "According to the old Keepers, the empty shaft was used for transport or something like a lift, but after the collapse of the cat civilization most of the machinery stopped working. We're walking through the dried bones of what was a thousand years ago a vibrant transportation terminal packed with cats traveling throughout the galaxy. This is a pale relic of a heavily-traveled hub of cat civilization; an abandoned, empty meeting place for beings that are long dead."

Amy flicked a cobweb from her fingers.

"So where'd all these cats go? Florida?"

"Much like other complex societies, the cats became so focused on their own pleasures that none became engineers, mechanics, or doctors, and instead yearned to be actors, musicians, and talk-show hosts. The creation of SpaceBook turned celebrity worship into a fever. When a deadly virus emerged, the cats were unable to stop the spread of the disease, having few scientists. The cats who could leave rushed to the past, unwittingly spreading the virus further. The cats who stayed eventually died, some from the disease, and others from the violence and starvation that follows a breakdown of society."

"Wow," said Amy. "You know a lot about it."

"The credit belongs to the old Keepers. They passed down the stories."

"Blum lum," said Baby Three.

"How's the child?" asked Philip softly. "Will she remain quiet for the rest of the journey?"

"I can't guarantee anything when it comes to babies," said Amy. "Anyway, I bet her screams will chase away the ugly, hairy things hiding in the dark."

"I wouldn't be so confident about that."

Amy followed him down another flight of damp concrete steps.

"Here's a question: if you've got this SpaceBook teleporter that can go anywhere in time or space, why don't you pop out to a supermarket and bring back a load of groceries instead of eating coconuts and fish?"

Philip sighed. "A trip to the green grocer's using a thousand-year-old machine designed by long-dead cats is not worth my life. The island and surrounding ocean provides everything that I and my companions need."

A dozen floors below, the glowing stick in Amy's hand was the only source of light, and the scrape of their footsteps the only sound. Shadows moved along the water-stained concrete walls; shadows from a darker pool of blackness than Amy had ever experienced. She smelled a faint odor of ammonia and shifted Baby Three to her other arm.

Philip led the way across the long half-circle of balcony and down another set of steps. At the bottom he stopped and held up a hand.

"What's wrong?" asked Amy.

"Hush."

A scrape came from the direction of a dark and empty doorway. Philip slowly raised his right hand to his shoulder and pulled the sword out of its scabbard. The polished steel gleamed blue in the light from Amy's stick-lantern.

A loud hiss came from the doorway and Philip lunged inside, his sword flashing overhead. Amy heard a wet smack and several thumps, and ran to the doorway. A large, coffee-colored lizard the size of an alligator lay on the floor of the room, headless and thrashing in a pool of blood. Philip kept the sword pointed at the lizard, and a hand raised to block Amy from walking inside. The scaly head of the lizard lay at his feet, its jaws open and loose, and full of sharp, triangular teeth. Although completely separated at the neck, the huge black eyes on each side of the head still blinked and twitched.

"Watch out," said Philip, breathing faster than normal. "The body keeps moving even after death."

"Good gravy!"

Amy and baby Three waited outside the room. After the scraping sounds faded, Philip joined them. He wiped the blood from his sword with a rag, and slid the sharp weapon back into the scabbard over his shoulder.

"Nothing to worry about," he said. "There was only one. The others would have attacked by now."

"I see why Blanca and Lannie don't come down here," said Amy. "That thing could have eaten us both!"

Philip rubbed his gray beard. "Not quite. At worst it might have taken a hand or a foot."

"I'm very attached to both those, thank you very much. What does a huge thing like that even eat down here? Don't tell me hands and feet or I'll smack you."

"Their diet consists mainly of spiders."

"Spiders? A lizard that size would have to eat thousands."

Philip grimaced. "Very, very large spiders. Imagine a cat with eight legs and sixteen eyes."

Amy stared at Philip for a second with her mouth open, and then walked briskly with Baby Three toward the next set of stairs.

"Nope. Nope. Nope. Move faster and bring that sword!"

They descended the next sixty levels without meeting hungry reptiles or spiders, although Baby Three began to whine and sudden noises in the dark caused Philip to stop and draw his sword a dozen times.

Amy's back and legs ached from the long climb down the eighty-plus flights of steps, and she felt the pain of blisters forming on her feet.

"Good gravy, little baby," she said. "Lose some weight already. I wish I had one of those baby-carrier things, because my arms feel like someone beat them with a rubber hose."

Below floor eighty-seven, the steps continued fifty meters through empty, pitch-black air without a railing and ended in a dusty floor with no walls in sight. The light in Amy's hand shone on nothing, as if she stood at the bottom of a cavern or a dry well. Her boots scraped away a layer of dust on the floor and revealed a mosaic of tiny white and black bricks in a curving pattern.

Philip waved her forward. "This way, please."

Amy pointed at her feet. "Nice floor. Hey! There's a fish."

"Those are directions, not decorations."

After a short walk, a tall, half-circular opening of a tunnel glowed ahead. Philip led Amy and Baby Three a few hundred meters through the tunnel to another large space, too wide for the blue light to reach the walls. A new pattern of black and white bricks covered the floor, whirling around a red oval in the center like the curved arms of a hurricane around an empty eye.

"You may take off the extra clothing and boots now," said Philip.

Amy stared at him for a second. "Oh, right! I guess you'll need them for the next Amy Armstrong."

She slipped her feet out of the boots and unzipped the jumpsuit.

Philip walked a few paces and placed his feet over a rectangular pattern of white bricks that contained a deep impression of two cat's paws. The air crackled, and a five-meter green hologram of a cat on its hind legs flashed into existence in front of Philip. The transparent cat bowed, and a diamond-shaped pendant dangled from its neck.

"Bon apremidi," said the hologram in a calm female voice. "Mete tike ou nan plas la, tanpri."

Philip took a polished metal square from his toolbelt and placed it on the cylinder.

"Mwen gen yon paspo diplomatik yo," he said. "Tout vol yo gratis."

The hologram bowed. "Mesi."

"That sounds familiar," said Amy. "Is it Cat French? Where did you learn how to speak it?"

Philip shrugged. "I've picked up a few phrases here and there. The machinery has always communicated in English, but we had an electrical storm last year and it began speaking this way. I'm not certain how to change it back."

"Kisaki destinasyon ou?" asked the hologram.

Philip pointed at the red oval in the center of the floor––the focus of the gigantic pattern of black and white bricks.

"Place the infant on the platform," he said. "I'll send her to Zeta Five."

Amy stepped away from him. "What? No! She's coming with me."

Philip frowned. "I'm afraid that's impossible. This node is designed for single-person transport. Don't worry––she'll be absolutely fine on Zeta Five. I've sent many young women through who will be overjoyed to take care of her."

"No! Send me first, and Baby Three to the same place, back to where Philip and my friends are."

"I'm afraid it's too dangerous. The precision of this transport node is not high enough to guarantee her arrival immediately after you. She may arrive moments later, or years, and suffer in the landing." He paused. "I didn't want to mention this in front of Blanca and Lannie, but any transport, even to Zeta Five, is perilous for the infant. This machinery is a thousand years old and designed for cats, after all."

"How do you know it even works? You think you've been helping these copies of me, but maybe you've been killing them!"

Philip held up a hand as if he were swearing on the Bible. "I promise you that is not the case, and I've tested the system myself." He rummaged through the large leather pouches on his belt, at last pulling out a gold bracelet covered in ridges. "This bracelet is a temporary pass. The old Keepers said that it was used by the maintenance workers in the old days to test the node."

"Test the node?"

Philip shrugged. "The universe is a complex system, with supernovas and shifts of dark matter. The bracelet automatically brings the traveler back to this node after sixty seconds."

"That seems awfully short."

"Not without oxygen, it isn't," said Philip. "One minute is the average time a cat can hold his breath or survive exposure to a vacuum. Let your mind be at ease——wear the bracelet and travel with the infant to Zeta Five. I assure you, sixty seconds is enough time to realize what a paradise it is."

Amy looked down at Baby Three and touched the soft blonde hair on top of her head. The baby giggled, and grabbed at the heart pendant dangling from Amy's neck. Amy gently pulled it away from the baby's pink fist.

"No," she said. "Not Zeta Five. I know a place where she'll have friends, a family who will love her, and where she'll have a chance to grow up happy."

"And where might that be?" asked Philip.

Amy looked up. "Earth. Pacific Grove, California. February 1, 1981."

"You're a very determined young woman," said Philip. "That's a very specific request, but I'm certain you have your reasons. In any case, the decision is yours."

He repeated the destination and date to the holographic cat, and it bowed again.

"The departure information has been accepted," said Philip. "I simply need a small sample of blood to focus on the proper dimension. Don't worry, it's less than a drop."

Amy held out a finger. "Use mine. It's my dimension."

"As you wish."

Philip guided Amy's hand to a flat green triangle on the patterned floor. The triangle flashed white and she felt a sharp pain on her middle finger.

"Ow! That hurt."

Philip smiled. "My apologies. I should have warned you."

He slid the golden bracelet onto Amy's wrist and waved her toward the center of the mosaic.

"Place your feet on the red oval and don't move, whatever happens."

Amy walked to the center and stood quietly, jiggling Baby Three a little to keep her from crying.

Philip murmured a series of phrases to the hologram. A blue light began to glow from beneath the floor, and burst through the cracks between the tiny bricks. A buzz like Mothra fighting a gigantic bumblebee grew from a whisper to a roar, so loud that Amy's teeth hurt. Baby Three's hair puffed out like a tiny Afro, and the hairs on Amy's arms stood out straight. A dizzying smell of lavender filled the air.

"I'll see you in sixty seconds!" shouted Philip. "Good luck!"

The bumblebee hum grew even louder, and a hurricane of blue lightning whipped around Amy, blowing up the hem of her cotton nightgown. The black and white bricks crumbled away, leaving the pair standing on a column topped by the red oval, in the center of a sphere of roaring blue energy.

With the snap-crack sound of a whip, the sound and fury disappeared. Amy stood under a star-filled sky, on the patched gray asphalt of a street lined with Victorian houses. Huge, gas-guzzling cars from Oldsmobile, Ford, and Buick were parked along both sides of the narrow lane. The oak trees beside the houses waved in a gentle breeze, their green leaves passing along the sound of waves crashing on the beach at the end of the street.

"Mum mum," said Baby Three.

"Holy crap!" Amy held the baby tight and sprinted up the street. "I'm nowhere near the police station!"

She raced as fast as she could through the sleeping city, her bare legs flashing and the rough asphalt burning the bottom of her feet. A line of bright blue lights around the edge of the bracelet had lit up when she arrived, and for each second that passed, a light turned dark.

Amy huffed up the sloping street to the back door of the Pacific Grove police station. The door was painted blue and made of reinforced steel, but from past experience Amy knew it was the door closest to the parking lot and would have more foot traffic as the officers came to work or changed shifts. At this time of night, someone would pass by here more often than the front door.

"They should … make this … an Olympic event," she gasped. "Basket … need … basket."

A dumpster stood nearby. Amy grabbed a cardboard box and gently laid Baby Three inside, sliding the box next to the door. She unfastened the heart pendant from around her neck and placed it down at the baby's feet, out of her reach.

"We don't want our little munchkin to choke to death, now do we?"

"Mum mum!" said Baby Three, and frantically waved her chubby arms.

Amy kissed the infant on the forehead.

"I love you, too," she said. "Be a good girl and don't get into trouble. Well, not too much trouble. Don't do anything I wouldn't do!"

She glanced at the blue lights on the bracelet.

"Ten seconds," she said. "Enough time for a little trouble."

Amy leaned into the dumpster and rummaged around, at last pulling something from the trash.

"Got it!"

The golden bracelet ticked from one to zero, and the gale of lavender whirled through the air. The back of the police station and the parking lot began to shiver and glow blue.

She waved at Baby Three. "Happy––"

With a loud crack, the building and the starry skies were replaced by the cavern and the dusty black and white mosaic.

"––Birthday!" shouted Amy.

The old version of Philip rubbed his fingers through his beard and stared at her.

"Are you quite all right? You seem pale."

Amy crossed her arms. "Oh, I'm fine. Do you think every woman has to faint at the drop of a hat? That's some old-timey Victorian values, mister. I'm a freethinking American girl who just realized that she's her own mom. Wait––that's not right. I'm not my own mother, I'm a trans-dimensional copy of myself who was shrunk down to a baby by another trans-dimensional copy of myself and left at the back of the police station by ... myself. Whoa, dizzy ..."

Philip ran up and caught her before she hit the floor. He rubbed her arms briskly for a few seconds, and Amy opened her eyes.

"Tattoos," she whispered. "Do I have any tattoos?"

Philip pushed up the sleeves of Amy's nightgown.

"None on your arms," he said. "I have to admit, this has been the strangest conversation I've had in years."

He helped Amy to stand and guided her back to the red oval in the center of the floor.

"Could I have my bracelet back, please?"

"Sure."

Amy handed him a circular piece of metal and Philip slid it into a pouch without looking. He stepped over to the "cat's paw" indentations in the floor and activated the giant hologram of a cat.

"Now, Miss Armstrong," he said. "Where would you like to go? I can send you anywhere in the universe. Remember, Zeta Five is quite literally a paradise. Two words: Chocolate river."

Amy stared at the floor. "I've been trying to get back home to my family ever since I got caught up in this crazy, dimensional-future mess." She took a deep breath and let it out slowly. "But I'd never be able to live with myself if I didn't try to help my friends."

Philip nodded. "I understand. Where would you like to go?"

"There's only one place in the universe for me. The morning of October 13, 1912. Same dimension."

Philip spoke to the cat hologram for a moment. The huge sphere of blue lightning hummed around Amy, whipped her blonde hair into a frenzy, and she popped out of existence.

The old man stretched with his arms above his head and sighed. He walked slowly over to the red oval in the floor, dropped to one knee, and spread a wrinkled hand across the stone.

"Peace be with you, Amy Armstrong."

18

On the dry yellow hillside a mountain jay chattered from his favorite lilac bush, which also happened to be the largest lilac bush he'd ever seen. At this moment, the jay was more interested in heavenly rather than earthly considerations, and tilted his blue head to keep an eye on the chaotic battle in the sky.

A blonde girl in a filthy nightgown popped into existence four meters above the bird and sent him fluttering away. The human landed in the lilac bush and tumbled down the hillside knocking purple flowers and stalks of dried grass into the air. She rolled slower and slower and at last stopped in a saltbush.

Amy hissed in pain and climbed to her feet. She rubbed at the scratches on her bare legs.

"Why does everything smell like cat pee? Thanks for almost killing me, old man! Ten feet higher and I'd be a squishy pile of broken bones."

A boom echoed through the mountains. Amy looked up to see three huge spacecraft shaped like bulbous submarines gliding through the clouds over the sea. Two of the ships––one maroon and the other dark blue––circled the largest of the three, like sharks around a wounded green whale. Dots flitted and buzzed like gnats around the long green ship, which trailed plumes of black smoke. A streaky haze floated below the ships, and Amy smelled an odor like bitter gasoline and burning rubber. A cluster of narrow white contrails flew from the side of the maroon ship and struck the nose of the green vessel with a bright flash. A few seconds later, a loud boom rolled over the sea.

Amy rubbed the back of her leg. "Good grief, they're fighting each other. That big pickle looks like

One's ship, the *Hare Twist*. Why would Two and Four turn on her? Wait a second––I'm the dumbest girl in the universe. Philip didn't come through the portal, so he probably escaped and took over the ship. They're not fighting One, they're fighting Philip!"

In the yellow hills to the north, silver glinted under the morning sun. The *White Star* lay hidden on a flat, grassy area between two mountains. Someone had half-heartedly covered the graceful, hundred-meter spaceship with swaths of brown fabric and the branches of fallen trees.

"I don't believe it," said Amy. "Blanche!"

She sprinted through the dry grass of the ridge and up the hill to the camouflaged spaceship.

"Awesome," she whispered, and ran her fingers over the smooth silver hull.

A pair of cat soldiers in dark green armor stepped out of hiding and aimed plasma rifles at Amy.

"Stop!" shouted one, a gray tabby. "Don't touch that!"

The black cat next to him nodded. "Yeah, Centauran scum."

Amy crossed her arms and glared at the two cats.

"Do I look like Centauran scum?" she snarled. "Think for a second exactly who I look like."

"Oh, poopie," said the black cat, and lowered his rifle.

The gray tabby shook his head. "Who are you? Identify yourself!"

Amy pointed a finger at him and did her best imitation of One's voice. "Me? I'm the last thing you'll ever see, you pair of slobbering, mange-covered morons! If you don't get out of my sight in the next two seconds, you'll spend the rest of your days in a punishment cube, picking up dog crap in the world's biggest dog kennel!"

The two cats glanced at each other, and then sprinted away as fast as their four legs could carry them.

Amy walked along the bottom hull of the huge ship, pulling on the landing gear and slapping the silver hull.

"Open up, Blanche! It's me, Amy!"

The boom of distant explosions echoed through the hills. Amy backed up and shaded her eyes to get a better view of the slow-motion battle in the sky. She ran forward and slapped the silver hull even harder.

"Come on, Blanche. Philip's in trouble!"

The outline of a large red circle glowed on the smooth silver skin of the ship above Amy's head. The starboard airlock hatch popped open and a ladder slid down.

Amy climbed up to the airlock and crawled inside.

"I thought you were at the bottom of the ocean," she said. "What happened?"

The airlock sealed behind Amy and crimson lights in the ceiling flickered to life.

"My data showed that you had suffered the same fate, my Lady," came the smooth, motherly voice of the ship. "I was lifted from the depths and drained by a host of very smelly cats and dogs, none of whom were crew members."

"Are you able to fly? What about the explosion?"

"I have repaired the damage to the cargo hold," said the ship. "As there was no apparent threat and no captain, I was simply taking a nap. It is quite pleasant when you are my age."

"Philip's in trouble and we have to help him. Warm up the engines and let's get up there."

"Affirmative, my Lady. Please change into a set of prophylactic clothing."

Amy rolled her eyes and sighed. "Really? Those stretchy red things again?"

"Yes, my Lady. Your present clothing is covered with microbes, plant pollen, and the fecal matter of twelve different species. I can feel a sniffle coming already."

Amy pulled the nightgown over her head. "I know I need a bath, but you don't have to rub it in!"

She jammed her legs into a pair of red spandex trousers and her arms into a long-sleeved top. Amy stretched a black cap over her blonde hair and sprinted out of the airlock and through the corridors of the ship to the navigation room, where the yellow mountains and the battle in the sky was projected floor-to-ceiling on every surface around her.

"Ready to go?" Amy pointed up. "Head for that big green ship. The one that looks like a giant pickle."

"Yes, captain."

The invisible floor vibrated below Amy's feet. The mountains dropped away, replaced by the foaming surf and the sun-sparkled Pacific Ocean.

"My Lady, if your intention is to engage these craft in combat, I would advise against such a course of action," said the ship calmly. "I detect the radiation signatures of high-powered weapons."

"It's my friends that I care about," said Amy. "If anything's happened to Philip or Sunflower or Betsy, I'll burn a hole through all three of these ships, radiation signatures or not!"

A missile streaked past Amy, curved around with a smoky contrail, and blew a smoking hole in the rear of *Hare Twist*. The nose of the long green ship dipped toward the ocean for a moment as it glided below the clouds, and then rose again, with its engines flaring white.

"My Lady, I have located crew members on the starboard side of the central vessel."

"Show me!"

A section of the sky above Amy's head magnified. Philip, Sunflower, Betsy, and Amy's other friends stood in a damaged section of *Hare Twist*, their backs to the jagged hole of blackened metal and their fur and clothing whirling in the breeze.

"What's going on? Philip! What's he doing?"

"From the elevated heart rate and position of the crew member's body, I estimate an eighty-nine percent chance that he is about to jump, my Lady. The impact with the ocean's surface will certainly be fatal, as Centaurans cannot fly."

"No! Catch him or something!"

"Of course, my Lady. Maximum atmospheric thrust imminent. Please hold on."

The *White Star* flashed through the chaotic battle, dodging tiny cat fighters and the smoking trails of missiles. She rolled beneath the wounded green ship and popped open her port airlock as Philip jumped. The teenager tumbled inside and was followed by a steady stream of Amy's other friends: Nick, Sunflower, Andy Nakamura, Doctor MacGuffin, Betsy, and One's first officer Wilson.

"Collision warning," droned the ship. "Taking evasive action."

She closed the airlock and shot away as the *Wits Hater* rammed the *Hare Twist* with a fierce crunch of twisting steel. The reactors of both ships overloaded with a blinding flash, and the heavy, smoking remains fell into the sea far below.

Amy picked herself up from the deck of the navigation room.

"Blanche, did everyone make it? Blanche!"

"Analyzing. Crew members have successfully boarded the ship and are waiting in port airlock. Some have sustained injuries."

She kept talking but Amy was already out the door.

AMY PALMED the hatch and rushed inside the airlock. Her friends lay in a furry pile of arms, legs, and angrily waving paws.

"Betsy!" screamed Sunflower. "Get your stinky butt off my face!"

"Oh, hey Sunnie," barked the terrier. "That's what that was! I thought it felt funny."

"My face is not funny when your butt is on it!"

Amy helped Betsy and the others untangle themselves. She found Philip at the bottom of the pile on his back. The teenager's eyes were closed and a trickle of blood dripped from his nose and across his cheek.

"Philip!"

Amy shook him by the shoulders, and kissed the boy hard on the lips. Philip laughed and kissed her back. He wrapped his arms around her and hugged her tight.

Amy slapped him on the chest. "You idiot. You were just pretending!"

Philip kissed her again and rested his forehead against hers. "I'm not pretending that I love you, Amy Armstrong. What happened? Did One's evil machine not work? I assume it simply teleported you back to the ship."

Amy hugged him around the neck. "It sent me far, far away, but I came back for you. I came back for all of you."

Andy Nakamura pointed at Wilson and hissed. "What's that thing doing here? He works for One—he's her right-hand cat!"

"Right," said Sunflower. "Explain yourself, traitor! Don't make us dump you outside with the rest of the trash."

Wilson bowed from the waist and grinned sheepishly. "Ensign Wilson, formerly of the *Hare Twist*, at your service. What can I say? I quit. I didn't like working for One, anyway. She was so mean! Right? Am I right, or am I right?"

"Wilson is a girl's name," said Sunflower. "What's the matter? Did you have hippie parents like me?"

"Certainly not," said the black cat. "Wilson is my family name. My given name is Eunice."

"Oh. That's okay, then."

"Sounds good to me!" Betsy jumped on top of the cat and licked him in the face. "You can be my new best friend!"

Wilson squirmed and tried to push Betsy off. "Please stop—I'm allergic to dogs. Allergic!"

Sunflower sighed. "Wow. This is the best day ever."

Andy hugged the orange tabby with her furry paws. "Why? Because we're together again?"

Sunflower shook his head. "No. Betsy has someone to play with and will finally leave me alone."

Nick buzzed into the air, her scarlet dress ripped and hair out of place. "Somebody pay attention to me! If I don't get a shower I'll murder all of you!"

Philip grinned. "Oh dear—someone said 'shower.'"

He reached for the decontamination button on the wall.

"Nooo!" screamed Nick. "Not that!"

A storm of antiseptic liquid soaked everyone and plastered them to the curved sides of the airlock, followed by a gale-force wind that dried their clothes.

Nick slid down the wall to the floor. "I'll get you for that," she whispered. "Someday."

"Yeah, bad boy," said Amy, and pinched Philip's cheek. "Maybe I shouldn't have rescued you."

The teenager shrugged. "Sorry. It was getting a bit whiffy in here."

Everyone changed into the required spandex uniforms and followed Amy to the navigation room. Plumes of black smoke and a large patch of oil on the ocean's surface were the only signs that a battle had taken place.

Amy shook her head. "What happened to One's ship?"

"A collision occurred between *Wits Hater* and *Hare Twist*," said the calm voice of the ship. "The impact caused a reactor failure. Both craft are now resting on the seabed, approximately one point two kilometers to the north east."

Wilson paced the transparent floor of the navigation room, rubbing his head. "That was me! I almost died!"

"There was another ship," said Philip. "The one captained by Four, I believe?"

Wilson held up a paw. "Yes—*Raw Tithes*! She was a meanie, too. I brought her the wrong bottle of coconut oil one time and she hit me with a stick."

"What happened to her, Blanche?" asked Amy. "Is she waiting around to capture us, or planning a sneak attack?"

"From the radiation trail of her engines, I believe *Raw Tithes* has left the atmosphere and entered orbit," said the ship. "Detecting a gamma particle surge––I estimate a seventy-three percent chance that it has performed a dimensional jump in the last two seconds."

Philip shook his head at the sparkling waves far below his feet. "Any survivors?"

"I'm not saving her, if that's what you're asking," said Amy. "She tried to kill both of us!"

Philip hugged her around the waist. "Not at all, dear heart. If that woman survived, I hope she's forced to don a milkmaid's bonnet and live her entire life in a barn. I simply meant any innocent cats or dogs from her crew."

"Right!" said Andy Nakamura, nodding her gray furry head. "Some of One's crew were forced to work for her. Not all of them were nasty pirates."

"I'm not a nasty pirate," said Wilson. "Just a normal cat on the run with a gambling debt longer than a sauro's tail. What? Woolongs don't grow on trees, you know!"

"Amy ... I notice you're not carrying a baby," said Philip. "I hope this isn't a bad time to mention the subject. What happened to Three?"

Amy stepped back and curtsied. "You're looking at her."

"Poppycock! You're not Three. You're the real Amy––MY Amy."

Betsy wagged his tail. "She's making a joke! Three was pretty and had bigger bump-things on her chest."

Amy kicked at the terrier with a bare foot and missed. "I'll show you a bump––on your HEAD!"

Philip pulled up the sleeve of Amy's uniform and stared at her arm. "You don't have any tattoos, either. Definitely not Three."

"I'm also not a baby. Let me sum up––no, that's too hard. Let me say this––I never had parents and I don't know who they were. I was abandoned behind the police station in Pacific Grove when I was just a baby, and that's when my foster mother adopted me. Three and I are exact genetic copies of each other. We're not twins––we're the same person." Amy shrugged. "I didn't have any way to change what happened to her, but I could choose to go anywhere, so I took her back to where I was found on my birthday–– the back door of the Pacific Grove police station."

"The circle is now complete," whispered Betsy, wide-eyed and drooling. "You're your own mommy!"

Sunflower snorted. "Only a dog would say something that stupid. She's not her mother at all."

Andy patted him on the head. "Sunnie, be nice."

"I think I understand," said Philip. "You're the real Amy, but also Three. Brilliant. Can I say I'm dating two girls at the same time?"

Amy crossed her arms. "Absolutely not!"

"Very well," said Philip, and kissed her. "Shall we fly down to the surface and find these surviving cats and dogs? Hopefully before anyone has captured the poor souls and put them in a zoo."

Amy nodded. "Blanche, take us down to the surface." She held up a golden bracelet covered in sixty fine ridges. "After that, how about a little trip to Fiji?"

Betsy jumped into the air and turned a somersault. "Yay!"

Epilogue

The pair of hulking sauropods––one brown and one green––wandered over the seaweed-covered rocks and dodged the occasional spray of surf. The larger, more muscular brown reptile stopped and bent over every few minutes, sometimes thrusting a claw into a dark place to pull out a red-shelled crab.

"I don't know why you keep doing that," said the smaller one. "My wounds have almost healed. Smearing more crab guts over them won't help."

"Sorry," said George. "I'm just bored. Can we murder some humans now?"

Nistra shook his scaly green head. "Absolutely not. Do you think I want to get captured again? Better for us to travel down the coast and find a cave where we can live out our natural lives, than to be locked in another cellar by those Centauran monsters."

"Okay. Can I at least have a human as a pet?"

"Maybe a small one, but you have to promise to feed it and clean its cage."

"Yay! Thanks, Nistra."

George reached down into the surf and picked up a large metal panel. The meter-wide square was dark green on one side and tarnished gray on the other, and covered in deep scratches.

"Hey! Look at what I found!"

Nistra rolled his eyes. "Ooo, pretty. A piece of alloyed titanium just like the fifty other pieces of alloyed titanium we just saw today. They're coming from the same place."

"From the ocean?"

"No, from the crashed ships, you idiot!"

George pouted. "You promised not to call me that. A promise is a promise, as my––whoa, look there!"

The giant sauro dropped the huge metal square and pointed down the beach.

A human figure lay facedown on a large couch cushion that washed in and out with the waves. Naked and covered with seaweed, the human female had pale legs, a back covered with bruises, and dozens of cuts dripping blood. Her right shoulder was almost entirely pink scar tissue, and the arm had been replaced with a mechanical limb, the chrome bones tangled with the same seaweed as everything else. Her wet hair had turned dark brown from the seawater, and was covered in sand from the constant pushing of the waves.

George clapped and giggled. "A pet! Egg bless us both!"

Nistra grabbed the larger sauro. "Stop! She might be dangerous. I've lost everything today––my comrades, my transport back home, and my actual home planet which is still spinning uselessly in the ship belonging to that egg-blasted Amy Armstrong. I don't want to lose my life as well."

He crept carefully across the sand to the seaweed-covered body, prodded it with a foot, and then pulled it and the cushion up to the high-tide line on the sand. The sauro knelt down and brushed sand-covered hair away from the face. A pink scar slashed the woman's left cheek from forehead to chin.

Nistra shrieked as the woman opened her eyes.

"Hello, boys," whispered One.

END

(To be continued in Book Four ...)

A Note From the Author

Thanks for reading *SpaceBook Awakens*! Please leave a positive review on Amazon if you enjoyed the book, and check out the other books I've written!

Cheers,
Steve Colegrove

SpaceBook Strikes Back
(Amy Armstrong Book Four)

Amy travels to a dead planet at the center of the universe where SpaceBook satellites were created, and fights to shut down the entire trans-dimensional network.

Available 2017

Made in the USA
Charleston, SC
07 November 2016